The Dreamer

Volume I

Dr. Shahzad Younas

Dedication

To all those who believe in humanity, equality, transparency, merit, justice, and self-actualization.

Preface

This book does not seek to glorify Imran Khan or portray him as a larger-than-life figure. Instead, it analyzes the facts that have influenced his successes, failures, triumphs, setbacks, and wrongful imprisonment. It offers a thorough and critical look at the character of this exceptional person, grounded in facts and evidence. Additionally, this book aims to examine the traits and circumstances that have enabled Imran Khan to garner lasting respect and admiration from the public over the past 54 years, in contrast to many of his political and non-political contemporaries who have lost public support and respect. It also examines how he has ignited a revolutionary democratic movement in Pakistan, fueled by the people's desires in the face of oppression and injustice.

In today's scientific era, our world, comprising seven continents, has transformed into a global village, all within a 227-gram mobile device that measures 16.3 centimeters in length. Regardless of how much one might assert their apolitical stance, it is nearly impossible to navigate life without engaging with social media through one's smartphone. Furthermore, it's difficult to stay indifferent to both local and global political events and developments.

Regardless of one's location globally, it is evident on mainstream and social media that Imran Khan is a central figure in discussions across various settings, both within and outside Pakistan, including offices, schools, colleges, universities, social and overseas gatherings. He frequently emerges as a prominent topic in everyday conversations,

WhatsApp groups, and popular talk shows. His presence is felt in editorial columns, analysts' commentary, and the headlines of both local and international media, where he garners a blend of admiration and criticism.

Some people refer to him as a player, while others see him as clumsy. Some connect with him, while others reject him. Many are pleased to see him, while others view him with skepticism. Some consider him a savior, while others see him as a scoundrel. Some refer to him as the "Taliban Khan" or "Jewish agent," while others honor him as a "brave heart patriot." Some call him an anarchist, while others regard him as a statesman. Some see him as a master of U-turns; others perceive him as a far-sighted politician. Many have placed their hopes in him, while others want to see him removed. Some consider him a Playboy, while others champion him as a great leader of the Muslim Ummah. Some people mock him, while others are willing to risk their lives for him. Many see him as a guarantor of Pakistan's prosperous future, while others view him as a threat to their power and Pakistan's integrity. Thus, after observing all those facts, it's natural for anyone to be curious about the reasons and personal qualities that have made Imran Khan a unique leader and the center of attention for millions of people in Pakistan and around the world.

On the other hand, over the past three years, we have witnessed long-standing rival political parties in Pakistan unite to form the Pakistan Democratic Movement (PDM) in opposition to Imran Khan. This illegitimate PDM government is violating the constitution, disobeying the law, and disregarding moral principles, as well as Eastern and

Islamic values. They are supported and facilitated by the powerful military establishment, the judiciary, the media, and other state institutions. In contrast, the public remains quietly yet steadfastly supportive of Imran Khan, opposing the PDM government and its allies. This situation brings to mind the famous saying: "You can fool all the people some of the time, and some of the people all the time, but you cannot fool all the people all the time."

The embarrassing defeat of the PDM alliance and its supporters by the Pakistan Tehreek-e-Insaf (PTI) in the general elections on February 8, 2024, is a clear indication that the Pakistani people have become aware of the true nature of those who have misled them for the past 78 years. These conventional dynastic political leaders and dictators have raised slogans about democracy, "bread, cloth, and house," Islam, and "Pakistan first." However, now the public is no longer willing to be deceived by such claims. This heightened awareness among the people is undoubtedly credited to Imran Khan's 29-year political struggle.

Since childhood, we have often heard that "Pakistan is going through a critical period in its history." However, the ongoing "Khan vs All" fight over the past three years has caused irreparable damage to Pakistan, its people, and its institutions—something that is hard to put into words.

Ironically, for the past seven decades, the people of Pakistan have placed their hopes in the military, dynastic political, and religious leaders whom they viewed as saviors. They have showered these leaders with love, even making personal and financial sacrifices when necessary. Rather than addressing the needs of the people, keeping their commitments, and paving a new way for the struggling Pakistani population caught in a cycle of issues and suffering, these leaders have prioritized their vested interests and those of their families, establishing themselves as the elite class of Pakistan. Meanwhile, Imran Khan, the most popular political leader who brought rare accomplishments to the nation—such as the Cricket World Cup, three free cancer hospitals, and Namal University—now endures the hardships of imprisonment.

Even three years after the successful regime change operation against Imran Khan, the PDM government and its powerful backers continue to engage in state oppression, violating both the constitution and the law. Despite this, Khan has steadfastly refused to make any deals or compromises. Surprisingly, instead of isolating him, the nation stands firmly by his side. This situation leads us to ponder and pose essential questions in our quest for understanding.

What qualities make Khan distinctive?

What flaws contribute to his failure?

How did the most stylish, favorite, and successful captain in cricket history become a prominent figure in Pakistani politics?

What led to the transformation of Shaukat Khanum's compassionate son into an authoritarian revolutionary leader?

How did this player, renowned for dismissing legendary batsmen, awaken a nation that had been previously indifferent, igniting a passion for change within them?

How did this previously unsuccessful politician manage to bring together a nation divided by various groups, sects, languages, castes, and provinces under the banner of his party (PTI) to create a new Pakistan?

What prevents Imran Khan from attaining genuine freedom, even with the backing of more than 80% of the Pakistani populace?

Why are the establishment and the PDM government's tactics to defeat Imran Khan and eliminate the PTI failing, despite all the state power, oppression, and fascism?

What could be the best solution to the three-year-long tension, conflict, and chaos of "Khan vs. All" that is acceptable to Imran Khan, the people of Pakistan, and the powerful military establishment?

Is it possible to overcome Imran Khan and take him out of the public spotlight? If yes, what steps would be involved?

Is Imran Khan truly a great, successful, and unique leader who accomplished what no one else could in 78 years?

Will Imran Khan, who has consistently achieved his dreams throughout his life, find true freedom in his later years and build a new Pakistan based on the principles of the State of Madina, or will this dream remain unfulfilled?

To explore the answers to these questions, we present the first volume of a three-volume series titled "The Dreamer." Volume One consists of seventeen chapters that examine Imran Khan's aspirations and the challenges he faced in sports, health, education, and politics. It also delves into his experiences, including his defeats and victories, as well as his faith, love, patriotism, ideology, endurance, and uniqueness, all supported by compelling arguments and facts.

The 1st volume outlines Imran Khan's 47-year journey, beginning with his early days in cricket and culminating in his inauguration as Prime Minister of Pakistan. It also incorporates brief references to pertinent current events. The 2nd volume will provide a constructive and critical analysis of Imran Khan's tenure as Prime Minister, spanning three and a half years, focusing on the steps taken and decisions made during that time. The 3rd volume will provide an in-depth examination of the reasons behind the regime change operation, its aftermath, and its effects on Imran Khan, the PTI, and the country as a whole. After reading these three volumes, you will find it much easier to understand the answers to the questions posed.

I hope that after reading this book, Imran Khan's supporters will reflect on his flaws and weaknesses instead of supporting him blindly. Similarly, I encourage his critics to reevaluate their preconceived notions and negative assessments by fairly considering his contributions to Pakistan and humanity, particularly in contrast to those of their traditional dynastic leaders. I also urge the military establishment, which played a role in removing Imran Khan from power and imprisoning him on dubious charges, to view him as a key figure for Pakistan's integrity, strength, and unity, rather than as a threat to their ongoing influence. Ultimately, it is essential for both current and future generations in Pakistan to recognize these aspects of this historical figure, as they are crucial for comprehending our present circumstances and the nation's history.

Dr. Shahzad Younas

Table of Contents

Introduction

The first volume of "The Dreamer" series consists of seventeen chapters.

It is essential to read the preface and the first chapter to grasp the distinctive aspects of Imran Khan and the motivation for writing the book; without engaging with these introductory sections, this understanding is difficult to attain.

Chapters 2 through 12 examine different phases of Imran Khan's life, showcasing his aspirations, practical challenges, achievements, setbacks, and trials, all supported by historical facts and substantial evidence.

Chapters 13 to 17 focus on Khan's genuine strengths, ideology, and traits, while also confronting the accusations, slander, and character attacks made by his opponents.

For a thorough understanding of this unique historical figure and to gain the maximum benefit from the book, it is essential to read it in order, from start to finish. This method will enhance your understanding of Khan's character and provide clear answers to any inquiries you may have about him.

Beyond Uniqueness

Among the 8 billion people in the world, every individual is distinct in their physical and mental traits, features, and abilities. This means that everyone can see themselves as the most unique person in the world, as their characteristics and talents differ from those of anyone else. However, this raises an important question: is being naturally unique sufficient for achieving success and fame on a global scale? The answer is a resounding "no." More critical than uniqueness is the ability to contribute something meaningful to the world by effectively understanding and using one's natural talents rather than leading a purposeless life.

Although every human being is unique in appearance and mannerisms, one commonality is the vast ocean of dreams and desires that lies within each person's heart and mind. The majority of people long to stand out in their chosen pursuits. Depending on their mood, preferences, beliefs, circumstances, and experiences, everyone seeks success and aims to achieve a prominent status by doing something remarkable.

Everyone has dreams, including you and I. Some aspire to be world champions, like Muhammad Ali Clay, while others hope to invent something special inspired by figures such as Thomas Edison, Marie Curie, and Alexander Fleming. Many aim to revolutionize the tech industry, following in the footsteps of Bill Gates, Steve Jobs, and Elon Musk. Many want to rule the playing field, like Ronaldo, Messi, Shane Warne, Vivian Richards, Virat Kohli, Roger

Federer, Martina Hingis, Michael Phelps, Jahangir Khan, Shahbaz Senior, and Samiullah Khan, who have dominated their respective sports. Some dream of becoming successful entrepreneurs like Warren Buffett and Jeff Bezos. Others are driven by the desire to serve humanity, following the examples set by Mother Teresa and Abdul Sattar Edhi. Many wish to heal patients, inspired by doctors like Dr. Adib Rizvi, Sir Alfred Cuschieri, and Harrison. Some individuals aspire to motivate their nations, like Allama Mohammad Iqbal. Lastly, some dream of being great leaders, following the paths of Nelson Mandela and Quaid-e-Azam Muhammad Ali Jinnah.

What is it that prevents most individuals from realizing their aspirations, while only a handful manage to succeed? Why do our goals often go unachieved? Why do we lose hope? If we have shortcomings, what is at their core? Those who have developed conveniences for humanity have made significant sacrifices and achieved numerous scientific breakthroughs. Those who have conquered space, explored the oceans, and discovered cures for multiple diseases. Those who have lifted their countries and nations out of crises and elevated them to the ranks of developed nations. Those who have demonstrated what it means to be among the best of creation. We find joy and inspiration in their stories through literature and films that celebrate their accomplishments. We admire them as role models and inspire our children to follow their example. Who are those people?

They are not aliens or beings with magical powers, but simply human beings like us. However, what do they have that we lack? If they can dream, then so can we. So, why do the dreams of billions like us often remain unfulfilled? Why do those who make grand claims become afraid of taking practical action? Why do so many hardworking, talented, and determined young people lose hope, stumble, and eventually fade into obscurity? Why do countless courageous and spirited people lose motivation just a few steps away from their destination?

To solve this puzzle, it is essential to reference the model created by American psychologist Abraham Maslow. In 1954, he published his book "Motivation and Personality", which introduced a prioritized list of human needs known as "The Hierarchy of Needs." Maslow initially presented his theory in 1943 under the title "A Theory of Human Motivation." This classification serves as a fundamental framework for understanding human psychology.

Maslow's theory suggests that when someone experiences hunger or thirst, their primary focus becomes fulfilling those fundamental needs. Once those needs are satisfied, their attention moves to concerns about safety and security. After establishing a sense of safety, individuals aim to cultivate love and connection in their relationships. Next, they shift their focus to building self-esteem. Ultimately, when all these needs are addressed, individuals pursue self-actualization and a deeper understanding of themselves.

Reflecting on Abraham Maslow's concepts, it is evident that most people spend their lives focused on fulfilling basic needs, such as food and water. Their primary goal is to support their families by working hard day and night. Those with greater resources tend to grapple with issues concerning their safety and security. Only a select few truly experience the joys of love, respect, and acknowledgment. Ideally, those fortunate enough to have wealth, protection, love, recognition, and respect should strive for personal growth, pursue their aspirations, and contribute to the betterment of humanity. Sadly, many of these privileged individuals become entangled in material comforts and luxuries. Instead of aiming for their full potential, they may become complacent, abandoning their high aspirations and dreams without fully tapping into their talents or quitting midway through their endeavors.

Life is a valuable gift from nature that allows us to innovate and make a positive impact on humanity. When we fail to embrace this purpose, our lives can seem directionless and unfulfilling, regardless of our wealth and social status. Therefore, it is essential to cultivate qualities such as courage, determination, resilience, and a strong belief in our ability to succeed while actively pursuing our dreams. Without dedication, our aspirations may turn into regrets. Remember that while having considerable talent is essential, effectively applying those skills is just as crucial for achieving success in life.

That's why, in a world with billions of people, only a few achieve accurate self-awareness and self-actualization. Furthermore, among those individuals, only a small number truly recognize their natural talents and use them to help humanity. Finding such unique individuals is like searching for a rare gem.

Contrary to Abraham Maslow's theory, a closer look at the lives of those who have achieved global fame, success, and even Nobel Prizes reveals a secret. These exceptional individuals, despite facing numerous challenges—be it economic, social, or personal—pursue their dreams by harnessing their unique abilities. Like everyone else, they experience fatigue, poverty, and worries. They face heartbreak, loss, and their lives are filled with grief. Yet, they continue to strive for their dreams, often sacrificing their time, energy, and resources. They push through difficulties, ignoring hunger, thirst, and safety concerns, driven by their commitment to their vision. Ultimately, they not only achieve their goals but also become role models for others.

Thomas Carlyle said, "World history is merely the biography of great men. A great man is like lightning from the sky, whose brilliance dazzles the eyes and astonishes the surroundings."

Let's discuss Imran Khan, a prominent figure from Pakistan.

Since gaining independence in 1947, many individuals from Pakistan have made significant contributions across various sectors, earning both national and international recognition. However, the global respect, fame, and achievements that Imran Khan has attained over the last fifty years are unparalleled among his fellow countrymen.

Prominent figures and leaders in every domain worldwide are acclaimed and admired for their expertise and enduring success in their respective fields. Imran Khan stands out as a unique individual whose fame and respect are not solely attributed to his cricketing career but also to his exceptional achievements in various fields, including health, education, social welfare, and politics. These accomplishments distinguish him from other notable personalities and leaders both in Pakistan and around the world.

Reflecting on Imran Khan's life journey—his goals, aspirations, grand dreams, and tireless efforts to realize them—reminds me of the famous saying by former President of India and scientist APJ Abdul Kalam: "A dream is not what you see in your sleep, but rather what wakes you up."

A brief overview of Imran Khan's life, spanning 72 years, reveals fascinating and impressive facts that are hard to deny. At just nine years old, Imran dreamed of becoming a test cricketer after watching his cousins represent Pakistan. Despite early setbacks, he captained Pakistan to its only ODI World Cup title in 1992. His contributions to cricket have earned him recognition as one of the greatest all-rounders and captains in cricket history.

At the peak of his cricket career, this exceptional captain decided to retire. After retiring, he had the opportunity to earn substantial money and enjoy luxurious travels, just like other legendary cricketers. However, instead of pursuing his lavish Playboy lifestyle, he surprised everyone by announcing an ambitious plan to build a world-class cancer hospital. This facility would provide free care and treatment for those suffering from cancer in his country.

Despite repeated advice and suggestions from friends and experts to abandon the idea of building a free cancer hospital in a poor country like Pakistan, Khan, with sincere determination, the grace of God, and the support and prayers of the Pakistani nation, turned this seemingly impossible task into reality by establishing the world-class Shaukat Khanum Memorial Cancer Hospital. Building the hospital was undoubtedly a significant challenge, but running it successfully proved to be almost impossible. While many were skeptical and predicted Khan's failure, he remained focused on his next goals.

After successfully managing the hospital, Khan decided to embark on a new journey into politics, aiming to rid his nation of oppression and injustice. This move surprised the world and disturbed the traditional dynastic politicians.

Khan began his political career with his emerging political party, Pakistan Tehreek-e-Insaf (PTI). Simultaneously, he achieved significant success in the field of education by being elected Chancellor of the University of Bradford and establishing Namal College. This college was established in the underprivileged area of his hometown, Mianwali, providing deserving students with access to free, world-class, and modern technical education.

Successfully confronting and combating the accusations and negative tactics of shrewd, opportunistic, corrupt, and traditional politicians in the political arena, building the Shaukat Khanum Cancer Hospital in Peshawar after its establishment in Lahore, and soon expanding to Karachi; gradually enhancing the quality, capacity, departments, and student enrollment at Namal College, ultimately elevating it to Namal University; defeating established dynastic political parties after 22 years of an incredible democratic struggle; and becoming the Prime Minister of Pakistan and the most popular leader in Pakistan and the Islamic world—especially after being ousted from power through a regime change operation—are all manifestations of the fact that Khan is on a profound journey of faith and self-actualization where one feels a divine calling to express his will.

While it's easy to narrate, listen to, read about, and write about such achievements, the reality of accomplishing them is nearly impossible.

Prominent individuals, including leaders, scientists, politicians, educators, writers, poets, athletes, artists, Nobel Prize laureates, and experts in various fields, have earned their recognition through exceptional skills and remarkable achievements, all of which are the result of a lifetime of hard work and dedication. Upon closer examination, it becomes evident that the honor, fame, and unique position conferred by nature on the exceptional son of Shaukat Khanum are probably unmatched by anyone to date. While a few prominent figures may have succeeded in politics alongside their primary fields, none have attained the remarkable international fame, success, and recognition in sports, health, education, social, and political realms that Imran Khan has.

Imran Khan is unique in that he has effectively merged the roles of athlete, philanthropist, influencer, politician, and widely admired leader. Even in the face of tough situations, perilous challenges, hardship, and criticism, he has realized every aspiration, reached every goal, and distinguished himself in all areas.

Jack Canfield's words resonate here: "Whatever you want to achieve is on the other side of fear."

Imran Khan has demonstrated unparalleled determination, resilience, conviction, and bravery, breaking through every barrier of fear. Despite being unjustly imprisoned at the age of 72, he endures challenges in solitude. He is dedicated to realizing his ultimate vision of a "New Pakistan," rooted in the ideals of the "State of Madina," and strives for genuine liberation from the corrupt forces that dominate the nation.

Research indicates that all successful and renowned individuals who have achieved global fame, respect, and recognition in their fields have primarily done so due to their intelligence, skills, performance, contributions, and inventions. The world often recognizes this success only after these individuals have fully utilized their talents and dedicated their lives to hard work, perseverance, and commitment in their respective areas.

Here, this question arises. How did Imran Khan rise to prominence as a renowned playboy, an outstanding cricket captain and all-rounder, a prominent philanthropist, the Chancellor of the University of Bradford, the Prime Minister of a significant nuclear nation, and a highly influential global leader—all in one lifetime?

To address this question, it's essential to examine Imran Khan's character, thoughts, beliefs, ideology, and the significant events that have shaped his life. The first part of the three-volume series "The Dreamer" aims to provide in-depth insights into this extraordinary historical figure. Readers who approach this volume with an open mind may find it helpful to evaluate, based on the evidence presented, whether Khan embodies hope or despair.

The Power of Passion

Success isn't a matter of luck, a coincidence, or a gift; it stems from relentless perseverance, substantial sacrifices, and the obstacles faced along the way. This kind of achievement is meant for individuals who are dedicated, energetic, and creative, driven by a strong enthusiasm for their aspirations. Everyone strives for success and pursues it. However, to be truly recognized as a winner, one must cross the finish line by skillfully using one's physical, mental, and emotional capabilities, outpacing one's rivals.

Can anyone believe that Imran Khan, who took a wicket on the last ball of his cricket career at the age of 40, won the game as captain and led his team to become world champions in the 1992 World Cup final? Interestingly, he had been out of the national team for three years due to a disappointing performance in his first international match. From dreaming of joining the national team to rising from obscurity and becoming a national hero, Khan faced numerous challenges and overcame significant obstacles throughout his journey. Ultimately, he earned the title of the most outstanding captain and all-rounder in cricket history, maintaining his charisma despite retiring three decades ago.

At the age of 9, he felt motivated to pursue a career as a successful cricketer after witnessing his cousins, Javed Barki and Majid Khan, play on the cricket fields and represent their nation. Over time, this desire evolved into an obsession, propelling him to prefer spending time with a bat and ball rather than focusing on his studies. As a result, by the age of 13, Imran Khan was playing cricket regularly.

He joined the Pakistan national cricket team at the age of 19 during the 1971 tour of England. His debut match, however, was quite disappointing. He bowled 28 overs in both innings but failed to take any wickets. With the bat, he managed to score just five runs. Following this poor performance, he was dropped from the team.

Imran Khan chose to stay in the UK for educational purposes instead of returning to Pakistan with the team. This decision prompted critics to question his selection and the Barki family's influence, and they made negative comments about the situation. Critics argued that the cricket board favored Imran Khan by arranging a free trip to England for him.

Instead of feeling upset and disappointed by his poor performance and the criticism he faced, Imran Khan chose to reflect on his shortcomings, improve his technique, and return to the team fully prepared. To achieve this, Khan dedicated himself to intensive practice and physical training, spending as much time as possible on the field. During this period, he was also honored to be elected captain of the Oxford University cricket team.

Initially, Imran Khan bowled at medium pace with a chest-on action, but this technique did not bring him much success. He then dedicated himself to improving his pace and style while strengthening his body fitness. Contrary to critics' predictions, he successfully enhanced both his bowling speed and technique.

After three years of tireless work and patience, he returned to the team in 1974. On July 26, 1974, during the second day of the Leeds test against England, Imran Khan achieved a significant milestone by taking his first international wicket, with Wasim Bari catching Tony Gregg. This match marked the beginning of an invaluable and unforgettable journey of success for him, as he took two wickets in the game.

Imran Khan was a member of the national cricket team during the 1976-77 tour of Australia and the West Indies. His exceptional fast bowling skills gained international recognition during this tour. Thanks to his outstanding performance, Pakistan achieved a historic milestone by winning its first test match against Australia on its home ground in Sydney, bringing pride to the entire nation.

At the 1978 Perth fast bowling contest, he delivered at 139.7 km/h, finishing third after Jeff Thompson and Michael Holding, while surpassing Dennis Lillee and others. As a result, Pakistan gained a new hero in the form of Imran Khan.

Imran Khan is recognized as the pioneer of reverse swing bowling and played a vital role in teaching this technique to Wasim Akram and Waqar Younas, who went on to popularize it further. His consistent all-around performance significantly contributed to Pakistan's success, resulting in numerous memorable victories and enhancing his fame. Due to his remarkable achievements, he was appointed captain of the Pakistan cricket team in 1982.

Imran Khan gained widespread respect and fame as a fast bowler from 1980 to 1988. During this period, he took

236 test wickets at an impressive average of 17.17 runs per wicket. He achieved the milestone of five wickets in a single innings eighteen times and ten wickets in a match on five occasions. Notably, his bowling average and strike rate were superior to those of renowned bowlers such as Richard Hadlee (19.03), Malcolm Marshall (20.20), Dennis Lillee (24.07), Joel Garner (20.62), and Michael Holding (23.68).

He became the second-fastest in history, after Ian Botham, to the all-rounder double of 3,000 runs and 300 wickets, accomplishing it in 75 tests. He has a batting average of 61.86, which is the second-highest for a batsman batting at number six in tests. His test career ended in January 1992 when he faced Sri Lanka at Faisalabad.

He concluded his career with 3,807 runs from 126 innings across 88 test matches, averaging 37.69. His career includes six centuries and 18 half-centuries, with a highest score of 136. As a bowler, he took 362 wickets in test cricket, becoming the first Pakistani and the fourth bowler worldwide to achieve this milestone. Khan played in 175 One-Day Internationals (ODIs), scoring 3,709 runs at an average of 33.41. His highest score was 102 not out, and his best bowling performance was six wickets for just 14 runs.

As captain, Imran Khan played in 48 test matches. Out of these, Pakistan won 14 games, lost eight, and drew 26. He also participated in 139 One Day Internationals (ODIs), with 77 wins, 57 losses, and one tied match. In his second match as captain, Khan led Pakistan to its first test victory on English soil at Lord's after a 28-year gap. He set a record for the best test bowling figures of his career by taking eight wickets for 58 runs against Sri Lanka in Lahore in 1982. That same year, he ranked first in both bowling and batting during the three-test series against England, achieving 21 wickets and a batting average of 56 runs.

Additionally, in the 1982 series against India, Khan captured 40 wickets in six Test matches, with an impressive average of 13.95. By the end of the 1982-1983 series, he had taken a total of 88 wickets in 13 test matches as captain within the year. Notably, during the same test series against India, he was sidelined from cricket for over two years due to a stress fracture in his leg.

After recovering by the end of 1984, he made a triumphant return to international cricket during the latter part of the 1984–1985 season. Shortly after rejoining the team and taking on the captaincy, Khan led Pakistan to another victory against the West Indies. He later described this performance as "the last time I bowled well." In 1987, Khan guided Pakistan to their first Test series victory in India. That same year, he achieved remarkable bowling figures of 10 wickets for 77 runs at Headingly in England, leading Pakistan to their first series-deciding victory.

Imran Khan announced his retirement from international cricket following the 1987 World Cup. However, Pakistan's President, Gen. Zia-ul-Haq, convinced him to continue playing and represent the country. In 1988, Khan was awarded the Man of the Series for taking 23 wickets in just three test matches against the West Indies. He also holds several world records, including the most wickets taken by a captain in test matches, the best bowling strike rate, the best bowling average, the best bowling figures of 8 wickets for 60 runs, and the achievement of five wickets in a match six times.

Captaining Pakistan to the 1992 Cricket World Cup title was the crowning moment of Imran Khan's illustrious career. He stated, "The team selected for the World Cup was strong, but unfortunately, two match-winners, Saeed Anwar and Waqar Younas, were unfit. When we arrived at the World Cup, Javed Miandad and I became unfit. However, we must commend the fighting spirit of this team, which embarked on its journey to victory from a point where most teams would typically give up. That was the greatest strength of our team."

When the 1992 World Cup began, the West Indies defeated Pakistan in the first match. A potential defeat against England was narrowly avoided due to rain; however, after suffering successive losses to South Africa and India, Pakistan's chances of success began to dwindle. Following a win against Zimbabwe, Pakistan found itself at the bottom of the points table, positioned only above Zimbabwe after playing 5 out of 8 matches in the group stage. Imran Khan emerged as a true leader and captain at that critical moment. He motivated his team to fight like a "cornered tiger," lifting them from despair. He boosted their morale and assured them that they would win the World Cup, God willing.

His leadership, combined with the nation's prayers during Ramadan, lifted the team's spirits and fueled a miraculous turnaround. With renewed enthusiasm, they stepped onto the field. They won their remaining matches, stunning the world and cricket fans alike by defeating Australia, Sri Lanka, and the previously unbeaten New

Zealand. A crucial point in a rain-affected game against England secured their place in the semi-finals. In the semi-finals, they not only ended New Zealand's hopes of becoming world champions but also delivered one of the biggest upsets in World Cup history. Then, in the final match held at the historic Melbourne Cricket Ground, a seemingly weak Pakistan team, led by Imran Khan, achieved the impossible by defeating England by 22 runs. Imran Khan's impressive innings of 72 runs and the decisive final wicket marked a memorable evening, as he received the crystal trophy from Sir Colin Cowdrey, proclaiming Pakistan as world champions. This moment is still celebrated as a pivotal milestone for both Pakistan and cricket fans.

The legendary captain, Imran Khan, retired from cricket gracefully while he was still at the peak of his career. He consistently captivated both rival teams and cricket enthusiasts with his bravery and integrity on the field during matches. During the Leeds Test in 1987, when wicketkeeper Saleem Yousuf appealed for Ian Botham's catch—despite the ball having hit the ground—Imran Khan scolded Saleem for making a wrong appeal.

Imran Khan has asked batsmen who were unhappy with the umpire's decision to continue batting on three occasions during his captaincy. One notable example occurred during the 1989 ODI against India in Lahore. When Srikanth expressed his dissatisfaction after being given out LBW, Imran Khan invited him to bat again, which Srikanth immediately accepted. However, Waqar Younas, proving his captain's trust, dismissed Srikanth on the very next ball, caught by Saleem Yousuf, leading to a disgraceful exit towards the pavilion. The second incident took place in the West Indies when Desmond Haynes was leaving the field after the umpire declared him out. Imran Khan called him back, insisting that the umpire had made a wrong decision. The third time it happened in New Zealand, where Imran Khan again summoned Jeff Crowe back to bat after the umpire ruled him out wrongly.

During Imran Khan's tenure, the umpires from the host country also served as match referees. Such practices frequently led to disputed calls that favored the home side, resulting in losses for visiting teams and frustration among their supporters. To address this issue and promote transparency in the game, Imran Khan proposed inviting foreign or neutral umpires to officiate all matches held in Pakistan. The International Cricket Council (ICC) not only praised this initiative but also made the use of neutral umpires a permanent practice in the sport of cricket.

Imran Khan faced a ban for participating in the Kerry Packer series at the height of his cricket career. Despite the ban and the criticism he received, he remained steadfast in his beliefs. Even after returning to the game, he continued to defend the Kerry Packer series, which notably transformed the sport of cricket. While addressing an ICC event in Mumbai on November 7, 2008, Imran Khan referred to Kerry Packer as a benefactor of the game of cricket. He stated, "He extended the life of cricket. I believe Kerry Packer's initiative was a turning point that fundamentally changed the game." Imran Khan said, "Because of Kerry Packer, one-day matches, night matches, and colorful uniforms were introduced to cricket, which ultimately improved the sport overall."

Even those who opposed him admit that Pakistan has never had another player or leader of his caliber. Khan's captivating bowling style, reverse-swinging Yorkers, formidable captaincy, and charismatic personality have contributed significantly to the popularity of cricket in the Indo-Pak subcontinent. Rather than fearing failure or being affected by criticism, Khan consistently focused on his fitness and technique, turning the impossible into reality.

In his book "Imperfect," prominent Indian batsman Sanjay Manjrekar beautifully recounts an interesting incident that illustrates Imran Khan's dedication and focus during a match. He described a moment from the 1989 Faisalabad test when a ball that had lightly touched Sachin Tendulkar's bat proceeded to the wicketkeeper. Surprisingly, no one from the Pakistani team, except for Imran Khan, appealed for the wicket because no one else had heard the sound of the ball hitting the bat. Although the umpire rejected the appeal, Imran Khan was convinced that Tendulkar was out. As he returned to his fielding position, he told his teammates, "The sound has come," emphasizing this claim. Tendulkar was aware that the ball had touched his bat. At the end of the over, he expressed his astonishment to Manjrekar about Imran Khan, saying, "What a man he is! What sharp ears." Manjrekar wrote that the sound, which went unheard by the wicketkeeper and the umpire, was audible to Imran Khan, positioned at mid-on.

Jeff Boycott has stated, "When it comes to great captains, Imran has always been my top choice."

Tony Greig stated that "under Imran Khan's leadership, there was never any question of someone else taking over the captaincy, which may have contributed to Pakistan's victory in the 1992 World Cup".

Viv Richards remarked on Imran's prowess as a competitor, noting, "No matter how well you were batting, he always had a tactic that would destroy you. I respect Imran and his cricketing ideas."

Martin Crowe regarded Imran as "the most superb all-rounder after Garry Sobers".

The BBC referred to Imran Khan as "one of the best fast bowlers in the world."

ESPN Cricinfo declared him "the greatest cricketer to emerge from Pakistan and the second-best all-rounder in the world after Garry Sobers."

In the ICC test bowlers' rankings, Imran Khan is ranked third overall and has been recognized as the best bowler of the last 100 years.

Throughout his cricket career, Imran Khan received multiple Man of the Match and Man of the Series awards, five of which were earned against the West Indies. He was inducted into the Wisden Cricketer of the Year award in 1989 and the ICC "Hall of Fame" in 2010. Additionally, the Government of Pakistan honored him with the Hilal-e-Imtiaz and the President's Medal for Meritorious Service.

In 2020, Imran Khan was honored with the Mohammed bin Rashid Al Maktoum Creative Sports Award for his significant contributions to the sport of cricket. In a poll conducted by the ICC in 2021, he received 47.3% of the votes and was recognized as the best captain among those included in the poll. Indian captain Virat Kohli came in second place with 46.2% of the votes.

Imran Khan is truly a king in the world of cricket. His captivating charm, strong leadership, bravery, intellect, and remarkable performances have left a lasting mark. He has captured the admiration of cricket enthusiasts worldwide. Although he retired more than three decades ago, Imran's legacy and impact on the game remain strong, driven by his memorable performances and significant accomplishments.

The True Taj Mahal

A mother commands the deepest love, honor, and dignity in all human bonds. She is the first person we connect with, feeling our earliest movements and kicks. After enduring many hardships, she carries and protects us in her womb with patience and calm. The term "Mother" represents unconditional love, kindness, grace, solace, support, authenticity, devotion, and bravery.

Taking care of one's parents, especially mothers, is seen by individuals as both a privilege and a crucial obligation. We strive to make our parents happy, honor their desires, heed their guidance, and do our best to alleviate their challenges and meet their needs. Yet, those who can demonstrate their profound love for their mothers by engaging in actions that benefit humanity and inspire those around them are genuinely lucky.

The Gulab Devi and Shaukat Khanum Hospitals in Lahore, founded by Lala Lajpat Rai and Imran Khan, represent a genuine embodiment of love, much like the Taj Mahal. These hospitals stand as living monuments to the profound love sons carry for their mothers. This sentiment resonates globally and is of greater importance than the marble Taj Mahal in Agra. As the renowned poet Sahir Ludhianvi remarked about the marble monument, "An emperor has mocked the love of us common folk by using his wealth to create it."

In memory of his mother, Shrimati Gulab Devi, who passed away from tuberculosis in 1927, Lajpat Rai founded the Gulab Devi Hospital in 1934. This hospital was established to treat tuberculosis patients and has helped millions recover.

In early 1984, when Imran Khan's mother was diagnosed with cancer, his family was overwhelmed with grief and concern. This painful experience prompted the cricket superstar to reevaluate his perspective on life and his daily routine. Witnessing his mother's agony, alongside the absence of proper cancer care in Pakistan, deeply shaped his outlook. He took her to London for treatment, but his heart ached at the thought of impoverished Pakistanis who have cancer without access to proper medical care.

While his mother was being treated at Mayo Hospital in Lahore, he listened to the distressing stories of cancer patients and their families. Hearing about their fears of the deadly disease, as well as the financial burdens it imposed, left him shocked and disturbed.

The pain of his beloved mother brought him to tears, while the death of his fellow countrymen from untreated illnesses tormented his soul. The weak voice of his brave mother filled him with anxiety, and the despair on the faces of impoverished cancer patients troubled him deeply. His mother tried to hide her suffering to spare him more pain, and in turn, her son's love and care strengthened her courage.

Khan watched in painful silence as his mother took her last breath. In that moment, he felt a passionate drive to ensure that cancer patients in his country would receive the best possible diagnosis and treatment. That painful experience turned his devotion to his mother into a mission to serve his people, which grew into a lifelong love for humanity. Driven by a dedication to fulfilling God's purpose and caring for His creations, Imran Khan set out to establish a top-tier hospital in Pakistan that would offer cancer treatment at no cost.

In his autobiography "Pakistan, A Personal History," Imran Khan reflects on a poignant moment: "When we returned to Pakistan on February 10, 1985, with my mother's body, my resolve to establish a cancer hospital for our nation grew even stronger. It would be my humble tribute to her. I repeatedly reaffirmed this determination."

Imran Khan experienced injuries and fitness issues multiple times during his cricket career, a common occurrence among athletes. However, watching his brave mother battle a severe illness and face the end of her life was a profound shock and a significant test of his patience. Cancer, being a life-threatening disease, poses a serious challenge not only for the patient but also for their family.

Imran Khan never imagined that the mother who once cradled him in her arms would no longer be able to place her loving hand on his head. The mother who once told him bedtime stories could no longer confide her sorrows to him. The mother who fed him would now need him to help her even drink water. The mother, who was always happy to see him, would forget to smile. The brave mother who encouraged him would herself become frail. In those tender moments, as the mother was walking away from her son's world, fate tested his strength and restraint.

Imran Khan did everything possible to ensure his mother's treatment and recovery. Despite his global fame, connections, immense effort, and access to excellent medical care, Shaukat Khanum ultimately lost her battle with cancer. However, through the establishment of the Shaukat Khanum Cancer Hospital, she became a source of hope for millions of patients. In this way, she achieved a form of immortality, remaining prominent both in this world and the hereafter.

Imran Khan grew up under his mother's influence, where he learned to live fearlessly, serve humanity selflessly, and never lose courage or give up. He was taught not to fear what tomorrow might bring and always to dream big, for Allah appreciates individuals who do so. As a result, Allah's help and grace are always with those who are determined.

Shaukat Khanum's dedicated education and training had a profound influence on her son. Instead of succumbing to the grief and shock of his mother's passing, he chose to honor her memory by following her advice and vision. He quietly shared his dream with friends and family: to build a cancer hospital in Pakistan that would meet a critical need. While everyone praised the idea, many raised concerns about its feasibility in a developing country, questioning its potential for success. Nevertheless, Khan remained resolute, driven by his strong faith, conviction, and determination. With unwavering belief, he took action and announced that, with public support, he would establish a premier cancer hospital in Pakistan, where 75 percent of cancer patients would receive treatment free of charge. His commitment surprised the world.

The majority of people described Khan's decision as emotional, while 19 out of 20 experts considered it impossible. Despite this, Khan remained steadfast and refused to change his mind. His mother's prayers and good wishes strengthened his resolve. The sighs, sobs, and tears of cancer patients fueled his determination to achieve his goal quickly. In pursuit of his dream, Khan bid farewell to the luxurious life of a prince, surrounded by beauty, and began collecting donations for the hospital.

In his quest to raise 550 million rupees, Khan used various methods to connect with both influential figures and common citizens. He also celebrated a World Cup victory during this time. When he faced challenges in reaching his goal, he sought assistance from innocent children and students. Khan relentlessly advocated for his cause by visiting schools, colleges, streets, and markets, even embarking on a 30-city tour by truck that lasted around the clock.

Pakistanis rallied behind Khan, pouring in their time, energy, and donations to support their hero. This collective effort led to the realization of his ambitious vision with the founding of the impressive Shaukat Khanum Cancer Hospital (SKMCH), which was inaugurated on December 29, 1994.

Indeed, Shaukat Khanum's extraordinary love, compassion, guidance, and encouragement played a crucial role in helping her son achieve this significant milestone—one that will be remembered by humanity for generations to come.

All over the world, countless individuals have established numerous hospitals to provide free treatment for those in need, fulfilling their duty to help humanity. However, Shaukat Khanum Hospital (SKMCH) is truly unique for several important reasons:

1. The hospital was constructed not by the wealth of an individual, ruler, or family, but through the donations and generosity of the people of Pakistan.

2. Its main focus is to provide high-quality, free treatment to underprivileged patients, funded through zakat and charity. The hospital is not intended to evade business taxes or conceal illicit income.

3. This hospital is unique as it provides free treatment to 75% of private-sector cancer patients without any government support.

4. Shaukat Khanum Hospital is dedicated not only to treatment but also to recognized research, education, and the global training of medical staff.

5. The hospital funds all operational costs through public donations and services from radiology, laboratory, and other departments.

6. Despite offering expensive cancer treatments at no cost to 75% of its patients, this charitable hospital consistently expands its capacity and services. The success of SKMCH in Lahore and Peshawar, along with the upcoming inauguration of Asia's largest SKMCH in Karachi, clearly demonstrates this growth.

7. The Shaukat Khanum Memorial Cancer Hospital and Research Centers in Lahore and Peshawar have received the Joint Commission International (JCI) Gold Seal of

Approval for establishing and maintaining international healthcare standards.

8. The organization's website offers an audit report from 1989 to the present, allowing anyone to review the donations received and how they have been utilized.

9. The SKMCH has obtained formal Sharia compliance certification, demonstrating that the collection, utilization, and management of Zakat funds strictly adhere to Sharia principles.

10. By establishing a world-class free cancer hospital and successfully operating it for the past thirty years, Imran Khan has demonstrated on a global stage that the Pakistani nation is capable of achieving seemingly impossible goals.

Between 1984, when Imam Khan first envisioned building a free cancer hospital, and its completion in 1994, he faced numerous challenges and hardships with remarkable patience and determination. Despite setbacks and discouraging advice, he never lost hope.

The SKMCH, which generated revenue of Rs 141 million in its first year, has seen its revenue grow to Rs 30,164 million by 2023. The hospital occupies 20 acres in Lahore and offers 195 beds, while its location in Peshawar covers 6.25 acres and has 60 beds. To date, Shaukat Khanum Hospital has treated 137,005 cancer patients and provided diagnostic services to millions of people. The institution employs 3,861 staff members and has spent Rs 96 billion on patient care and services.

In 2023, a total of 13,483 new cases of cancer were registered. Additionally, 328,741 patients visited outdoor clinics, and 15,645 patients were admitted to the hospital. Throughout the year, 17,917 surgeries were performed, while 6,139,492 pathology tests and 228,224 radiology tests were conducted. Furthermore, 79,998 patients received chemotherapy, and 80,544 patients underwent radiotherapy. The overall expenditure for these services amounted to Rs. 22,744 million.

The figures underscore the unwavering trust that the Pakistani nation has in this hospital, which has been delivering world-class cancer treatment for the past three decades. It is the only hospital in the world that operates solely on public donations, offering free cancer treatment to 75% of its patients, and consistently sets new standards of success.

Despite facing accusations, slander, obstacles, and even imprisonment, Imran Khan remains committed to working for the betterment of his country and its people. His deeds and words reflect his mother's teachings and keep alive the vow he once gave her.

If the intention was to honor his mother, the establishment of the hospital in Lahore has already fulfilled that aim. However, the plans for additional cancer hospitals in Peshawar and Karachi suggest that Imran Khan has broader ambitions, reflecting a commitment to aiding humanity and bringing joy to people. The Shaukat Khanum Hospitals in Lahore and Peshawar, with a new facility set to open in Karachi, symbolize a pledge to offer care and support to those in need. They will serve as a genuine symbol of everlasting love for humanity, dedicated to celebrating the spirit of motherhood forever.

The Shining Star

Imran Khan frequently visited his ancestral home in Mianwali during his free time. However, during the 2002 election campaign, he had the opportunity to witness, for the first time, the backwardness of his hometown. He witnessed the widespread joblessness, limited education and technical expertise, as well as the deep frustration and hopelessness of the youth. The genuine love, respect, and sincerity he received from the community, along with the hopes they placed in their national hero, compelled Imran Khan to seriously consider how he could improve the lives of the people in his area.

If Imran Khan had wanted to, he could have deceived them with fake reassurances, false promises, and unrealistic visions. However, instead of offering temporary and superficial solutions, Khan sought a permanent, sustainable, and practical approach to ensure the bright future of his region and its underprivileged youth. His efforts could transform the fate of Mianwali and uplift its impoverished residents, enabling the youth to emerge from the depths of despair. This would enable them to experience a sense of relief in an uplifting atmosphere and showcase their skills on an international level, thereby gaining recognition for Pakistan.

As Khan battled with his inner turmoil and quest for meaning, he found himself captivated by the stunning scenery of Namal Lake, surrounded by the hills of the Salt Range in his hometown region. This moment sparked an idea that had long eluded him in his dreams. Instead of merely providing food, Khan aimed to ease his community's struggles by equipping them with the skills of fishing. He envisioned imparting skills that would enable them to live independently and with dignity, rather than succumbing to starvation and unemployment.

Khan sought to revolutionize knowledge, technology, and research by establishing a world-class, sustainable education project for present and future generations. With a focus on sports and health behind him, he made a bold decision to enter the realm of education and technical skills, aiming to brighten the future of underprivileged youth. He planned to establish a premier educational institution near Namal Lake, where the underprivileged class could receive free, high-quality education, technical training, and skills development. His goal was to empower his people to secure prominent positions in society and earn a respectful livelihood.

Imran Khan, who has always had grand ambitions, accomplished many of his dreams with the prayers and support of the people. This time, he set himself a formidable target: to create the nation's first world-class knowledge city in the remote and underdeveloped region of Mianwali, to transform the lives of the local community.

During his time as a student, Khan assessed the educational quality at Oxford University, acknowledged its academic significance, and recognized its importance for both personal and national growth. This inspiration led him to establish Namal College in 2002, with the vision of elevating its standards to match those of the University of Oxford.

The advancement and development of nations fundamentally rely on research, knowledge, and skills. The economic success, social progress, technological advancements, and scientific innovations observed in developed countries largely stem from the educational and research efforts of prestigious institutions such as Oxford, Harvard, MIT, and Cambridge. Such universities are acknowledged as centers of learning, providing vital insights and a strong foundation for advancement. Consequently, educational institutions and teachers are held in high esteem and respect across all developed nations. Imran Khan, a student at the University of Oxford, has experienced this reality firsthand.

Among roughly 25,000 universities globally, Oxford, established in 1096, is distinguished as the leading institution, celebrated for its high academic standards, strong principles, and its impact on shaping influential leaders and researchers. Remarkably, the university has been attended by 28 British Prime Ministers, 72 Nobel Prize winners, 160 Olympic medalists, and various notable figures, including Imran Khan. These accomplishments highlight Oxford's prestigious reputation. The faculty includes Nobel laureates and prominent researchers across numerous disciplines. The university comprises 39 semi-independent colleges, six permanent private halls, and a comprehensive array of academic departments, which are generally divided into four divisions, offering programs across all fields of study.

Oxford boasts the world's oldest university museum and the most extensive academic library system in the UK. Established in 1586, Oxford University Press serves as the official press of the university and holds the title of the world's largest university press. Over the years, it has published numerous research papers and books, with a distribution network that spans nearly every continent. Among its numerous publications, the Oxford English Dictionary is its most famous work.

Oxford University's endowment funds exceed £6.1 billion. This substantial financial support enables the university to offer scholarships to a majority of its students. Students enjoy complete freedom and support in designing and completing their research projects. They receive funding for research trips and substantial financial assistance for their start-ups.

Imran Khan's ambition to establish a knowledge city in Pakistan, modeled after the University of Oxford, is often dismissed by his opponents as mere idealism. When a journalist from Newsweek sarcastically asked him, "Are you kidding about building an Oxford University in Pakistan, the most dangerous country in the world in terms of terrorism?" Imran Khan responded with admirable seriousness and politeness, saying, "No, I want to build a successful university like Oxford and Cambridge on this beautiful land."

Khan, who was deeply involved in political and social activities, often found himself preoccupied with thoughts about his constituency's circumstances and his vision of making Namal College a reality. On one hand, he felt a profound joy at the prospect of building a world-class knowledge city in his area. On the other hand, friends and experts considered this idea impractical, given the challenges of Mianwali's underdevelopment and remoteness.

Once more, Khan encountered the same challenges that had tested him during the building of Shaukat Khanum Hospital. Nevertheless, he consistently refused to surrender and remained resolute in his pursuit. Despite the harsh realities surrounding him, Khan clung to hope. Even amidst the chaos and ongoing setbacks in his personal and political life, he kept the vision of Namal College alive in his heart and mind. His past successes, including winning the World Cup and founding the Shaukat Khanum Hospital under seemingly insurmountable conditions, inspired Khan and reinforced his belief in the construction and future success of Namal College.

Paulo Coelho, the author of "The Alchemist", famously stated, "When you want something, the whole universe conspires for you to achieve it."

A French proverb also says, "He who is determined to reach his goal considers every obstacle insignificant."

Imran Khan's dedication to his nation's welfare and the accomplishments he has attained serve as clear proof of the validity of Paulo Coelho's quote and the French proverb.

It is a natural principle that anyone committed to serving God's creation will ultimately succeed. However, Imran Khan never imagined the path and status that awaited him in the pursuit of his dreams this time. No player in the world or any Asian individual had previously achieved such a feat. This accomplishment stands as a historic record and honor. In 2005, Imran Khan was nominated for the position of Chancellor of the University of Bradford in the UK, based on established rules, regulations, and merit. The university is highly regarded for its engineering and management programs, as well as its research initiatives.

To become the Chancellor of the University of Bradford, one does not need to be a British citizen or have an academic background. The Chancellor does not engage directly in teaching or learning activities. Instead, the role requires a strong leader and an effective administrator.

Imran Khan's leadership skills and achievements are reflected in several notable accomplishments, including winning the Cricket World Cup, founding a free cancer hospital, providing a wide range of welfare and social services, combating corruption, promoting the rule of law and justice, and encouraging political engagement among young people. With his extensive experience and natural talents, he was appointed Chancellor of the University of Bradford.

On the auspicious occasion of his appointment as Chancellor, Chris Taylor, then Vice-Chancellor of the University of Bradford, remarked in 2005, "With his charismatic personality, international reputation, outstanding achievements, and charitable activities, Imran Khan will not only enhance the reputation, quality, and performance of the University but will also continue the tradition of electing distinguished and qualified individuals as Chancellors of the University of Bradford. He will serve as a role model for the University and the city's youth. Furthermore, he will strengthen our connections with South Asia and act as a valuable bridge between the East and the

West. Mr. Khan will be formally appointed as Chancellor on December 7. His primary duties will involve awarding degrees to graduates of Bradford and establishing the groundwork for the University's new Institute of Cancer Therapeutics.

Imran Khan was elected as the first and fifth international Chancellor of the University of Bradford in the United Kingdom on December 7, 2005. Before his appointment, the following individuals served as Chancellors: Lord Wilson of Reuvilles from 1966 to 1985, Sir John Harvey Jones from 1986 to 1991, Sir Trevor Holdsworth from 1992 to 1997, and Baroness Betty Lockwood from 1997 to 2005.

Shortly after being elected Chancellor, Imran Khan seized the opportunity to establish a partnership between his proposed Namal College and the University of Bradford. His vision and dedication were recognized, leading to an agreement in December 2005 that granted Namal College associate status with the University of Bradford. A resident, Ghulam Muhammad Silo, generously donated 20235 square meters of land for the college. Construction began in 2006, with significant contributions from both local and overseas donors.

In July 2006, Imran Khan, the Chancellor of the University of Bradford, shared his vision in an interview with the Telegraph and Argus. He expressed his hope that his role at the university would contribute to establishing a center of excellence for technical education in Pakistan. Khan emphasized that this college would focus on serving the country's poorest districts. The University of Bradford is collaborating in the development of the curriculum for this initiative. His primary objective is to build a technical college to address youth unemployment. However, he also aspires for Namal College to become Pakistan's most significant and finest university. With the state education system in decline and high unemployment rates in rural areas, he aims to make young people more employable and equip them with the necessary skills to secure jobs. A delegation from Bradford University is working in Pakistan to assess the local economy's needs.

In 2007, Imran Khan invited ten students from Bradford to participate in a week-long program at Namal College in Pakistan. This initiative aimed to educate participants about Pakistan's economic, cultural, and social challenges and observe the effects of globalization on developing countries. The Yorkshire regional team of the Young Enterprise Organization organized the program, which was supported by the Bradford Council's Bradford Kickstart initiative.

On Sunday, April 27, 2008, the most-awaited moment finally came when Imran Khan officially inaugurated Namal College in Mianwali. This event marked the fulfillment of his commitment to the nation and transformed a seemingly impossible dream into reality. A large crowd attended the inauguration ceremony, including Prime Minister Yousaf Raza Gilani, who served as the chief guest, as well as government ministers, educators, philanthropists, and residents of Mianwali. During the event, Prime Minister Gilani and Imran Khan welcomed Professor Mark Cleary, the Vice Chancellor of Bradford University, and Alison Darnborough, the Director of Academic Administration.

In his inaugural address, Imran Khan stated, "During my campaign in Mianwali for the 2002 elections, I was deeply concerned about the high unemployment rate among the youth. As a result, I decided to establish a technical college to help these young people become employable. Now, my dream is to transform this college into a world-class university. The goal is to provide the youth of Pakistan with a quality education supported by high-quality facilities and research from the University of Bradford." Students from various regions, including South Waziristan, Swat, Bannu, Mianwali, and their neighboring districts, have received scholarships. Those studying at Namal College in Mianwali district will follow the same courses as those at the University of Bradford and will graduate with degrees from the University of Bradford."

Mark Cleary, the Vice-Chancellor of the University of Bradford, emphasized the significance of the partnership with Namal College in 2008. He stated, "The University does not grant Associate College status lightly. In our 42-year history since receiving our Royal Charter, we have only granted this status to eight Associate Colleges in the UK and three worldwide. However, we have been deeply impressed by Namal College's vision and values, which align closely with our own high standards." He cited the Shaukat Khanum Memorial Hospital, another partner of the University, as an example of these shared values and standards. Cleary remarked, "We are committed to a long-term engagement that will facilitate the development of a first-class higher education campus at Namal, capable of offering high-quality diplomas and degrees to as many people in the region as possible."

Jeff Lucas, the Deputy Vice-Chancellor of the University of Bradford, responsible for Strategic Partnerships, stated, "We are thrilled to announce that Namal College has officially become an Associate College of the University of Bradford. The university will actively participate in designing and developing the curriculum, as well as creating an educational plan tailored to meet the needs of the Mianwali district. We hope this partnership will enhance young people's employment opportunities upon graduation."

The first development phase will focus on establishing specific subject areas in automotive engineering, information technology, and the construction industries. The second phase will involve developing courses and curricula at Bradford University, improving the training and performance of teachers and staff, and ensuring the implementation and regular use of world-class standards and regulations. Namal College will offer courses in four phases. Phase I will include certificate courses, Phase II will consist of diploma courses, Phase III will feature degree programs, and Phase IV will offer research degree programs. All courses will be taught in English. The initial curriculum will emphasize the following areas: construction (including carpentry and electrical work), automotive engineering, equipment repair, electrical engineering, agricultural equipment manufacturing and maintenance, and work in the cement industry. Additionally, Namal College will engage with primary school children to promote literacy.

The University of Bradford will provide training and degree courses to support the cancer hospital established by Imran Khan. This hospital is forming close connections with the Institute of Cancer Therapeutics at the University of Bradford. The university will offer a BSc in Diagnostic Radiography to students in Pakistan, supporting the hospital that treats 5,000 patients annually. Additionally, a program is being developed to enable sponsored research opportunities for Pakistani students. Initially, two postdoctoral students from Pakistan will come to Bradford to study at the Institute of Cancer Therapeutics. The University of Bradford is actively seeking support from business institutes to fund scholarships that will enable more Pakistani students to study at Bradford.

In 2009, 68 students enrolled in various courses, including computer science, software engineering, web engineering, software development, and network administration. Namal College started its journey with just one degree program. The vision is to transform it into a research university of Oxford quality and to develop a knowledge city where future architects and scholars can study and work in an educational environment reminiscent of Oxford.

In December 2013, during the institution's first convocation ceremony, Imran Khan awarded B.Sc. degrees to 60 engineering students at Namal College. In his speech, Khan emphasized the importance of providing equal educational opportunities to all citizens. He pointed out the prevalent double standard in the country, where children from elite families receive high-quality education in English while those from poorer backgrounds are taught in Urdu. He stated, "The quality of education provided at Namal College is comparable to that of British universities, and the degrees awarded meet international standards." Khan highlighted that this is the only private-sector university in rural Pakistan where the majority of students receive free education through scholarships. He expressed a commitment to attracting more talented students, announcing that agents would be sent to various locations to identify and recruit bright students for the university. To support this effort, the Imran Khan Foundation has been established to provide financial assistance to over 90% of deserving students.

After the historic rally on 30 October 2011, Imran Khan's growing popularity, along with organizational issues and political commitments, made it impossible for him to attend the convocation at the University of Bradford. In February 2014, the university newspaper "The Bradford Student" remarked that "the time has come for senior management to make a decision, and Imran Khan himself should seriously consider whether he can properly fulfill his responsibilities in the prestigious position of Chancellor." Due to his continuous absence from every convocation held since 2010, on 26 February 2014, the University of Bradford Union introduced a motion of no confidence to remove him from the position of Chancellor. As a result, Imran Khan resigned from the chancellorship on 30 November 2014, citing his increasing political commitments.

Imran Khan, upon resigning, stated, "It has been an honor for me to serve as Chancellor of the University of Bradford. This role has been both rewarding and informative, and it is an experience I will always cherish. However, increasing political commitments and the challenges of fundraising for Shaukat Khanum Hospital and Namal College have made it extremely difficult for me to fulfill my responsibilities as Chancellor and to dedicate the necessary time to the position."

The university's vice-chancellor, Brian Cantor, described Mr. Khan as "a wonderful role model for our students." Mr. Khan, the leader of the opposition in Pakistan, faced criticism from some students earlier this year for not attending graduation ceremonies. Professor Cantor emphasized, "Imran Khan has played a key and important role for us as Chancellor of the university. He has awarded degrees to many students here in Bradford. He has also established Namal College, one of the fastest-growing colleges in Pakistan, which awards degrees in partnership with the University of Bradford. Khan's global recognition and commitment to education have not only enhanced the University of Bradford's prestige but have also encouraged our students and strengthened connections between the university and the wider community."

Student Union officer Sam Butterworth stated, "We were saddened to learn of Imran Khan's resignation. He has been a significant figure for both the university and the city. His contributions to politics and philanthropy will always be appreciated."

Imran Khan resigned from his role as Chancellor of the University of Bradford to concentrate on his political activities. Nonetheless, he remained committed to the growth and development of Namal College. In 2016, Namal College established an affiliation with the University of Engineering and Technology Lahore. By early 2019, it was upgraded from a college to the Namal Institute after receiving degree-awarding powers. Over time, Khan's vision for an educational institution evolved into the ambitious goal of creating Namal Knowledge City, the largest university town in Pakistan. The groundbreaking ceremony for Namal Knowledge City took place in 2020, attracting friends and supporters from around the world to help bring Khan's vision to life. The event was a significant success, reaffirming Imran Khan's commitment to establishing a vast consortium of knowledge, skills, and research in a remote, underdeveloped region of Pakistan.

In 2021, Namal Institute reached a significant milestone by becoming Namal University after receiving a charter from the Punjab Assembly. On this historic occasion, Imran Khan stated, "If we want to build a balanced society, we must provide equal opportunities for everyone to progress and thrive. Access to quality higher education creates these opportunities. Making higher education available and affordable for our talented youth will lay the foundation for a vibrant and developed society, enabling us to stand among the ranks of developed nations. Namal University Mianwali aims to provide equal opportunities for the youth in underprivileged rural areas. Establishing a Center of Excellence in such a remote location poses a significant challenge. It will require substantial funding to achieve international standards for the university. I imagine students from underprivileged backgrounds receiving scholarships at the university, students who are currently unable to afford a high-quality education within our prestigious education system. With the provision of financial assistance for the educational expenses of most students, an increasing number of PhD faculty members, and the enthusiastic response from companies and institutions hiring our graduates based on merit, Namal University is rapidly progressing toward our vision of becoming a hub of higher education in the region and fostering development in rural areas. The success of Namal University marks a key milestone in our ultimate goal of creating the largest knowledge city in Pakistan."

Namal University is situated on the scenic banks of Namal Lake, at the foothills of the Salt Range, approximately 30 km from Mianwali City. The institution began its journey in 2008 as a vocational college. From its inception until 2015, Namal College was affiliated with the University of Bradford. From 2016 to 2018, it was affiliated with the University of Engineering and Technology (UET), Lahore. In 2019, it was upgraded to Namal Institute, acquiring degree-awarding status, and by 2021, it was officially renamed Namal University.

In addition to offering undergraduate programs, the university has established two research centers: the Nisar Aziz Agri-Tech Research Center and the Namal Center for Artificial Intelligence. These initiatives have laid the foundation for creating Pakistan's first knowledge city in rural areas, inspired by the model of Oxford University in the UK.

Namal University represents a significant step toward Imran Khan's vision of creating Pakistan's first Knowledge City, known as Namal Knowledge City. Spanning 1,000 acres along the banks of Namal Lake and set against the stunning backdrop of the Salt Range, Namal University is not only beautiful but also rich in diverse wildlife. It is the largest university town in Pakistan, featuring academic buildings, student hostels, faculty apartments, a central library, a mosque, an enterprise hub, and various commercial centers.

Namal University is a hub for a vibrant community of teachers, students, and staff characterized by strong collaboration and unity. This environment is built on high values, including competence, integrity, tolerance, merit, commitment, and social responsibility, all of which aim to establish the university as a center of excellence.

Namal University's primary objective is to empower capable youth to make significant contributions to the country's development, its institutions, and society through education and skill development. The university seeks to develop innovative solutions to the challenges faced by rural areas by leveraging the expertise of highly trained academics. It is designed to integrate education with employment, enabling talented youth to become economically self-sufficient and socially responsible citizens of Pakistan. The goal is to equip students with essential knowledge and professional skills by creating a collaborative framework that fosters public-private partnerships. Both the Namal Education Foundation and Namal University are focused on developing strategic linkages with educational institutions and the industry to promote a culture of collaboration between academia and the workforce. The objective is to promote a culture of research and innovation by integrating creative, technical, and entrepreneurial skills on a shared platform through collaboration between university researchers and businesses. Part of the university's mission is to develop technically skilled individuals who embrace these values. LUMS is a local partner of Namal College. LUMS faculty members offer guidance and advice in managing Namal College and its curriculum.

Students at Namal University come from diverse regions and socio-economic backgrounds across Pakistan. The capable, dynamic, hardworking, and dedicated faculty members conduct research that expands the boundaries of knowledge and imagination. Their teachings equip students for success in both academic and practical fields, fostering a commitment to lifelong learning and teaching. At present, the university comprises four academic departments: Business Studies, Computer Science, Electrical Engineering, and Mathematics. Through these departments, it offers higher education in four undergraduate degree programs: BBA, BS in Computer Science, BS in Electrical Engineering, and BS in Mathematics.

Namal University offers complimentary education to 96% of its student body through a scholarship initiative. The student-to-teacher ratio stands at 12:1, with a current enrollment of 633 students and a staff of 52 teachers. The employment rate for graduates from Namal University is 86%, with 900 alumni successfully entering the workforce. After achieving the status of a degree-awarding institute and university, Namal University is no longer affiliated with the University of Bradford.

Namal University has launched a time bank to impart important social values to students, in addition to providing them with the knowledge and skills needed to build a welfare society and shape their future. The unique aspect of this bank is that it operates without money. Instead, each student is required to deposit 320 hours of their time each year into a social account and a practical work account. These 320 hours must be dedicated to community service activities, which include garbage collection, providing free tuition to school children, participating in tree-planting campaigns, and various projects associated with Namal University's industrial and agricultural institutions. These projects focus on areas such as renewable energy, waste recycling, olive cultivation, and the cultivation of various fruits and vegetables. The Time Bank aims to benefit the country and its citizens in the long term by instilling in students the six core values of Merit, Integrity, Tolerance, Excellence, Commitment, and Social Responsibility.

The university library houses over 12,000 books covering a wide range of subjects, including computer science, electrical engineering, literature, history, religion, and social sciences. Additionally, the magazine section features over 35 international journals and provides access to a variety of digital resources. The library also features a book bank, where students can borrow textbooks for all available courses throughout the semester. There are four computer labs equipped with over 200 computers, available for student use. All computers in the labs are connected to the campus local area network and can be accessed via the Internet and other services.

Namal University provides eight student societies and clubs to enhance leadership skills, education, and training.

1. Namal Environmental Club (NEC): This club promotes awareness of environmental issues and organizes tree-planting campaigns.

2. Namal Idea Club (NIC): The NIC focuses on improving entrepreneurial skills, promoting research ideas, and enhancing students' market understanding.

3. Namal Society for Social Impact (NSSI): This society encompasses the Blood Wing, Education Wing, and Emergency Medical Services Wing. It encourages members to contribute to societal welfare and serve those in need.

4. Namal Literary and Debating Society (LDS): The LDS aims to develop students' creative, literary, writing, and oratory skills.

5. Namal Sports and Adventure Club (NSAC): The NSAC promotes a healthy balance between sports and education, fosters a positive competitive environment among students, nurtures natural talent, and encourages participation in sports activities.

6. Namal Dramatic Club (NDC): This club promotes the arts, music, and acting skills among students.

7. Namal Media Club (VON): The VON covers events happening on and off campus, encourages student participation in photography and videography competitions, and promotes the Namal brand.

8. Skill Development Society (SDS): The SDS focuses on helping students learn English fluently, hone their creative writing skills, and explore developments and innovations in English literature.

Rumi House serves as the headquarters for the Namal Societies. It houses various clubs, including the Rumi Debating Club, Rumi Art and Calligraphy Club, Rumi Reading Club, Rumi Decor Club, and Rumi Writing Club. The editorial board of Rumi House regularly publishes the Rumi Newsletter, which includes reports on significant events, visits, and society activities organized throughout the academic year. This board monitors the progress of each society and club and organizes various events in collaboration with them.

A Quality Enhancement Cell (QEC) has been established at Namal University to transform it into a center of excellence and contribute significantly to the country's development and prosperity. The QEC aims to introduce and implement internationally recognized quality educational standards gradually. It has been functioning at Namal since the institution was an affiliated college of the University of Bradford and later became affiliated with the University of Engineering and Technology (UET), Lahore. After gaining degree-awarding status in 2019, the QEC was accredited by the Higher Education Commission (HEC) by the Quality Assurance Agency (QAA) policy guidelines.

Namal Knowledge City is a project inspired by Imran Khan's vision, and it is being realized through the collaboration of prestigious institutions, including Shaukat Khanum Hospital, LUMS, and Descon Engineering. The facility features a two-story building spanning 62,500 square feet, which houses administrative offices, faculty offices, classrooms, laboratories, and a cafeteria. Additionally, the project encompasses 1,000 acres of land dedicated to the development of Namal Knowledge City. There is also a new academic block adjacent to the main building that features lecture theaters, a main library, two research centers, and a professional development center. Furthermore, a high-quality residential facility has been constructed to provide accommodations for participants attending courses, workshops, and conferences at the university.

The master plan and design for Namal Knowledge City were developed by the renowned American architect Tony Ashai, following approval from the Board of

Governors. Construction on the infrastructure and several essential buildings is set to begin soon. The Namal Education Foundation (NEF) provides both financial and logistical support to Namal University. A Board of Governors oversees all affairs related to Namal University and Namal Knowledge City.

Namal Knowledge City is an innovative project in Pakistan designed to promote a knowledge-based economy by creating the largest consortium in the country focused on stable, sustainable, and meaningful scientific and technological development through education and research. This initiative is the first of its kind in Pakistan, aiming to empower talented students from underprivileged areas by providing them with quality education through scholarships. With the guidance of highly trained educators, these students will be equipped to take on essential roles in developing various institutions, organizations, and communities while also finding innovative solutions to the challenges faced by rural areas.

Namal Knowledge City will feature various facilities, including Schools of Science and Engineering, Medicine, Business, Humanities, and Agribusiness. It will also have libraries, technology parks, business centers, dairy farms, primary and secondary schools, sports facilities, hospitals, shopping centers, hotels, and housing communities for staff, faculty, and students.

The initial stage of building and developing Namal Knowledge City was scheduled to be completed by 2023, with the majority of the project expected to be wrapped up by 2027. However, significant delays have occurred due to the regime change operation against Imran Khan's government and his subsequent arrest. Still, the foundation laid by Imran Khan with the establishment of Namal College in the underdeveloped rural area of Mianwali—aimed at fostering knowledge, skills, and scientific research for the nation's advancement—has started to show positive outcomes. Despite facing various challenges, the Namal Institute is expanding and evolving into a university.

Imran Khan stands out as the sole political leader in Pakistan who not only conceived the idea of a global hub for knowledge and research but also showed a strong dedication to investing in the education and training of both current and future generations. His goal was to empower the youth with the necessary skills to transform the nation's future and elevate it to the level of developed countries. He realized this vision by founding Namal University. In contrast, throughout Pakistan's history, military dictators, political figures, and rulers have generally prioritized their vested interests over the nation's needs.

Despite their various periods in power, Pakistan's military rulers and prominent political families, such as the Bhuttos, Sharifs, and Zardaris, have failed to establish a single world-class educational institution that can effectively educate and train the populace for contemporary scientific needs and future challenges. In contrast, Imran Khan, even before taking office, not only proposed the groundbreaking concept of creating such a technical and educational institution but also successfully established and operates Namal College and University in partnership with Bradford

University in his underserved home region—a feat that many viewed as unimaginable.

Imran Khan, who has studied at Oxford and mainly lived in Europe, recognizes that Pakistan's advancement does not depend on empty promises, false claims, foreign loans, or tall tales. Instead, he asserts that it is crucial to obtain modern scientific knowledge, engage in research, and develop skilled and capable individuals in multiple areas.

The most challenging phase—establishing and successfully launching the university in a remote, underdeveloped area—is now accomplished. It is currently inspiring and enlightening the Mianwali region. However, to position Namal University as a global institution, it needs to make significant advancements in various developmental areas. As time passes, the university will progress through the remaining stages of its growth, with a vision that will ultimately achieve worldwide recognition, respect, and acceptance. Eventually, Namal University will gain global recognition as a beacon of knowledge, shining brightly like a star and fulfilling a role similar to that of Oxford, God willing.

Field of Thorns

He aspired to be a cricketer, driven by his ambition to excel as a fast bowler and a strong wish to win the World Cup. Imran Khan is one of the few individuals who have turned their dreams into reality, earning lasting admiration and global recognition that many can only aspire to. As the only son in a household of four sisters, his upbringing was filled with comfort and joy, free from the typical challenges often associated with being the only boy in a family. Having grown up in a wealthy and influential family, he had a limited understanding of the challenges faced by ordinary people in Pakistan. Although he was a highly regarded cricket captain, celebrated by fans and attractive women alike, his true dedication was to easing human suffering and serving his nation—a path he had never expected to pursue.

Khan never imagined he would abandon his princely life to take up a shovel and dedicate himself to the sake of humanity. Rather than feeling shy and nervous when speaking in front of people, he will confidently address rallies of millions regularly. Beyond cricket, he would not only excel in human welfare and politics, but he would also aim to deepen his understanding of Islam. Instead of being an ordinary Muslim, he will read and interpret the Holy Quran and study the biography of the Prophet Muhammad (peace be upon him). He will also combat Islamophobia around the world as a devoted follower of the Prophet (peace be upon him). However, the illness of his beloved mother profoundly changed Imran Khan's perspective, behavior, and life.

When asked about politics, Khan previously stated he had no interest or intention of getting involved. Later, in 1994, motivated by his ambitions, Khan joined the Jamiat Pasban, a splinter group formed by Hamid Gul and Muhammad Ali Durrani that broke away from Jamaat-e-Islami to help develop his political thinking. However, two years later, on April 25, 1996, he founded Pakistan Tehreek-e-Insaf at Zaman Park and entered the political arena.

The popular Australian TV program "60 Minutes" produced an extraordinary documentary about Imran Khan following his victory in the 1992 Cricket World Cup. The documentary was titled "Imran Khan: A Living God." A significant moment in this documentary showcased a luncheon with former Prime Minister Nawaz Sharif, Imran Khan, and the World Cup-winning team. During the meal, Imran Khan introduced the host, Richard, to Nawaz Sharif, saying, "Sir, this is Richard. He came from Australia to record the '60 Minutes' documentary.

Nawaz Sharif inquired about Richard's well-being, and Richard then asked, "Are you proud of this young man?" Nawaz Sharif replied, "Yes, very much." Richard questioned, "If he decides to enter politics, would he be the right choice for your team?" Nawaz Sharif responded, "I offered him this opportunity long ago, but he refused. I do not know why. However, my offer still stands." The scene then shifted to Imran Khan sitting in a room with Richard, where he stated, "I was offered the chance to enter politics twice. However, everyone recognizes their limitations, and I know that I cannot become a politician." Considering this perspective from 1992, what prompted Imran Khan to establish the Pakistan Tehreek-e-Insaf (PTI) four years later?

During the fundraising campaign for Shaukat Khanum Hospital, Khan saw firsthand the inequality, corruption, poverty, illiteracy, and various forms of social and economic injustice in Pakistan. Rather than ignoring these issues and feeling sorry for himself, he decided to take action to help alleviate the suffering of his country and nation. While building the cancer hospital, Khan also committed to the vision of transforming Pakistan into an Islamic welfare state, inspired by the model of the State of Madina. Those who supported him during the fundraising efforts noted that the overwhelming reception he received demonstrated that much more could be achieved. Thus, when circumstances forced Imran Khan to engage in politics—despite his repeated refusals to accept government and party positions from General Zia-ul-Haq and Nawaz Sharif—he chose to enter the political arena with determination, courage, and mission rather than relying on external support or vested interests.

If Khan's only goal had been to gain power, he could have easily achieved it by subordinating himself to military dictators like Zulfikar Ali Bhutto or Nawaz Sharif. Alternatively, like many traditional politicians, he could have accepted Nawaz Sharif's offer to join the PML-N and secured a position of influence. However, instead of opting for an easy route, Imran Khan chose a demanding and challenging path: confronting powerful family-controlled parties like the PML-N and PPP, dismantling their alliances, and ultimately breaking their political monopoly, thereby leaving a significant impact on the political landscape.

In June 1996, Imran Khan established the first Central Executive Committee of Pakistan Tehreek-e-Insaf (PTI). The committee included members Naeem ul Haque, Ahsan Rashid, Hafeez Khan, Mowahid Hussain, Mahmood Awan, and Nausherwan Barki. Naseem Zahra was appointed as the party's central information secretary, while Hassan Nisar drafted the PTI manifesto.

Imran Khan's objective in entering the political arena is to ensure that every Pakistani has equal access to justice. He aims to establish a free and transparent justice system, promote meritocracy, and harness the talents of the Pakistani people. Additionally, he seeks to provide healthcare, education, social welfare, freedom of expression, and employment opportunities for all citizens.

He seeks to raise awareness about religious freedom, interfaith harmony, and a fair tax system. His focus is on eliminating corruption through government transparency and holding leaders accountable. Imran Khan envisions liberating the country from corrupt, inept, and tyrannical rulers to establish a genuinely independent welfare state, one that guarantees political freedom, equal opportunities for economic development, and social justice.

Although Pakistan is rich in natural resources and populated by hardworking, capable, and sincere people, these assets have not been fully utilized due to injustice and corrupt leadership. Imran Khan wants to see Pakistan as an independent nation that prioritizes the interests of its people and makes autonomous decisions.

In reflecting on the early days of the party, Naseem Zahra shares, "We used to engage directly with the public. We would stand on ladders in the markets with baskets of mangoes and vegetables, while Imran Khan delivered speeches. Occasionally, we organized meetings at Karachi Company and other locations around the city, where we set up a small stage. Imran Khan was always full of energy. After these events, he would excitedly say, 'Look at how many people have come.' In reply, we would point out that the crowd was not very large, consisting of only one or two hundred individuals. But Imran Khan would counter, 'Did you notice the passion in their eyes? The enthusiasm was incredible!' This sense of enthusiasm was present from the very start. Imran Khan consistently expressed, 'I will become the Prime Minister one day.' At that time, it was not about the large number of supporters; when we convened, he stressed that the spirit of the people was what truly mattered."

Imran Khan's fame, prestige, World Cup victory, and the establishment of a free cancer hospital raised hopes that the Pakistan Tehreek-e-Insaf would soon gain public acceptance, allowing it to compete with traditional dynastic political parties and defeat them in elections. However, contrary to expectations, the party struggled to achieve immediate popularity. The political landscape in Pakistan is tightly controlled by influential figures, including feudal landlords, industrialists, and investors. Different linguistic, provincial, sectarian, and caste-based groups have formed a system that holds the populace in a tight grasp, making it difficult for the average person to escape this control.

Pakistanis viewed Imran Khan as a national hero but hesitated to accept him as a politician. They would gladly contribute to his causes but were reluctant to vote for him. While voters admired Khan's words and ideas, they were unwilling to change their political beliefs or party affiliations. Although people praised Khan for his victories, good intentions, and honesty, they did not support his bid to become Prime Minister. Khan did not lose heart despite these challenges, fears, and uncertainties. Instead, he continued his political journey with courage, determination, and faith.

Due to his simplicity and political inexperience, Imran Khan believed he would quickly overcome and defeat his strong and experienced political rivals, just as he had in cricket. His political opponents, especially the PML-N, viewed him as a significant threat to their future. Rather than competing democratically, they resorted to immoral, undemocratic, and illegal attacks on Khan's character and his spouse.

Khan consistently operated within moral, democratic, and political boundaries, focusing his criticism on the politics, merit issues, institutional decay, and corruption associated with the Sharif and Zardari families rather than on personal matters. In contrast, his opponents targeted his personal life and his ex-wife, Jemima, slandering him as a Playboy and a Jewish agent. Khan never expected that the Sharif brothers—who had previously invited him to join their party—would descend to such depths of political opposition, even filing a case against Jemima for tile theft and issuing a non-bailable arrest warrant for her.

He encountered numerous challenges, including ridicule from the "Tanga Party," teasing about his clumsiness, the distress of divorce, and the ongoing pain of being permanently separated from his children. Additional burdens include the bomb explosion at Shaukat Khanum Hospital and allegations of corruption. Hostage situations at Punjab University, instigated by Jamiat students during Musharraf's rule, coupled with early electoral defeats and a boycott of the 2008 elections, have further compounded his difficulties.

He has faced disconnection from his family, betrayal by trusted partners, the illegal seizure of the PTI's mandate, and pressure from allies. Challenges such as electoral fraud, vote theft in the Senate, biased judicial actions, and actions by the establishment to weaken the Constitution present considerable hurdles. Furthermore, he faces resistance from media outlets, institutional rigidity, a no-confidence motion, and the successful execution of a plan to alter the regime.

The party has endured severe crackdowns, forced press conferences for its leaders, violent police raids on the Zaman Park residence, and even threats of assassination at the Islamabad High Court. Over 200 fabricated cases have been filed against him, including unjust penalties that affect his family members. The violent attack in Wazirabad and his experiences of solitary confinement in Adiala Jail highlight his ongoing struggle.

Various political, military, judicial, domestic, and international adversaries have employed numerous tactics and committed acts of aggression to intimidate, defeat, and eliminate him from the political sphere. Nevertheless, they have failed to suppress him or diminish the affection he commands among the people.

Imran Khan and his party, Pakistan Tehreek-e-Insaf, have been navigating the challenging landscape of politics for the past 28 years. They have faced constant hardships and significant obstacles. Despite their efforts to succeed, they are still far from achieving their ultimate goal: the vision of "New Pakistan". However, Khan's unwavering dedication has empowered the Pakistani nation, fostered awareness, and laid the groundwork for genuine freedom and lasting success. This journey will ultimately lead to the realization of "New Pakistan", inspired by the principles of the "State of Madina". God willing

Childhood

With Father and sons

Sisters

With Sons

On the day of marriage with Jemima

With Jemima in London

On the day of marriage with Reham Khan

Nikah with Bushra Bibi

With Queen Elizabeth

Bowling

Bowling

Bowling

Batting

Victory Moment: 1992 World Cup

World Champion

Celebration of World Cup Victory

Fund Raising For SKMCH

Construction phase SKMCH

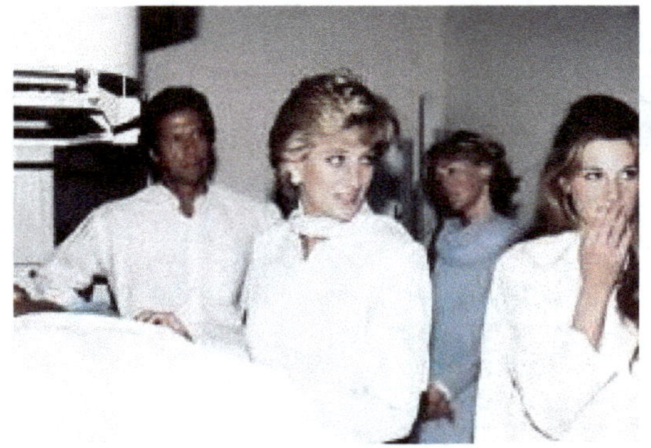

Princess Diana Visits SKMCH

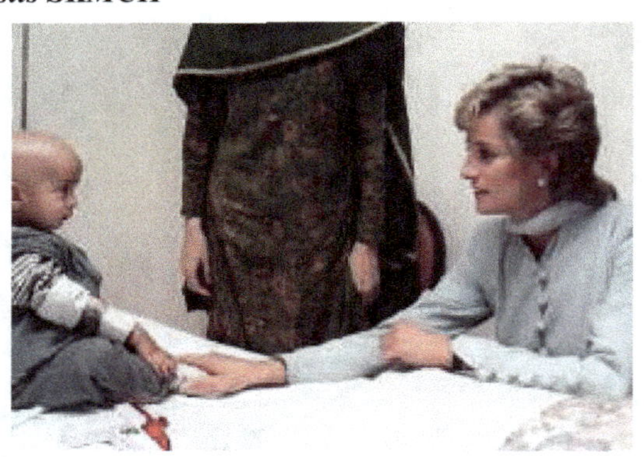

Princess Diana Visits SKMCH

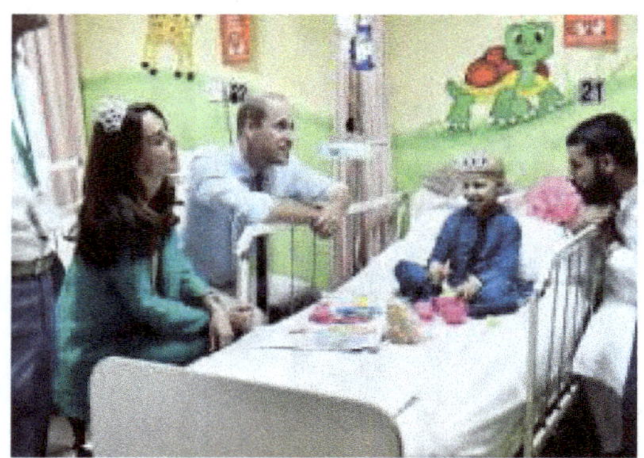

*Prince William and Kate Middleton visit
SKMCH*

Amir Khan visits SKMCH, Lahore

Children donating for SKMCH

SKMCH Lahore & Peshawar

Inauguration of Namal College

Namal Knowledge City, Mianwali

Convocation Bradford University

Convocation Bradford University

Convocation Namal University

*Mother of the Namal graduate
expressing gratitude*

Crushing Defeat

Following the 11-year rule of General Zia-ul-Haq, there were high expectations for the flourishing of democracy and democratic values in Pakistan. However, during the 1990s, rather than fostering a transparent democratic environment, the Pakistan People's Party (PPP) and the Muslim League-Nawaz (PML-N) became entrenched in a recurring power struggle. Both parties frequently accused each other of corruption and misconduct. Each time one party assumed power, it would initiate legal actions against the other based on various allegations. After a time in governance, they often faced dismissal due to charges of corruption, nepotism, and incompetence. They would subsequently revert to opposition, attempt to destabilize the current government, and eventually regain power. This continuous cycle of conflict and toxic politics between the two main parties has significantly harmed Pakistan and undermined its democratic framework. The relentless pursuit of power, neglect of merit, degradation of institutions, and the suffering experienced by the people led Imran Khan to enter the political arena, despite it being against his usual inclination.

In 1996, Imran Khan founded the Pakistan Tehreek-e-Insaf (PTI) while Benazir Bhutto was serving as the Prime Minister of Pakistan, leading the Pakistan People's Party (PPP). During this period, Imran Khan concentrated on organizing his party. On November 5, 1996, President Farooq Leghari dismissed Bhutto's government, citing allegations of corruption and misuse of authority. Numerous PPP members, including Benazir Bhutto's husband, Asif Ali

Zardari, were arrested for corruption linked to government institutions and for taking kickbacks on contracts. Consequently, the national and provincial assemblies were disbanded, and a caretaker government was formed under Malik Meraj Khalid. General elections were later scheduled for February 3, 1997.

This posed a considerable challenge for Imran Khan and his newly formed party. Due to his lack of political experience and organizational structure, party officials and family members suggested that he focus on strengthening the party and increasing its visibility nationwide, rather than entering the elections. They contended that Pakistan Tehreek-e-Insaf should not participate in the polls without sufficient preparation, experience, and organization, as an inevitable defeat could adversely affect the party's prospects. Nevertheless, Imran Khan felt that even though defeat was likely, it was essential to capitalize on this unique opportunity to gain insights into electoral politics and compete against established family-run parties. As a result, he chose to enter his nascent party in the 1997 general elections against the PPP and PML-N, despite being underprepared.

The initial and most challenging phase involved identifying candidates for the National and Provincial Assembly seats nationwide. Except for a few constituencies, the PTI faced challenges and did not experience considerable success, despite its dedicated efforts. Instead of feeling disheartened and withdrawing, Imran Khan chose to run for elections himself in eight National Assembly constituencies.

This move added more excitement to the elections. The PTI campaigned using the lamp as its symbol.

On February 3, 1997, elections were held in Pakistan. More than 6,000 candidates participated, with 1,758 contesting for the National Assembly and 4,426 for the four provincial assemblies. However, voter enthusiasm was low, resulting in a turnout of only about 36%. The PML-N achieved a landslide victory, receiving 8,751,793 votes and securing 135 seats. This marked the first time the PML-N won an election without an alliance. Meanwhile, the PPP faced a significant setback, garnering only 4,152,209 votes and winning just 18 seats, reflecting its growing unpopularity. Contrary to expectations, the PTI was unable to challenge the traditional family-run parties and suffered a crushing defeat, failing to win a single seat.

Pakistan Tehreek-e-Insaf secured eighth place, receiving only 314820 votes compared to other parties nationwide. Imran Khan not only lost to Fazlur Rehman in NA-18 Dera Ismail Khan, but also to PML-N candidates Mian Gul Aurangzeb in NA-21 Swat, Syed Zafar Ali Shah in NA-35 Islamabad, Maqbool Ahmed Khan in NA-53 Mianwali, and Mian Ijaz Shafi in NA-184 Karachi. Additionally, he lost to MQM candidate Dr. Farooq Sattar in NA-190, Karachi, PML-N candidate Tariq Aziz in NA-94, Lahore, and to Nawaz Sharif in NA-95, Lahore. PTI also forfeited their deposits in most constituencies, finishing last in many of these races.

The key highlight of the February 1997 elections was the debut clash between Nawaz Sharif and Imran Khan in Lahore's NA-95 constituency. This election drew significant attention, as many anticipated an exciting contest between the two candidates. Imran Khan had garnered considerable popularity, especially among the youth, thanks to his outstanding World Cup win and his dedication to building a cancer hospital.

In an attempt to secure Imran Khan as a political ally rather than a rival, Nawaz Sharif offered him an alliance for the 1997 elections, proposing to grant PTI 20 seats if he won. However, Imran Khan rejected this offer. Consequently, the rivalry between the two political leaders intensified. PML-N leader Pervez Rashid raised objections to Imran Khan's nomination papers, citing a controversy published in a British magazine regarding his undisclosed domestic and foreign assets and allegations of tax evasion. Nonetheless, the Returning Officer accepted Khan's nomination papers. In the election, Nawaz Sharif won the NA-95 constituency with a total of 50,592 votes. The PPP candidate received 9,623 votes, whereas Imran Khan obtained just 5,365 votes.

Sardar Ayaz Sadiq, the current Speaker of the National Assembly, was a close friend and classmate of Imran Khan at Aitchison College. He initially joined the Pakistan Tehreek-e-Insaf. Their political journeys began in Ayaz Sadiq's constituency of Garhi Shahu in Lahore. In their first electoral contest, Ayaz Sadiq aimed for a seat in the Punjab Assembly, while Imran Khan sought election to the National Assembly; however, both faced defeat. After this initial loss, they diverged in their political paths. In later elections, they found themselves competing against each other in the same constituency where they had once run together as PTI candidates. Each time, Ayaz Sadiq came out on top against Imran Khan.

It's important to highlight that the bat symbol was not part of the Election Commission's official symbols until after the Pakistan cricket team won the World Cup. This symbol first appeared during the 1997 elections. Interestingly, it was initially assigned to the Pakistan Nijat Party, which fielded only two candidates nationwide and garnered just 648 votes. In the 2002 elections, the Pakistan Nijat Party withdrew from the race, allowing other political parties to use the bat symbol. After a lackluster performance in 1997, Tehreek-e-Insaf opted to switch its symbol from a lamp to a bat. Today, the bat is widely recognized as the emblem of Tehreek-e-Insaf.

Although Khan entered these elections as a trial, he had hopes of securing one or two seats. His party was optimistic that the Pakistani public would rally behind their national hero. They believed that the voters would not only cast their ballots for him and help him enter parliament but also support his political success, express dissatisfaction with traditional political dynasties, and embark on a journey towards liberation. However, the election results shattered the expectations of Khan and the Pakistan Tehreek-e-Insaf party. The outcome not only shook their confidence but also provided their rivals, especially the PML-N, an opportunity to mock and criticize them. Additionally, these results inflicted considerable harm to the young party, which was still in its formative phase.

Jemima once tweeted that she remembers Imran Khan's election in 1997. At that time, three-month-old

Suleman was in my lap, saying he would achieve a clean sweep. I sighed and started laughing.

Imran Khan was well acquainted with defeat and criticism, having faced both many times during his 21-year cricket career. Instead of being disheartened by these challenges, Khan chose to reflect on his mistakes and strive to improve, eventually achieving notable successes. He took a similar stance in his political career. Naseem Zahra recounted, "After the party did not secure a single seat in the 1997 elections, Khan Sahib brought everyone together and asked, 'Aren't you all feeling anxious?' He motivated the team, reassuring them that everything would turn out fine."

Imran Khan's notable defeat in his first election, coupled with his grasp of the intricacies of electoral politics, uncovered a stark reality: the political environment in Pakistan is profoundly shaped by biases tied to caste, community, language, province, and class. It is almost impossible to free the average voter from the grip of these influences.

Khan came to understand that people were willing to support him with donations. They were happy to receive his autographs, yet they did not view him as deserving the right to vote. More than simply securing a victory in the election, the actual test for Imran Khan was to enhance awareness about individuals' rights and motivate them to stand up for those rights. Although he could have advanced his political aspirations by accepting Nawaz Sharif's proposal or choosing a more comfortable life with his family in London, he opted to face the challenges of political life head-on. Rather than backing down, he undertook this challenging endeavor to realize his vision of welfare, development, and prosperity for his country and its citizens. He started his political path with a strong commitment to succeed in the political arena.

Fighting Against Odds

Every success tends to overshadow the challenges encountered on the journey. Yet, when someone rises to the status of world champion and serves as an inspiration for others, it motivates them to strive for even higher goals. Imran Khan, after excelling in sports and charitable efforts, has taken on the daunting task of realizing his vision for a New Pakistan. This ambition is fraught with numerous challenges and risks.

Envisioning the challenges and obstacles that Imran Khan faced over a span of 15 years, from founding his party in 1996 to October 29, 2011, is no easy task. Many individuals in his situation might have lost hope in politics, discouraged by the tactics of their rivals, and stepped back from the fray. However, fueled by a profound love for his country, Khan chose to persevere, compete, and make sacrifices in pursuit of his objectives.

On February 17, 1997, Nawaz Sharif was elected Prime Minister for the second time, securing a three-fourths majority with 177 votes. During his administration, he forced Army Chief General Jahangir Karamat to resign due to disagreements over the National Security Council. On October 12, 1999, Army Chief Pervez Musharraf was dismissed due to conflicts related to the Kargil War. In response, Musharraf overthrew Nawaz Sharif's government, imposed the country's fourth martial law, assumed the self-proclaimed position of Chief Executive, and imprisoned Nawaz Sharif.

In his first address to the nation, General Pervez Musharraf presented a seven-point agenda aimed at restoring the country's stability and unity. His key points included:

1. Rebuilding the nation's confidence and spirit.

2. Enhancing the federation and promoting national unity by resolving inter-provincial discord.

3. Ensuring law and order while providing speedy justice.

4. Revitalizing the economy and boosting investor confidence.

5. Depoliticizing government institutions.

6. Devolving powers to the local government level.

7. Eradicating corruption and ensuring immediate accountability for corrupt politicians nationwide.

Opposition leaders, including Benazir Bhutto, Maulana Fazal-Ur-Rehman, Altaf Hussain, and Tahir-ul-Qadri, who were dissatisfied with Nawaz Sharif's ambitions to become Amir-ul-Momineen and his policies, welcomed the martial law imposed on October 12. The public celebrated this move by distributing sweets. Imran Khan openly supported Pervez Musharraf's martial law, particularly because of the seven-point agenda, which included a commitment to eliminate corruption and dismantle corrupt mafias.

On December 10, 2000, Pervez Musharraf exiled Mian Nawaz Sharif and his family to Saudi Arabia as part of a deal. General Pervez Musharraf announced a presidential referendum during his address to the nation on April 5, 2002, to extend his rule. The question posed to the public was, "To ensure the preservation of the local government system, support for democracy, ongoing economic reforms, the elimination of sectarianism and extremism, and the fulfillment of Quaid-e-Azam's vision, it is essential to vote for Army Chief President Pervez Musharraf to extend his term by an additional five years.

Imran Khan publicly announced his support for the referendum, despite strong opposition from all other political parties, which deemed it unconstitutional and illegal. Khan justified his support for Pervez Musharraf's military government and the referendum by citing Musharraf's promises to eradicate corruption and the corrupt elite. There are probably two main reasons for his position. Firstly, Khan frequently brings up Musharraf's proposition to appoint him as Prime Minister in 2002. Secondly, after his party's decline following the 1997 election loss, Imran Khan may have adopted a more pragmatic approach to politics, opting for a more straightforward route rather than facing an extended struggle.

A controversial referendum took place on April 30, 2002, in which General Pervez Musharraf was the sole candidate and won the presidency with an "overwhelming majority." He secured 42.8 million votes, while the opposing side managed only 883,676 votes. There were 282,676 votes deemed incomplete, bringing the total votes cast to 43,907,352. The voter turnout was registered at 56.10 percent, with an impressive 97.97 percent of voters supporting Musharraf. This vote count was unprecedented, as no candidate from any party had achieved such a high total in previous general elections. Musharraf asserted that the referendum was in accordance with democratic principles, even though the Constitution of Pakistan does not permit presidential elections to be conducted via a referendum. The opposition chose to boycott the vote, deeming it unconstitutional. Furthermore, the Human Rights Commission of Pakistan voiced criticism regarding the referendum process.

While casting his vote in the referendum, Imran Khan expressed hope that General Musharraf would keep corrupt politicians and parties out of politics. Subsequent events demonstrated that Khan's support for Musharraf was misguided and detrimental to his political career and party. Imran Khan has openly acknowledged this mistake on several occasions.

After winning the referendum, instead of implementing his 7-point agenda, Pervez Musharraf established the King's Party, also known as the Muslim League-Q, through political maneuvering. General elections were announced for October 10, 2002. This situation led to disagreements between Imran Khan and Pervez Musharraf, resulting in Khan withdrawing his support for Musharraf. At that time, both Nawaz Sharif and Benazir Bhutto lived in exile.

Approximately 70 political parties participated in these elections, among which 18 managed to secure seats in parliament, including the Pakistan Tehreek-e-Insaf. The voter turnout was 41.8%. The Pakistan Muslim League Quaid-e-Azam won the most seats, securing a total of 118.

The Pakistan People's Party Parliamentarians (PPP) followed with 81 seats, while the Muttahida Majlis-e-Amal Pakistan (MMA) won 60 seats. The Pakistan Muslim League (N) secured only 19 seats. In contrast, the Pakistan Tehreek-e-Insaf won just one seat in the National Assembly, finishing in 10th place.

Imran Khan contested the elections for four seats in the National Assembly but lost all of them, except for his home constituency in Mianwali. The Pakistan Tehreek-e-Insaf party, aside from securing one seat in the provincial assembly through Mian Nisar Gul Kakakhel, did not perform well in the 2002 elections. Instead of supporting Pervez Musharraf's candidate, Mir Zafarullah Jamali, for the position of Prime Minister, Imran Khan voted for Maulana Fazal-Ur-Rehman. Khan has repeatedly stated that Pervez Musharraf offered him the role of Prime Minister, which he declined.

Despite being relatively weak in organization and candidate presence during the 2002 elections, there were considerable hopes within the Pakistan Tehreek-e-Insaf for better electoral performance and the possibility of securing multiple constituencies. However, the actual results were a major disappointment for both the party leadership and its support base. Differences arising from Imran Khan's decision-making, along with his apolitical mindset and approach to politics, led many leaders to feel it was safer to resign from their party positions and distance themselves from politics altogether.

In contrast to what was anticipated, six years after its establishment, the PTI found it challenging to position itself as a significant political entity and experienced a downturn, predominantly becoming associated with Imran Khan's charisma. Opponents ridiculed Khan, labeling him politically clumsy and referring to his party as the "Tanga Party." They even advised him to leave politics and pursue cricket commentary or continue his charitable work. Additionally, the PTI faced internal challenges, including high party expenses, a lack of funding, concerns among its members, and voter dissatisfaction.

Even though he encountered many obstacles and hardships, securing a single seat in Mianwali instilled a renewed sense of hope in Khan. Rather than feeling disheartened by the loss, he stayed true to his nature and reiterated his dedication to his political ambitions and ongoing battles. This commitment is evident in how Khan not only accepted his party's loss openly but also embraced the position of a formidable opposition leader, becoming an influential voice in Parliament despite winning only one seat.

Imran Khan, renowned for his captivating personality and international recognition, garnered considerable media coverage, which opened up numerous opportunities for him. As the primary representative of his party, he actively participated in discussions with the government and other opposition groups across different platforms and talk shows. Khan expressed a bold and insightful perspective on the fight against terrorism, both domestically and globally. He raised awareness among the Pakistani people about issues like injustice, corruption, and unfair practices. Additionally, he motivated the youth to pursue their aspirations, emphasizing the importance of self-fulfillment and hard work in achieving those goals. In conclusion, despite facing detractors, character attacks, and setbacks in elections, Imran Khan continued to show remarkable resilience in the political landscape.

During a time when Khan was struggling to maintain his political position, he was also facing a major personal crisis. Jemima became unhappy with his constant focus on politics and the various obstacles he encountered. Although she initially backed him, the complex dynamics of Pakistani politics, along with allegations related to antique tile theft against her, non-bailable arrest warrants, and damaging claims by his political opponents branding Khan as a Jewish agent, led to her considerable distress. In the end, Jemima opted to leave Pakistan with their children. She had converted to Islam before their marriage, and together they had two sons in Pakistan: Suleman Isa Khan, born in 1996, and Qasim Khan, born in 1999.

During this time, Jemima not only learned Urdu and Pashto but also made significant efforts to immerse herself in these languages. She wanted Imran Khan to leave politics and Pakistan to settle in England permanently with his wife and children. However, Imran Khan, driven by patriotism and a desire to bring change to Pakistan, was convinced that he would one day become the Prime Minister. For this reason, he was unwilling to leave his country. Conversely, Jemima found it challenging to live in Pakistan, which may have led them to choose separate paths.

Imran and Jemima Khan, who married in 1995, separated permanently on June 22, 2004. This decision was made despite their reluctance to part ways, and it was announced in a London court during their divorce proceedings. The news was officially communicated in Pakistan by Akbar S. Babar, the Information Secretary of the Pakistan Tehreek-e-Insaf. In his statement, Imran Khan expressed, "I am saddened to announce that Jemima and I have divorced. This decision is mutual and is a source of great sadness for both of us. Imran Khan stated that his home and future are in Pakistan, while Jemima made significant efforts to stay here. However, my political life made it challenging for her to settle in the country."

Jemima Khan explained in an interview with the British magazine Vanity Fair that the reason for her divorce was the difficult health situation she encountered while living in Pakistan. She noted that her husband's busy political career often meant he was only available to talk on the phone after 2 a.m. Additionally, she mentioned that she and their two children frequently fell ill, and Imran Khan was away from home for most of the time.

Inam-U-Allah Khan Niazi, Imran Khan's cousin, stated that Imran and Jemima have been facing challenges for the last six years. It was evident that Jemima was unhappy with Imran's political involvement, and over the past year, she had been attempting to convince him to exit the political arena. She felt increasingly isolated, especially as Imran intensified his focus on practical politics. Inam-u-llah Khan also pointed out that Jemima would inherit a considerable amount of her father's estate on her 33rd birthday, but Imran appeared uninterested in this inheritance.

Sheikh Aamir Hassan, a fashion designer and Jemima's friend, reveals that she has made significant efforts to adapt to Imran Khan's family environment. Out of love for him, she learned the Urdu and Pashto languages and embraced the local dress culture. Many of Jemima and Imran's friends believe that a key factor in their divorce was Jemima's mother, who always felt that Jemima would not find comfort living in Pakistan.

According to Ashiq Qureshi, a longtime friend of Imran, he tried diligently to keep the marriage intact. However, he often felt sad about his inability to spend enough time with Jemima. As a result, he allowed her considerable freedom. When Jemima expressed a desire to attend university in London for her studies, Imran supported her decision. After their separation, Imran Khan acknowledged his mistakes, stating that he bore full responsibility for the breakup, attributing the strain on their marriage to his political commitments.

Imran Khan was known among his close friends for his profound affection for his family. Despite his demanding political career, he consistently prioritized time for his loved ones. After attending various political events and meetings, he would hurry home whenever possible. Even when he had to travel to another city, he made it a point to return before nightfall. Each evening, he would share stories with his children and tuck them in at bedtime. Imran made every effort to nurture his marriage and encourage Jemima to remain by his side. However, when confronted with the tough decision between his wife, kids, and his homeland, he faced a heartbreaking choice. He chose to forgo the love of his family and a life of comfort for the sake of his motherland, crafting a poignant narrative of patriotism during a difficult period.

On March 9, 2007, President Pervez Musharraf dismissed Chief Justice Iftikhar Muhammad Chaudhry and filed a reference against him. In reaction, lawyers throughout the country launched a large-scale protest movement against Musharraf. On October 2, 2007, General Musharraf announced his intention to seek re-election as president while still holding the position of army chief. Imran Khan, along with 85 other assembly members, led a campaign against this decision under the All-Parties Democratic Movement. Despite the backlash, General Pervez Musharraf was re-elected as president during the elections on October 6, 2007. On November 3, 2007, he declared a state of emergency in Pakistan, suspended the higher judiciary and the constitution, and administered the oath of office to judges under the Provisional Constitutional Order (PCO). After the emergency was declared, attempts were made to arrest Imran Khan, but he successfully evaded capture.

On November 14, 2007, Imran Khan unexpectedly emerged from hiding and visited Punjab University at the invitation of the Joint Action Committee of students to lead a protest against the Emergency. Jamaat-e-Islami Ameer Qazi Hussain Ahmed approved his visit. Upon his arrival at the university, students supportive of Imran Khan warmly welcomed him, lifting him onto their shoulders and chanting slogans in his honor. However, shortly thereafter, a group of students from the Islami Jamiat-e-Talaba, the student wing of Jamaat-e-Islami, surrounded him. They verbally assaulted

Imran Khan and forcibly confined him in a room at the Center for High Energy Physics for approximately 45 minutes. A cameraman from a private TV channel, who managed to enter the building, was informed by a teacher that the students had misbehaved towards Imran during this time. Subsequently, the assailants placed Imran Khan in a van and took him to Gate No. 1 of the university, where he was handed over to the police.

Amir-Ul-Azeem, the Information Secretary of Jamaat-e-Islami, observed the event and described it as a blemish on the party. He voiced that the treatment of Imran Khan was disgraceful. He criticized the behavior of the Jamiat students, arguing that it damaged the party's image in the eyes of international media and jeopardized their shared mission.

In response, Muhammad Ayub, the Nazim of the Islami Jamiat Students at Punjab University, claimed that the university administration mistreated Imran Khan. He insisted that their party had no involvement in detaining him or handing him over to the police. Furthermore, he and other Jamiat students denied having invited the PTI chief to the university. They stated to the media, "We do not want any politician to hijack the students' movement against the imposition of emergency; they should stay away from the campus."

University Registrar Dr. Muhammad Naeem Khan stated that the university administration did not assist the police in arresting Imran Khan. "We had provided him with safe passage," he remarked. PTI Secretary General Shahid Zulfiqar and other leaders accused members of the Islami

Jamiat-E-Talaba organization of involvement in the incident. PTI Media Advisor Naseem Zahra claimed that Jamaat-e-Islami students kidnapped and assaulted Imran Khan before handing him over to the police. She alleged that intelligence agencies had employed certain members of the Islami Jamiat-E-Talaba to carry out this act, noting their presence during the incident. SSP Aftab Ahmed Cheema confirmed Imran Khan's arrest.

Following this incident, Pakistani newspapers and international journals widely condemned the manner in which Imran Khan was treated. They lauded his bravery and criticized both the character of Jamaat-E-Islami and the actions of its student wing. In reaction to these developments, Jamaat-E-Islami launched an investigation and decided to suspend the memberships of several Islami Jamiat-E-Talaba members. During that period, Qazi Hussain Ahmed and Imran Khan were very close friends. The late Qazi Sahib penned a column regarding this incident, where he expressed his deep sorrow and also critiqued the student wing of the Jamiat. This was an unusual event, as it was uncommon for any Ameer to admonish the student branch of his Jamaat.

The police filed a case against Imran under several legal provisions, including sections 124, 353, 149, 186, and 148 of the Pakistan Penal Code, section 16 of the Public Order Act, and section 7 of the Anti-Terrorism Act. Initially, Imran Khan was taken to the Iqbal Town police station. He was then transferred from the Sabza Zar and Civil Lines police stations to Kot Lakhpat prison, and subsequently, he was sent to Dera Ghazi Khan prison.

In his autobiography " Pakistan, A Personal History," Imran Khan recounts an incident at Punjab University, emphasizing that movements are most effective when youth and students play a central role. He compares this to the involvement of the new generation in America during the Vietnam War in the 1960s, the Indonesian youth uprising against President Suharto in 1990, and the student protests during the "Arab Spring" in the Middle East in 2011. Khan expresses his desire for students to take action at that moment, believing it was essential for the arrest to be witnessed by the international press and the student body, rather than happening in silence. He recounts how he confronted the Jamiat rioters, telling them he intended to surrender to the police. Instead, they aggressively pushed him into a car and brought him to the gate, where a police inspector was waiting for him.

He was looking me up and down repeatedly. I asked him what the matter was, and he replied that he was pleased to see me. Curious, I wondered why he was happy. He responded, "I'll tell you this when I reach the police station." He continued, "We have been in contact with them since last night. They were supposed to hand you over to us in such a way that I would have taken you straight to the hospital from there. They intended to break some of your bones." That was the plan. However, this inspector took a risk and deployed some of his colleagues in plain clothes at the university to protect me. He couldn't have done more than that, and I then realized how painful an ordeal I had narrowly escaped. Furthermore, Imran Khan could never have imagined that he would have to endure the hardships of imprisonment in DG Khan Jail and face the painful experience of a hunger strike for raising his voice in favor of restoring the rule of law and democracy in his country.

Newspapers around the world praised Imran Khan's struggle against the military dictator Pervez Musharraf. His ex-wife, Jemima Khan, attended a protest in London calling for his release, and the British media provided special coverage of his arrest. On November 18, Imran Khan began a hunger strike in Dera Ghazi Khan Jail, vowing to continue until death. Four days later, on November 22, he was unexpectedly acquitted of all charges and released from jail. When asked about the alleged involvement of the Islami Jamiat-e-Talaba in his arrest, he refrained from answering, stating that he held no grudge against Qazi Hussain Ahmed.

On 15 November 2007, President Musharraf dissolved the National Assembly after its constitutional term expired and announced general elections for January 2008. However, following the assassination of Benazir Bhutto, the elections were postponed and eventually held on 18 February 2008. All parties within the All-Pakistan Democratic Movement (APDM), including Imran Khan, decided to boycott the elections. In contrast, after Bhutto's assassination, Asif Ali Zardari and Mian Nawaz Sharif opted to participate in the polls.

On February 15, 2008, just three days before the elections, Imran Khan published an article in the Taipei Times titled "Why Boycott Pakistan's Elections?" He elaborated on his perspective in it, stating, "Many observers hope that the elections on February 18 will herald a new era of democracy and stability. However, sometimes boycotting elections while adhering to one's principles can serve democracy better. The emergency imposed by Pervez Musharraf on November 3, along with the issuance of the PCO, are unconstitutional and illegal actions, which is why my party and its allies are boycotting the elections.

Democracy is not merely about holding elections, as demonstrated by Zimbabwean President Robert Mugabe, who has frequently conducted elections, or Egyptian President Hosni Mubarak, who has held power for 30 years. Similarly, Uzbekistan's Islam Karimov has been in power for 30 years and has just been "re-elected" for another seven-year presidential term. True democracy can only be achieved when elections are free and fair, supervised by independent ombudsmen.

When my party was founded 11 years ago, we named it the Movement for Justice. We advocated for an independent judiciary because we believed that democracy and prosperity are impossible without the rule of law. Therefore, it is shocking that the U.S. State Department continues to discuss free and fair elections and the lifting of the emergency while failing to mention the reinstatement of judges, including the Chief Justice of the Supreme Court, whom Musharraf unlawfully dismissed. How can we expect free and fair elections if the judges are not reinstated? With the reinstatement of the Chief Justice and other judges, we could make progress towards a genuine democratic system. However, if Musharraf manages to retain his PCO judges, we are likely heading into a turbulent era. After all, how can a party led by a man who has less than 5% support win an election without resorting to rigging?

Unfortunately, most political parties have not supported the democratic process. The Pakistan Muslim League (N) has chosen to participate in the elections following the leadership of the late Benazir Bhutto's Pakistan People's Party. Among the major parties contesting the polls, only the PML-N is calling for the reinstatement of judges. Fortunately, the people of Pakistan—students, observers, and lawyers—are standing up for the judges, taking action that political parties should have undertaken. The real dividing line in Pakistan is not between liberals and extremists; rather, it is between those who support the status quo and those who oppose it. The so-called democratic parties are not only backing Musharraf in this rigged election but are also contributing to the restoration of the status quo.

The solution to a dysfunctional democracy is not a military dictatorship but rather an increased commitment to democracy. Pakistanis understand democracy because we have a culture that values democracy. Our founder was a remarkable constitutional expert, and Pakistan was established through a democratic voting process. The primary issue is that we lack an independent Election Commission, as our judiciary also lacks independence. Consequently, except for the 1970 election, all of our elections have been rigged.

India has experienced 40 years of ineffective democracy dominated by a single-party system. However, in the past 16 years, the country has begun to enjoy the benefits of genuine democratic competition. An independent judiciary and an Election Commission instill confidence in the people that their votes can lead to change. Until Pakistan achieves a similar situation, no election can be considered free and fair.

For two and a half years, I supported Musharraf and believed in his promises to bring genuine democracy to Pakistan. I've learned my lesson about him. More importantly, no military dictator can succeed where Musharraf has so clearly failed. As Georges Clemenceau once said, "War is too serious a matter to be entrusted to generals," and the same can be said for democracy."

Thus, despite the growing popularity of his party and predictions of better election results, Imran Khan chose to boycott the elections and remained out of parliamentary politics for another five years. This decision demonstrates his commitment to the politics of values rather than merely seeking power. If Khan had wanted to, he could have accepted offers from Zia-ul-Haq, Nawaz Sharif, and Pervez Musharraf to launch his political career from the halls of power.

However, Khan consistently opted for the more challenging path. He embraced the challenge of turning the impossible into reality because true success lies in swimming against the current, growing flowers in the desert, cultivating barren land, igniting hope in times of despair, and confronting challenges with courage instead of succumbing to panic.

This is why, despite facing failures in the first three elections of his political career and challenges in his private life, as well as mistreatment by university students and unjust imprisonment, Imran Khan did not choose to quit politics out of frustration, hopelessness, or heartbreak. Instead, he faced all these trials with patience and perseverance. Despite the dangers, troubles, failures, and challenges, he continues to make progress to this day.

The Rise of Khan

Following the 2008 election boycott, the Pakistan Tehreek-e-Insaf appeared to fade from the political landscape. In the realm of television discussions and various media outlets, the leading spokesperson was Imran Khan. Despite encountering ongoing challenges, setbacks, and mockery, as well as family issues—such as separation from his partner and children during the initial 15 years of his political journey—Khan remained resolute and determined not to lose hope.

At a time when political opponents dismissed him as a formidable contender, he faced them single-handedly in every forum. When rulers and prominent politicians hesitated to address national and international issues during talk shows, Khan astonished everyone with his bold, factual, and clear positions. Even when mocked for his political failures, he consistently silenced critics with his reasoned arguments and unwavering self-confidence.

Khan has dedicated the past 15 years to raising political awareness among the nation. He has focused on exposing corruption, injustice, and mismanagement at all levels of government. His efforts aim to unite the youth and instill a sense of patriotism in them, while genuinely expressing public sentiments. Khan seeks to engage educated individuals disillusioned with traditional dynastic politicians and politics, encouraging them to participate actively. He aims to communicate the party's message to every household and unveil the Sharif-Zardari nexus. Determined to return to the political arena, he has relentlessly continued his struggle, strategic planning, and progress without wasting a moment.

During this challenging and prolonged political turmoil, Khan traveled from one city to another, overcoming obstacles and learning from his mistakes. He diligently worked to address his weaknesses and effectively sparked political awareness. Recognizing that the time was right for action, Khan, driven by an intense instinct for critical decisions and unwavering resolve, devised a strategy to capitalize on the increased political awareness. This tactic rejuvenated the Pakistan Tehreek-e-Insaf, lifting it from a state of obscurity and failure and guiding it toward the success that Imran Khan and his party had long sought.

Khan once again set an ambitious goal for himself, aiming to organize a rally for the Pakistan Tehreek-e-Insaf at Minar-e-Pakistan on October 30, 2011. Political parties typically demonstrate their level of support in two ways: by winning the most electoral seats or by organizing sizable political events, such as rallies and demonstrations. While elections were set for 2013, political parties can conduct rallies at any time. The selected venue for a political event also signifies a party's popularity. Hence, Imran Khan chose to hold a major rally at Minar-e-Pakistan, a site renowned for its historical importance and ample space. This rally aimed to highlight the popularity of PTI and the public's support for it.

In Lahore, significant historical gatherings have taken place at Minar-e-Pakistan, Mochi Gate, and Nasir Bagh at various times. However, Minar-e-Pakistan holds a unique historical significance. The events hosted here have influenced the direction of political parties in the region. Its prominence stems from the historic gathering of the All-India Muslim League, which took place on March 23, 1940, and was attended by the Father of the Nation, Quaid-e-Azam Muhammad Ali Jinnah. During this two-day gathering, a resolution was presented advocating for the establishment of Pakistan. At that time, the area was known as Minto Park. After the formation of Pakistan, during General Ayub Khan's administration, the construction of a monument named Minar-e-Pakistan was initiated on March 23, 1960, to commemorate the Pakistan Resolution. The monument was completed on October 21, 1968.

The Pakistan People's Party is proud to have hosted the first political gathering at Minar-e-Pakistan. Its founder, Zulfikar Ali Bhutto, held a significant rally there following the 1970 elections. On April 10, 1986, after her exile, Benazir Bhutto returned to Minar-E-Pakistan, arriving in a large rally from Lahore Airport. This event is regarded as one of the most important rallies in Lahore's history, marking a significant moment. After becoming Prime Minister, Benazir Bhutto held another rally at Minar-e-Pakistan in 1989.

When Nawaz Sharif was first elected as Prime Minister, he held a rally at Minar-e-Pakistan under the banner of the Islamic Democratic Alliance (IJI). While the rally garnered a good turnout, it was smaller than previous rallies held by the Pakistan People's Party (PPP). Following that event, there was a long hiatus of nearly ten years, during which no rallies were held at Minar-E-Pakistan. Eventually, the Alliance for the Restoration of Democracy (ARD), comprising the PPP and other political parties, including the Pakistan Muslim League-Nawaz (PML-N), organized a rally at the same venue. Additionally, former military dictator General Pervez Musharraf held a rally at Minar-e-Pakistan ahead of the presidential referendum on April 30, 2002. During Musharraf's rule, the Mutahida Qaumi Movement (MQM), a key ally of the ruling party, also hosted a rally there on August 13, 2006. Over the years, various political and religious parties have demonstrated their popularity and strength by organizing gatherings at Minar-e-Pakistan at different times.

Keeping this historical background and significance in mind, Imran Khan chose the iconic location of Minar-e-Pakistan to demonstrate his political strength and popularity at a time when no one took the PTI seriously in the political arena. Khan was well aware of this perception. However, after observing public sentiments and the realities on the ground during 15 years of tireless political struggle, he became confident in his success. At that pivotal moment, true to his nature, Khan boldly decided to aggressively challenge his political opponents at the Minar-e-Pakistan ground, aiming to take down the wickets of his rivals and apply political pressure on them. His political rivals and analysts mocked this decision, claiming it was unnecessary and akin to political suicide. PML-N leader Pervez Rasheed even described filling the chairs at the rally as a significant achievement.

On the night of October 30, 2011, a significant milestone was reached—the moment that Imran Khan had envisioned since he began his political journey. He had invested his entire fortune and reputation in the hope of fostering political awareness among the public. The vast Minar-e-Pakistan square was packed with people. The youth, educated middle class, and especially the passionate residents of Lahore, who had previously been indifferent to politics, attended the event with their families and children. Their enthusiasm provided Imran Khan with the courage, strength, and confidence that are essential for any successful leader.

The event was a political rally, but it felt more like a massive wave of passionate voices. A strong sentiment of discontent towards self-serving and dynastic politicians was evident. This assembly marked a pivotal moment in the political and democratic landscape, showcasing a growing trust in Imran Khan's leadership. People of all backgrounds—children, the elderly, women, and youth—came together to raise their voices with joy and optimism, chanting PTI slogans, singing anthems, waving flags, and warmly welcoming Imran Khan. This remarkable display of support not only caught the ruling class, opposition parties, and political analysts off guard but also affirmed the rightful recognition of Pakistan Tehreek-e-Insaf as a legitimate political force. As a result, PTI reshaped the nation's political dynamics and signaled alarm for the PML-N, PPP, and other political entities.

Imran Khan's happiness was evident. His hard work and dedication had paid off. After winning the World Cup and establishing a hospital, he was looking forward to achieving a lasting victory in the political arena. His party was thriving, and the captain was back in his prime. He strongly connected with the people, fully understanding their emotions, feelings, and aspirations. He pledged to bring about change in his beloved motherland and to create a new Pakistan. The excited audience and millions of viewers nationwide were eagerly anticipating Khan's address. As he made his way to the stage, the atmosphere buzzed with slogans, PTI songs, and joyful applause.

He opened his speech with the Quranic verse, " إِيَّاكَ نَعْبُدُ وَ إِيَّاكَ نَسْتَعِينُ" (O Allah, we worship You and only seek Your help). In addition to presenting his objectives, manifesto, ideology, and future plans for the country, he also challenged his political opponents.

Imran Khan, while delivering an impassioned speech at the rally for about forty-five minutes, stated, "If politicians do not declare their assets, we will launch a civil disobedience movement." He announced that the Pakistan Tehreek-e-Insaf would establish a cell to investigate the assets of politicians. Based on the findings of this investigation, all politicians, including President Zardari, will be required to declare their assets. If they refuse, the PTI will initiate a civil disobedience movement and shut down cities. Khan insisted that change is not just coming to the country; it has already arrived. He urged the people of Raiwind and Islamabad to listen, proclaiming, "This is not a flood; it is a tsunami." He added, I assure you that Zardari and Nawaz Sharif cannot stop this revolution. The Pakistani nation knows how to dismantle the Zardari-Nawaz partnership." He emphasized that this "in-swinger" will bring down Zardari and Nawaz. Khan criticized Asif Zardari for allegedly using Bhutto's name unjustly, questioning the fate of the slogan for "bread, cloth, and house," and pointed out that hundreds of people have committed suicide due to his policies. He dismissed the Muslim League rally in Lahore as one composed of "patwaris," stating, "If there was to be a rally, why was it filled with jackals? Nawaz Sharif cannot even fight mosquitoes; how can he confront Zardari?"

Khan expressed his views to the residents of Lahore, mentioning that they tend to be slow to react initially. However, once they commit fully, they become a formidable force. He conveyed his happiness about the change in direction among the people of Lahore, highlighting that Allah has endowed humans with the ability to set intentions and strive for their goals. He believes the objective is to disrupt the partnership between the two factions, and he feels that Allah has heard their pleas.

He announced plans to approach the Supreme Court against those who have failed to declare their assets and advocated for the establishment of an independent election commission. Khan also highlighted Pakistan's potential, noting that the country possesses 185 billion tons of coal and generates more electricity than Iran, Iraq, and Saudi Arabia. He claimed Pakistan could generate 60,000 megawatts of electricity, but this capacity will not be realized as it would not yield a commission for specific individuals.

Imran Khan stated that "Pakistan's biggest problem is corruption, costing the country Rs 3,000 billion. Tehreek-e-Insaf will put an end to this corruption. We will demonstrate this by eradicating corruption and tax evasion. A law will be introduced that requires individuals to declare their assets to engage in politics. Once assets are disclosed, the truth will come to light. We have been trying for 15 years to bring about change in the country and dismantle the partnership between the two dominant parties. Today, Allah has heard our call. I congratulate the youth, my sisters, and the workers of Tehreek-e-Insaf, ISF, along with those from the PPP and the Nawaz Sharif party who are present, for correcting your direction. I want to extend special recognition to the media for raising awareness among the people of Pakistan, particularly those in Lahore. From this point, we are beginning a new chapter in Pakistan. There has only been one greatest leader of Pakistan: Hazrat Quaid-e-Azam, who initiated the Pakistan Movement from here in 1940. My ideological leader, Allama Iqbal, expressed similar sentiments: 'Winning Lahore is essential for success.' How can I forget Hazrat Data Ganj Bakhsh? He was in Afghanistan when Allah instructed him to come to Lahore and raise the flag of Islam from here."

Challenging Zardari and Nawaz Sharif, Khan stated, "Nawaz Sharif and Zardari cannot stop this storm. Listen, people of Raiwind and Islamabad, this is not a flood; it is a tsunami. Whoever stands in its way will be swept away. The youth of Pakistan know how to break partnerships. An in-swinger is coming; this will be the first ball that will knock down the wickets of both batsmen. Asif Zardari, how much injustice have you done by using Bhutto's name? Where is Zulfikar Ali Bhutto, and where is Zardari? Bhutto was a nationalist; he opposed imperialism and raised the slogan of 'Bread, Cloth, and House.' Zardari, you talk about 'Bread, Cloth, and House,' but you have forced people to despair." He added, "A letter was given to the Pakistani ambassador in America, who is essentially the American ambassador, informing them to save me from the Pakistani army. I cannot serve you well. I will bring my generals and polish your shoes!" Khan challenged, "Mian Sahib, first tell me, for God's sake, what happened the day before yesterday? What was that rally? If there was going to be a rally, it should have been a show of strength. Instead, what we witnessed was a gathering of jackals. You cannot even compete with mosquitoes. How will you compete with Zardari?"

Discussing the internal and external challenges facing Pakistan, Khan stated, "Due to load shedding in the cities, the youth are unable to study, and factories are shutting down. The country is quickly descending into darkness. If we come to power, our first action will be to increase the capacity of all WAPDA generation plants, which are currently operating at only 25% to 70% of their full capacity. This will eliminate the need for load shedding. Pakistan's biggest issue is corruption, which has led to our subservience to America. We are losing Rs 3,000 billion every year due to tax evasion and corruption. We will put an end to this theft. We will demand answers from those who have suddenly become billionaires. For instance, one minister claims he does not know where Rs 40 million came from in his account. Why is so much money from politicians held abroad? Occasionally, Zardari visits Pakistan. We will demonstrate our resolve by collecting all due taxes, God willing."

The Khan asserted that both Zardari and the circus lion of Raiwind are incapable of addressing the critical issues that confront the populace. He stressed the need for

India to withdraw its military presence from Kashmir. Additionally, the PTI founder vowed to eliminate corruption and ensure accountability, asserting that they would hold all central officials accountable for corruption. It is estimated that Pakistanis have around $100 billion stashed in Swiss banks, while the country faces a foreign debt of $60 billion. He proclaimed, "Insha Allah, we will retrieve this money." He also mentioned that wherever there are patwaris, land-grabbing groups will emerge.

Khan said, we need to change the culture of the police stations and ensure that the police force is depoliticized. When political parties recruit their workers—who may include terrorists, thieves, and robbers—into the police force, how can we expect peace to prevail? After we depoliticize the police, elections will be held for the leadership of police stations. An elected police chief will be accountable to the people and will not be able to oppress them.

We also need to empower the people in our villages. We will establish a local government system that provides free justice at the village level. We plan to construct health units and primary schools under the auspices of local government bodies. People shouldn't have to run to top officials like the "chief minister (Khadim Aala)" out of desperation; we will bring these services to them.

Moreover, we recognize that the Balochi community has faced a great deal of injustice, and we will work to unite with them. We will embrace the Balochi people as our brothers and provide them with a status in Pakistan that has never been afforded to them before.

America's war was fought for profit by our leaders. You should be ashamed of sacrificing the lives of your people for financial gain. Those responsible for this will be held accountable. Thirty-five thousand Pakistanis lost their lives, including women and children. To those who worship money, we will ensure you face justice. We aspire to be friends with everyone in the world, including America, but we refuse to be subjugated.

We will assist you in finding a safe way to exit Afghanistan, but we will not conduct any military operations on your behalf. Tehreek-e-Insaf is committed to ensuring that the Pakistani army will never be used against its citizens.

Pakistan will never resort to begging. Just as Quaid-e-Azam did not beg, Imran Khan will also uphold this principle. We are determined to restore the dignity of Pakistan's green passport globally by eliminating corruption and establishing an independent judiciary system, with God's help. This will lead to a surge of investments flowing into our country. I pray that Pakistan becomes a destination where people from around the world come in search of jobs. I have informed all our supporters that we will support you and ensure that your rights are recognized. We will declare an emergency for women's education.

Christians and all minorities will also be free, and no one will be able to abuse them. I want to convey to India that the seven hundred thousand troops it has stationed in Kashmir cannot suppress anyone through military force. If America could not subjugate anyone with its army, how can India succeed? Tehreek-e-Insaf will stand with the

Kashmiris and support their rights. We will foster friendship with China and seek its assistance.

Imran Khan paid tribute to all his colleagues, stating that no one can stop them now. He addressed Asif Zardari, saying that he wants to send a message to his government urging them to declare their assets within a few months. We will investigate the assets of all politicians ourselves. Finally, Imran Khan concluded with a smile and a sarcastic tone in Punjabi, saying, "Mian Sahib, Jan Devo, Hun Sadi Wari Aan Devo (Nawaz Sharif, please quit and let us take our turn)."

Contrary to expectations, the tremendous success of this rally, along with the diverse representation of all sections of the public, created a significant impact in the political arena and the halls of power. The resonance of the slogans, the enthusiastic participation of children, youth, and women, and Imran Khan's confident and detailed speech stirred the political landscape. This event garnered global media attention to the growing political influence of the PTI in Pakistan.

Analysts began to acknowledge Imran Khan's political journey, while columnists treated the Sharif and Zardari families as mere side notes. Key political figures and influential elites started to align with the Pakistan Tehreek-e-Insaf. Political commentators deemed PTI the foremost contender against the PML-N and PPP, with Imran Khan being positioned as a likely future prime minister. Despite not being present in parliament and the absence of an election campaign, he showcased his persistent resolve and readiness by organizing a landmark rally at Minar-e-

Pakistan, suggesting that PTI was poised for success in the forthcoming elections.

The dramatic resurgence of PTI in Pakistan's political landscape has brought about a notable shift in the country's political culture. This remarkable rally exhibited a variety of features that were unprecedented in previous political gatherings. For example, the event began with the national anthem, and the DJ showcased exceptional talent, creating a lively atmosphere with energetic music. There was a plentiful display of party anthems and flags, and the widespread use of hats, badges, and mufflers established a fresh trend for political rallies.

Other political parties may not have recognized this trend immediately and therefore did not change their rally formats. However, over time, they began to adopt this approach as well, incorporating party anthems, music, DJs, and various accessories into their events. Throughout history, symbols have played a crucial role in bringing groups together, with flags being a prime example of identity representation for millennia. Social ideologies also recognize the significance of symbols, a concept that has persisted over time. The PTI recognized this and addressed the sensitivity of the circumstances. As a result, other political parties felt the need to implement comparable strategies.

The remarkable rise of Imran Khan and the Pakistan Tehreek-e-Insaf in the national political landscape can undoubtedly be linked to the rally that took place on October 30, 2011. Today, PTI is recognized as the largest political party in Pakistan and has successfully held numerous rallies at Minar-e-Pakistan.

A New Life

On May 7, 2013, during an election rally in Lahore, Imran Khan, along with three security guards, fell approximately 15 to 20 feet from a forklift. He sustained head injuries from the steel grill of the lift. After the incident, bystanders, not adhering to Advanced Trauma Life Support (ATLS) guidelines, lifted Khan by his arms and legs to get him into an ambulance. Despite the inherent risks of this action, Khan's survival and the fact that he avoided lifelong disabilities—including severe brain injuries, neurological damage, spinal cord injuries, and other organ injuries—can be considered nothing short of a miracle.

In May 2013, Imran Khan was actively campaigning for the national elections under the blazing sun. While members of the Sharif and Zardari families addressed a single rally in multiple cities on the same day, Imran Khan ran a solo campaign on behalf of the Pakistan Tehreek-e-Insaf. He held a series of energetic rallies at various locations throughout the day. On May 7, 2013, Imran Khan was scheduled to speak at eight different locations in Lahore, which included Ghalib Market, Railway Ground, Defense, Garhi Shahu, Baghbanpura, Sant Nagar, Gowalmandi Chowk, and Shahdara.

According to the schedule, Imran Khan arrived at NA-126, Ghalib Market, to address his first rally. He was ascending the stage via a lifter, accompanied by two security guards. In an attempt to join them, a third security guard also climbed onto the lifter, causing Imran Khan and the three security guards to lose their balance and fall from a height of approximately 15 to 20 feet. Imran Khan landed on his head, and the steel grill of the lifter also struck him, resulting in a head injury that began to bleed. Immediately following the accident, a stampede broke out among the rally attendees. PTI workers, including women, the elderly, children, and youth, were shocked to see their leader injured. Many began to cry and gathered around him frantically to help.

Imran Khan collapsed on the ground in a semi-conscious state, and there was no system in place for emergency first aid. In a state of panic, people lifted him by his legs and arms and rushed him to the ambulance. Without taking any safety precautions, he was placed in the ambulance and transported to a private hospital in Gulberg for immediate medical attention. There, he received first aid and had 11 stitches applied to his head wounds.

Dr. Faisal Sultan, the Chief Executive Officer of Shaukat Khanum Hospital, arrived promptly. Under his supervision, Imran Khan was transferred to Shaukat Khanum Hospital by ambulance. To ensure comprehensive care, the hospital also enlisted the services of expert neuro and orthopedic surgeons from Lahore General Hospital and the military, alongside local surgeons and physicians.

The PTI has canceled all its rallies, while PML-N leader Nawaz Sharif has announced the suspension of his election activities. Imran Khan's accident and health have taken center stage in Pakistan and worldwide, overshadowing discussions about the elections. A continuous flow of breaking news has emerged on both local and international media, and this story is spreading rapidly worldwide.

Residents began gathering in large numbers at Shaukat Khanum Hospital. At the same time, Imran Khan's supporters worldwide, as well as political leaders, including the President and the caretaker Prime Minister, expressed their sympathy and hopes for his swift recovery. Jemima Khan kept everyone updated on her ex-husband's condition through Twitter. Thousands of PTI supporters gathered outside the hospital, raising their hands and praying with tearful eyes for Imran Khan's health and longevity. The atmosphere was filled with sorrow, driven by concerns and fears about his well-being.

After the initial assessment and CT scan, Dr. Faisal Sultan informed the public through the media that "Imran Khan's tests are completed, revealing a minor spinal fracture. Thankfully, his brain, spinal cord, and other organs remain unaffected. He can move his hands and feet and actively communicates with his doctors and friends. However, due to the injuries to his neck and back, he will need to rest in bed for eight weeks." In response to this news, thousands of supporters gathered outside the hospital, expressing their gratitude and deep emotions, and began chanting slogans in support.

After waking up, Imran Khan demonstrated commendable sportsmanship by announcing through a message that the election rallies would proceed as planned. He encouraged his supporters to stay calm and composed, urging them not to get upset. His sister spoke to the press, sharing that he is concerned about the country and the upcoming elections, and noted that he intends to address the public soon. A Pakistan Tehreek-e-Insaf spokesperson confirmed that the rally in Islamabad on May 9 will proceed as scheduled, and Imran Khan is expected to address the event.

On the evening of May 9, Imran Khan addressed the nation via video link from the hospital. He bravely motivated his fellow citizens, stating, "Until he brings change to Pakistan, nothing can happen to him, by the grace of Allah." He urged the nation to come out on May 11 to change their circumstances, emphasizing that they should focus on the ideology rather than the individuals standing before them. Imran Khan remarked, "I have fought for Pakistan my entire life and have done what I could. Now, it is up to the people to decide on May 11 whether they want a new Pakistan. If you do not vote for change, I will endure what is coming next, but you will not be able to." His bold speech ignited a renewed enthusiasm and excitement among the workers, voters, and supporters of the PTI. Disappointment gave way to hope, and sadness gave way to joy.

Imran Khan's doctors, Dr. Kamran and Dr. Ahsan Shamim, describe the pace of his recovery as satisfactory. They note that bone injuries typically take longer to heal; however, Imran has recovered remarkably well due to his sports background and regular exercise. Dr. Faisal Sultan reflected on Imran's treatment as a memorable experience. He will never forget the harrowing moments when a bloodied Imran Khan was brought to Shaukat Khanum Hospital in an ambulance following the accident. "We wanted to reach the hospital quickly, but we were also concerned that any jolts from the vehicle could worsen Imran's spinal injuries. After a complete scan, we determined that the situation was not as alarming as we had feared, and everyone began to feel more at ease."

On May 22, 2013, after two weeks of treatment, Imran Khan returned to his ancestral home in Zaman Park. He wore a spine protection vest and was joyful at the sight of the trees and greenery. While there, he met with relatives, friends, party leaders, and workers. He reflected on the party's defeat in the elections, the formation of the government in KPK, and his plans for the future.

After thoroughly analyzing the events of May 7, 2013, from different angles—medical, spiritual, and more—it becomes clear that this incident not only provided Imran Khan with a new life but also deepened his faith, courage, and determination. This enhanced resilience played a crucial role in his ability to successfully tackle subsequent challenges.

As a trauma surgeon, I was shocked when I witnessed Khan's head-first fall from a lifter on television. Such a fall from a significant height can be perilous and may result in severe, permanent injuries to the brain, spinal cord, or other vital organs. Transferring a patient in this condition to a hospital without adhering to Advanced Trauma Life Support (ATLS) protocols is particularly risky. My concern about the way bystanders assisted Imran Khan into the ambulance was heightened by the lack of adherence to ATLS protocols, which poses significant risks.

However, following Dr. Faisal Sultan's media briefing, a wave of relief and reassurance swept through PTI leaders, supporters, voters, and Imran Khan's fans worldwide. In light of these events, one can only reflect: "When Allah grants protection, nothing can harm a person."

Following the accident, Imran Khan demonstrated remarkable courage and wisdom by uniting and mobilizing his party and supporters. He instilled hope in the nation for a transformed Pakistan, demonstrating his resoluteness and courage by speaking to the public during his hospital stay. He candidly acknowledged his defeat in the elections and expressed his dedication to continuing to fight for the country's welfare and the well-being of its citizens. This illustrates that Imran Khan is consistently prepared to confront challenges, make sacrifices, and engage in an ongoing struggle to realize his vision.

Incomplete Victory

Imran Khan's 17-year political journey, highlighted by his influential rally at Minar-e-Pakistan on October 30, 2011, significantly boosted public support and the popularity of the Pakistan Tehreek-e-Insaf party. The movement gained traction with the entrance of notable political figures like Shah Mehmood Qureshi and Makhdoom Javed Hashmi. Khan's opposition to drone strikes and his firm stance on counter-terrorism resonated with the majority. His groundbreaking manifesto, which focused on change and the slogan "New Pakistan," established him as the popular leader in the nation, ultimately leading PTI to become the dominant political party. A survey by the International Republican Institute showed that PTI was the most popular party across Pakistan, both on a national and provincial scale.

The term of the Pakistan People's Party government ended on March 16, 2013, after five years in power. According to Article 52 of the Constitution, the National Assembly was dissolved on March 17, and the Provincial Assemblies were disbanded on March 19. General elections were announced for May 11, 2013. On March 23, 2013, Khan introduced the "New Pakistan" resolution at the beginning of his election campaign.

On April 9, 2013, during the launch of his election manifesto, Imran Khan emphasized his dedication to eradicating corruption and promoting accountability. He vowed that his party would truly decentralize power to the village level, keeping only seventeen ministries within the federal government. Upon assuming office, he committed to stopping drone strikes and building relationships with all nations, including the United States, founded on mutual respect. Khan aims to create a new Pakistan that embodies the principles of both welfare and adherence to Islamic and democratic values.

He aims to foster peaceful and friendly relations with neighboring countries based on equality while taking immediate steps to eradicate terrorism and promote tolerance within society. He also plans to implement large-scale reforms across various sectors, allowing communities to decide on education, health, and development projects at the village level. He emphasized that he is not seeking alliances with other political parties, as he entered politics not for personal gain but to bring change. His policies will focus on supporting farmers and laborers, providing relief to the common man, and reducing poverty. Khan noted that no political party in Pakistan has historically conducted internal elections, but he intends to set a new precedent. He expressed his desire to move away from selecting candidates who repeatedly win elections and instead support the youth. He aims to allocate more than 25% of his party's tickets to candidates under the age of 35. Additionally, his party will develop an independent foreign policy, with Parliament playing a central role in the decision-making process.

On April 29, the Observer magazine identified Imran Khan and his party as the main rivals to the Pakistan Muslim League-Nawaz (PML-N). Between 2011 and 2013, harsh words, accusations, and criticisms were escalated between

Imran Khan and Nawaz Sharif, alongside their respective party leaders and supporters.

During the election campaign, Imran Khan concentrated on the regions of the Punjab and Khyber Pakhtunkhwa provinces. As a result, the PTI faced tough competition from the PML-N in Punjab, while in Khyber Pakhtunkhwa, it emerged as the most popular party. However, the PTI struggled to gain significant support in Balochistan and Sindh. In the 2013 elections, the party adopted the slogan "change," which Imran Khan described as a "tsunami," emphasizing that this change represented a shift away from dynastic and family-oriented politics. Numerous analysts also characterized PTI's movement as a "tsunami."

The 2013 election was notably distinct from all earlier elections in various important aspects:

1. This time, the competition was not limited to the two traditional dynastic political parties, the PML-N and the PPP. Instead, a third political force, PTI, emerged to provide robust competition.

2. Imran Khan, once considered clumsy and a failed political figure, rose nationally as a major challenger to the Sharif and Zardari families.

3. Imran Khan and the PTI garnered strong support from the public, particularly educated individuals and enthusiastic youth who felt alienated from traditional politics and were hopeful for a "new Pakistan."

4. The Election Commission successfully published approximately 86 million verified voter registrations by eliminating 37 million fraudulent votes and incorporating 36 million new voters, most of whom are young.

5. The election campaign was marred by the threat of attacks on political leaders from the Taliban, as well as the repercussions of various terrorist incidents.

6. Social media emerged as a powerful influence in conjunction with private media channels and talk shows.

7. For the first time in Pakistan's history, an elected government completed its term and peacefully transferred power to a newly elected government.

8. On May 4, 2013, Maulana Fazal-Ur-Rehman issued a political fatwa declaring that voting for Imran Khan was a "sin."

9. Imran Khan made a national address from his hospital bed, where he was recovering from injuries, while giving instructions to his party for the election.

On May 11, 2013, simultaneous elections took place across Pakistan for both the National and provincial assemblies. This significant event marked a milestone in the country's history, with approximately 86 million registered voters participating to elect nearly 1,000 representatives for the national and provincial assemblies for the first time. In these elections, the PML-N emerged as the frontrunner, garnering 32.77% of the votes, followed by the PTI in second place with 16.92%, and the PPP in third with 15.32%.

After abstaining from the 2008 elections, PTI garnered 14,302,302 votes in 2013. The party emerged as the second-largest vote recipient in both the national and Punjab assemblies, while taking the lead in the Khyber Pakhtunkhwa (KPK) assembly. In KPK, PTI captured 19.6 percent of the total votes and had a significant impact in Sindh with over 600,000 votes. In Punjab, PTI received 4,951,216 votes, ranking as the second-largest party in the region in terms of both votes and seats. However, its performance in Balochistan was relatively weak, receiving only 24,000 votes, or 1.8 percent of the total.

During the National Assembly elections, the PML-N won 166 seats, while the PPP received 42 seats. The PTI secured 35 seats, and the MQM achieved 23 seats. The JUI claimed 15 seats, and the Pakistan Muslim League-Functional (PML-F) obtained six seats. Both the Jamaat-e-Islami (JI) and the Pakhtunkhwa Milli Awami Party (PkMAP) won four seats each, whereas the National People's Party (NPP) secured three seats. The Pakistan Muslim League-Quaid (PML-Q) earned two seats. Additionally, several parties, including the Awami National Party (ANP), Balochistan National Party (BNP), Qaumi Watan Party (QWP), National Party (NP), PML-Zia, All Pakistan Muslim League (led by Musharraf), Awami Muslim League (AML), and Awami Jamhoori Ittehad, each secured one seat. Moreover, 28 candidates were elected as independents. With support from these independent candidates, the PML-N achieved a simple majority, allowing

Mian Muhammad Nawaz Sharif to be elected as Prime Minister of Pakistan for the third time on June 5, 2013.

In the 2013 national elections, PTI engaged in intense competition against established political parties. Despite their expectations, promises, and support from voters seeking change, PTI was successful only in KPK, where they established a provincial government. In the other three provinces and at the national level, they ended up as an opposition party, losing to PML-N and PPP.

Imran Khan ran an extensive and demanding election campaign. Although he was unable to achieve a complete victory for his party, the Pakistan Tehreek-e-Insaf performed well in Khyber Pakhtunkhwa, which provided a renewed impetus for the party to enhance its competitiveness in the future. Many analysts consider this a significant achievement for him. Building on this momentum, Imran Khan was expected to expand his influence in various regions of Punjab, particularly in areas where PTI garnered considerable support but only won a small number of seats.

On May 12, Imran Khan delivered a video message from the hospital to discuss the election results. He remarked, "A significant democratic process has unfolded in our country. This year's voter turnout was the highest in Pakistan's history. I want to congratulate our nation as we advance in the evolution of democracy." Khan expressed his satisfaction with the increasing political participation, noting that many who had never voted before are now engaged in the process. This highlights a growing awareness among the public and a commitment to influence their own futures. He mentioned that witnessing the enthusiasm of the youth during the elections has helped ease his feelings of loss, stating, "The happiness I've gained from the enthusiasm of young people in politics has outweighed the sorrow of losing." Additionally, he expressed gratitude to the youth for their support of the New Pakistan ideology and thanked women for their remarkable participation, saying, "Never before have so many women voted. This demonstrates that women are now playing a vital role in reshaping Pakistan's future and contributing to the creation of a new Pakistan."

The Pakistan Tehreek-e-Insaf (PTI) won a total of 55 seats in the Khyber Pakhtunkhwa Assembly. The Jamiat Ulema-e-Islam (F) and the Pakistan Muslim League (N) each secured 17 seats. The Qaumi Watan Party captured 10 seats, while Jamaat-e-Islami obtained 8. The Awami National Party gained five seats, and both the Awami Democratic Alliance and the Pakistan People's Party garnered 5 and 4 seats, respectively. The All-Pakistan Muslim League secured one seat, while independent candidates collectively won two seats.

Despite predictions, high hopes, and sympathy votes, the PTI did not achieve the expected victory in the 2013 federal and Punjab elections. However, rather than dwelling on this setback, Imran Khan seized the opportunity afforded by their partial success in Khyber Pakhtunkhwa. He embraced the responsibility of forming a coalition government in the province and focused on its reconstruction following the destruction caused by terrorism.

The voting for the Chief Minister position in the Khyber Pakhtunkhwa Provincial Assembly took place on Friday, May 31, 2013. The Pakistan Tehreek-e-Insaf candidate gained support from several parties, including Jamaat-e-Islami, the Qaumi Watan Party, the Awami Jamhoori Ittehad, and various independent members. Consequently, Pervez Khattak was elected as Chief Minister, obtaining 84 votes and forming a coalition government in Khyber Pakhtunkhwa. The opposition candidate, Maulana Lutf-Ur-Rehman, who is the brother of Maulana Fazal-Ur-Rehman, received 37 votes. Although Wajih-Uz-Zaman was nominated by the Pakistan Muslim League-Nawaz for the Chief Minister position, he withdrew his candidacy in favor of Maulana Lutf-Ur-Rehman.

During his first address to the assembly after being elected as Chief Minister, Pervez Khattak emphasized the importance of transparency and accountability in governance. He mentioned, "We will ensure a government that is clean and transparent. We will activate the Provincial Finance Commission and create District Finance Commissions." Khattak encouraged newly elected officials and representatives to quickly submit their asset details to the government. This information will be posted on the website, enabling the public to compare governance over time. He pointed out that while there is a law guaranteeing access to information, it has not been effectively enforced. His administration intends to publish all pertinent information online, allowing citizens to track how funds are allocated across various projects, particularly in the education sector.

He pledged to take concrete steps to combat corruption and improve the culture within police stations. Acknowledging that law and order are significant challenges, Khattak assured the public that his government would work closely with all political forces to address these issues and combat terrorism in the province. He concluded by stating, "We will not disappoint the people. They will notice the difference between our current administration and previous governments, and we will completely eradicate corruption by establishing justice and fairness in the province."

Despite facing challenges such as inexperience, terrorism, internal party divisions, and pressure from allies, the PTI provincial government implemented several historic and revolutionary measures aimed at enhancing public welfare and the province's development. The public responded positively to these initiatives, which also gained acknowledgment from other provinces and the international community.

Police Reforms

Establishing law and order and the authority of the government in the terrorism-ravaged province of Khyber Pakhtunkhwa (KPK) was the biggest challenge for the newly formed provincial government of the PTI. In response to this problem, the government directed the provincial assembly to approve the Police Reforms Bill. This legislation was designed to enhance the effectiveness of the police force, introduce structural changes within the police department, and promote increased citizen involvement.

As part of the new initiative to enhance law and order, around 150 police checkpoints and posts were removed from various cities, which had caused significant traffic congestion and long wait times for the public. In response to the persistent threat of terrorism, 94 new checkpoints were set up across eight cities. Moreover, 120 high-quality CCTV cameras were installed in key areas to bolster security. Furthermore, Chief Minister Pervez Khattak and other officials decided to reduce the number of staff assigned to personal security, enabling those officers to be redirected toward initiatives focused on combating crime and eliminating extremism.

Six exceptional training institutions have been established to enhance the skills of the police force. Among these are the Investigation School, the Bomb Disposal Training School, the Cellular Forensic Laboratory, and the Internal Command Access Line.

The provincial assembly approved the KP Police Act to reform the police department. By giving full authority to IG Police Nasir Durrani for implementation, the provincial government made the police department entirely apolitical. As a result, appointments and transfers were conducted based on the institution's needs rather than political interests, and new recruitments were carried out based on merit through the NTS.

A Council for Dispute Resolution was established to promote community participation and has successfully resolved thousands of cases in a harmonious manner.

The government, in partnership with the UNDP, launched a counter-terrorism program to enhance police capabilities in this area. Additionally, a counter-terrorism school and a bomb disposal unit were established.

Establishment of a cellular forensic lab to bring about structured reforms,

KP Restriction of Rented Building Act 2014

KP Restriction of Hotel Business Act 2014

KP Security of Sensitive and Vulnerable Places and Establishment Ordinance 2014

With UNDP support, the forensic lab was upgraded in May 2017, and within a brief six-month period, it successfully profiled 25,000 cases. According to UNDP, this lab is the largest forensic institution in Pakistan, following the Punjab Forensic Lab. Additionally, a new forensic lab was established in Swat.

The outcomes of these reforms were very positive and promising. The KPK Police demonstrated outstanding professionalism and efficiency, successfully combating terrorism and earning a strong reputation for integrity and respect nationwide. In a brief timeframe, the KPK Police Department emerged as a benchmark for police forces in the other three provinces, surpassing them in effectiveness.

Health Card

The health card represents a pioneering and exemplary flagship initiative by the Pakistan Tehreek-e-Insaf government, with no prior equivalent in Pakistan's history. Launched in 2015, the program initially provided healthcare coverage to 3% of the population in Khyber Pakhtunkhwa (KPK). In 2016, it entered its second phase, and by 2017, coverage had grown to encompass 64% of the population. By 2020, the Health Card had expanded to provide benefits to the entire population.

The health card initiative in Khyber Pakhtunkhwa has been successfully launched for the public. So far, billions of rupees have been allocated to the State Life Insurance Corporation and various private hospitals as part of this program. At present, 46 government hospitals and 127 private hospitals in KPK are participating in this scheme. The implementation of the health card has notably alleviated congestion and pressure on government hospitals. Moreover, it has provided the general public with access to medical services in private hospitals that were once only accessible to the affluent. The Khyber Pakhtunkhwa government has invested approximately 110 billion rupees in the health card initiative to date.

Political instability in Pakistan frequently leads to delays in the completion of major projects. Nonetheless, amidst a significant economic crisis, this public welfare initiative has had a profoundly positive impact on the lives of many individuals. Both critics and observers have recognized it as a key achievement of the Pakistan Tehreek-e-Insaf (PTI) government. In the 2018 and 2024 elections, PTI secured a two-thirds majority in Khyber Pakhtunkhwa, with the implementation of health cards being instrumental in this victory.

Billion Tree Tsunami

Over the past decade, our nation has been consistently identified as one of the ten countries most affected by rising global temperatures and their associated risks. According to the Global Climate Risk Index report published by German watch, we currently rank eighth in terms of our vulnerability to climate change. From 1998 to 2018, we suffered a heartbreaking loss of 9,989 lives due to natural disasters, which also had an economic impact of about $3.8 billion.

Pakistan's strategic location offers a variety of resources, but it also comes with considerable dangers. Our country is rich in diverse ecosystems, ranging from oceans to northern highlands. It features coastal zones, fertile agricultural lands, deserts, rivers, and more than seven thousand glaciers. Additionally, we are situated at the intersection of three major mountain ranges: the Hindu Kush, the Himalayas, and the Karakoram. While this geographical diversity is an important asset, it brings along various challenges. For example, the melting of glaciers and the potential for glacial lake outburst floods heighten the risk of flooding.

On the other hand, droughts pose a significant threat as well. Other hazards, such as cyclones and coastal erosion, further endanger communities. Tackling these issues is a formidable challenge for Pakistan, particularly given its struggling economy.

Environmentalists and scientists universally acknowledge that widespread deforestation is a primary contributor to many of the environmental challenges we face today. We might unknowingly be contributing to our own downfall through our actions. Notable examples of deforestation include Lahore, which is losing its trees and becoming a "smog trap"; Karachi, transforming into a "heat trap"; and Islamabad, which is evolving into a "pollution trap." Nonetheless, the Pakistan Tehreek-e-Insaf government has made significant strides in promoting awareness about forests and tree planting nationwide through its Billion Tree Tsunami initiative, a key component of its green agenda.

The Billion Tree Tsunami project was launched during the initial provincial government of the Pakistan Tehreek-e-Insaf in Khyber Pakhtunkhwa. Although a task force for the initiative was established in 2013, it was officially inaugurated by Imran Khan in 2015—the project aimed to plant one billion trees across 35,000 hectares of forested and barren land.

Starting in 2013, the regional 'Billion Tree Tsunami' initiative has quietly brought transformative changes to the country. Initially introduced in Khyber Pakhtunkhwa, it soon garnered recognition both within Pakistan and internationally. It was celebrated as a pivotal endeavor by environmental groups, including the Bonn Challenge, the World Bank, and the IUCN, owing to its remarkable results. Over time, foreign diplomats based in the Diplomatic Enclave of Islamabad took notice, which led to heightened awareness of the project through their visits and evaluations. Consequently, international media outlets began to report on the initiative, showcasing it as a notable effort by a developing nation in tackling climate change.

After completing the Billion Tree Tsunami project at the provincial level, the Pakistan Tehreek-e-Insaf sought to launch a nationwide environmental movement following its assumption of power in the central government in 2018. This initiative was primarily motivated by Prime Minister Imran Khan's commitment, leading to the introduction of the ambitious Ten Billion Tree Tsunami project. The goal was to restore, promote, and extensively plant trees across one million hectares of forestland in the country. Pakistan's dedication to this initiative has received commendation from organizations such as the United Nations and the World Economic Forum. Furthermore, countries such as South Africa, Bangladesh, and Saudi Arabia also expressed plans to initiate similar projects in their areas.

World Environment Day is observed every year on June 5th worldwide. The proposal to establish this day was presented during a session of the United Nations General Assembly in 1972, with the first global celebration taking place in 1974. In 2021, the theme was 'Ecosystem Restoration,' and this year was significant for Pakistan, as it had the privilege of hosting the worldwide celebrations. This recognition highlighted Pakistan's dedication to environmental improvement despite facing considerable climate challenges.

During a speech at the United Nations General Assembly on global climate change, British Prime Minister Boris Johnson praised Imran Khan's eco-friendly initiative, the Billion Tree Tsunami. He urged all nations to emulate

Imran Khan's commitment to planting a total of 10 billion trees in Pakistan.

Local Governments

According to the manifesto, the Local Government System Bill was passed in the initial year of the PTI's administration to empower local governance. In 2015, local government elections took place in KPK, which the PTI considers one of its key accomplishments.

The provincial government allocated 10% of the district development budget to local governments to improve tehsils and basic health centers, aiming to provide better healthcare services for residents in those regions.

The majority of the local government's development budget was allocated to education, accounting for 20 percent of the district's overall development budget. District officials stated that these resources were used to establish crucial facilities in elementary, middle, and high schools. A report from the Independent Monitoring Unit revealed that over 95 percent of schools across different districts in the province have access to water, more than 96 percent are equipped with toilet facilities, and over 90 percent have electricity.

Peshawar BRT Project

The contemporary Bus Rapid Transit (BRT) project in Peshawar was launched during the final six months of the Pakistan Tehreek-e-Insaf government's initial term. However, the project was not completed within the initially promised six months. The original estimated cost was Rs 49 billion, but due to multiple design alterations, the project faced unnecessary delays, and the projected cost escalated to approximately Rs 70 billion.

On August 13, 2020, Prime Minister Imran Khan launched Khyber Pakhtunkhwa's first modern BRT system, which is also the fourth of its kind in Pakistan. During the inauguration, Prime Minister Khan proclaimed that this initiative represents the finest metro bus service in the country. It is noteworthy that he, along with other PTI leaders, had previously criticized the metro bus projects in Islamabad, Lahore, and Multan established by former Prime Minister Nawaz Sharif and former Chief Minister of Punjab, Shehbaz Sharif, labeling them as "Jangla buses." Nonetheless, the successful realization of the BRT project in Peshawar stands out as a significant achievement for the PTI provincial government.

BRT is a third-generation initiative featuring a primary corridor that stretches 27 kilometers from Chamkani to Karakhano Crossing. This primary route is supported by five off-corridor links that connect different areas of the city. Among these, the Kohat Adda Shah Alam off-corridor route along Charsadda Road is 18 kilometers long, while the section between Chamkani and Pashtkha Chowk is 19 kilometers. Furthermore, three additional routes connect various neighborhoods in Hayatabad to Karakhano Crossing.

BRT Peshawar serves approximately 300,000 passengers daily and received significant recognition in 2022, winning three international awards from various American organizations. These awards were presented following a comprehensive assessment that considered factors such as innovation, safety, convenience, sustainability, customer satisfaction, bus durability, and environmental impact. In July 2022, BRT Peshawar was honored with the 'Best Smart Ticketing Program' award from Transport Ticketing Global, recognizing its innovative ticketing system that greatly enhanced the travel experience for over 200,000 users.

In 2024, Peshawar's Bus Rapid Transit (BRT) initiative earned international recognition when the Bus Industry Restructuring Program (BIRP) received an honorable mention at the Sustainable Transport Awards 2024. Trans Peshawar was recognized for its efforts to retire over 500 outdated buses and wagons, thereby contributing to the modernization of its transportation system. Officials from Trans Peshawar stated that this marks the fifth global award for the BRT project, a significant achievement for both Pakistan and Khyber Pakhtunkhwa. The initiative included scrapping more than 500 old buses and wagons, with compensation offered to their owners. The BRT project has previously been awarded a gold standard, along with other prestigious international honors.

Institutional reforms

The Access to Information Bill has been passed to help discourage corruption.

To enhance public convenience, several services have been streamlined: land transfers can now be completed within seven days, birth and death registrations within two days, issuance of domicile certificates within ten days, and

First Information Reports (FIRs) can be registered immediately.

There has also been a strong focus on girls' education and the construction of new schools.

Additionally, the Revenue Department successfully recovered Rs 70 million that had been extorted from the public by government officials in the form of bribes.

When the Pakistan Tehreek-e-Insaf came to power in Khyber Pakhtunkhwa, it encountered significant challenges, including terrorism, corruption, institutional decay, internal party divisions, the establishment of a forward bloc, and pressure from allied parties. Taking advantage of these issues, the opposition released a white paper on the performance of the Khyber Pakhtunkhwa government, covering the period from May 2013 to September 2014. This document was titled "A Grand Deception in the Name of Change."

On this occasion, Marvi Memon, a leading member of the PML-N and a member of the National Assembly, stated that the PTI government has spent only 25 billion out of the 83 billion allocated for the people in KPK during the current financial year. Following the adoption of the 18th Amendment, the provincial government has been unable to fulfill its duties or honor its commitments. The KPK government has also lagged behind Punjab in revenue generation and has not been successful in attracting investments to the province. Furthermore, Memon highlighted that work has yet to commence on 23 major new projects. Although PTI often criticizes foreign aid, she pointed out that the KPK government relies on foreign assistance for up to 20 percent of its development budget. According to a white paper prepared by the PML-N, the adult education program has not been initiated in KPK, and plans to double the number of women's schools have not materialized. Memon also expressed concern over the health situation in Khyber Pakhtunkhwa, noting that salaries are not being paid to health workers.

Despite facing criticism from the PML-N federal government, the provincial opposition, and the media regarding its governance and policies, the PTI-led provincial government, under the leadership of Imran Khan and Pervez Khattak, persisted in enacting various reforms. These initiatives included police reforms, the distribution of health cards, the Billion Tree Tsunami project, local government reforms, and institutional improvements, all carried out with a commitment to transparency and accountability. Due to this effective governance, the residents of KPK demonstrated their trust in Imran Khan by re-electing the PTI for a second and third consecutive term in the 2018 and 2023 elections, achieving an over two-thirds majority. This result highlighted their rejection of rival propaganda and established a new historical milestone in Khyber Pakhtunkhwa.

The Pathans are known for their strong political insight, often refusing to give a provincial government they disapprove of another opportunity. Thus, the consecutive three victories of Pakistan Tehreek-e-Insaf with a solid majority highlight not only the political savvy of the proud citizens of Khyber Pakhtunkhwa but also their unwavering trust in Imran Khan's leadership.

The Umpire's Finger

Immediately after the 2013 elections, Imran Khan demonstrated sportsmanship by acknowledging his party's defeat and accepting the election results. In contrast, Asif Zardari referred to it as an election orchestrated by the Returning Officers (ROs). A few days later, as further details emerged, all political parties, including Pakistan Tehreek-e-Insaf, began to raise allegations of electoral fraud.

In the first assembly session following his recovery, Imran Khan reiterated his allegations of election rigging and called for an audit of four particular constituencies: NA-125 in Lahore, where Khawaja Saad Rafique of PML-N emerged victorious; NA-110 in Sialkot, where Khawaja Asif from PML-N won; NA-122, where Sardar Ayaz Sadiq of PML-N triumphed; and NA-154 in Lodhran, where independent candidate Siddiq Khan Baloch defeated the PTI candidate.

Khan persistently urged the scrutiny of these four constituencies and the verification of thumb impressions. Despite his ongoing demands, protests, and warnings, he did not receive any justice from the Election Tribunal, nor did the government offer any support. After enduring over a year and two months without hearings, Imran Khan ultimately chose to announce the Azadi March, also known as the Tsunami March, in protest against the election rigging that favored the PML-N government.

On August 3, 2014, Imran Khan called on all party members to gather in Islamabad on August 14, highlighting the importance of thorough preparations for the Azadi March. He indicated that a critical confrontation was expected on that date and suggested that arrests might occur. Khan urged the party's backup leadership to prepare for this possibility. Additionally, he requested the formation of a group of 100,000 motorcycle riders for the occasion. The services of the Insaf Youth Wing and the Insaf Student Federation were to be enlisted for this purpose. He advised that buses, vehicles, trucks, and cars be arranged in advance to ensure a smooth operation on the day of the march. Imran Khan stated that this was a crucial phase in Pakistan's history and asserted that this struggle would lead to genuine democracy and true freedom. He encouraged everyone to participate in the movement, arguing that change would undoubtedly come to the country. To apply further pressure on the government, Khan also requested the resignations of party members serving in the National Assembly.

During a press conference on August 11, 2013, Imran Khan accused the PML-N government of coming to power through electoral fraud. He expressed that, after 14 months of seeking justice through various legal channels—such as the Election Commission, the Tribunal, the Judiciary, and Parliament—his concerns had been ignored. As a result, he argued that their only recourse was to take to the streets to push for reforms in Pakistan's governance. Khan highlighted that the primary goals of the PTI's long march and sit-in were to demand the resignation of Prime Minister Nawaz Sharif, call for transparent mid-term elections, and ensure accountability for those responsible for electoral rigging. He assured the government that the PTI would conduct its protests peacefully, refraining from any illegal or destructive actions.

Ameer Jamaat-e-Islami Sirajul Haq expressed his condemnation of electoral fraud and made attempts to initiate discussions between Imran Khan and the government, but these efforts yielded no results. Jamaat-e-Islami decided not to take part in the Azadi March. Haq cautioned that this scenario could potentially open the door for military intervention, posing a risk to democratic processes. Prominent political parties, such as the PPP and MQM, acknowledged that some of Imran Khan's claims of rigging had merit; however, they also refrained from backing the Azadi March.

After Imran Khan's announcement, the PTI began preparations in full swing to ensure the success of the Azadi March. Supporters from across the country started gathering at Zaman Park in Lahore. The atmosphere in Zaman Park was festive, with the entire area adorned with colorful banners. The enthusiasm of the workers was palpable as they sang, danced bhangra, and played national songs along with PTI anthems. It felt more like a celebration of victory than a preparation for protest. The workers expressed that they had overcome numerous obstacles to reach Lahore, and they were determined to march to Islamabad.

In a national address on the evening of August 12, Prime Minister Nawaz Sharif discussed the country's political situation and reviewed the government's performance over the past year. He announced that the government has decided to establish a three-member Supreme Court commission to investigate allegations of rigging in the 2013 elections. He requested the Chief Justice to form this commission, which will provide a final report after thoroughly examining the claims of election rigging.

Sharif emphasized that he will leave it to the nation to determine whether there is any justification for a protest movement following this governmental action. He pointed out that both domestic and international media, as well as observers, monitored the elections in Pakistan, and no one deemed the elections non-transparent. He expressed his concerns about a particular party's continued allegations of rigging, stating that these baseless claims are creating an atmosphere of uncertainty. The Prime Minister assured that his government is open to discussions on all national issues and recognizes the constitutional right to peaceful protest. However, he declared that anarchy would not be tolerated. He emphasized that decisions need to be made in Parliament and that a few individuals should not be permitted to compromise the will of millions.

He also pointed out that despite the government's efforts to promote the country's development, specific individuals are obstructing progress by spreading baseless claims and staging protests. He encouraged the public to critically evaluate the motivations behind these demonstrations and understand the reasons fueling the current unrest. Additionally, he called on the media to consider its influence in the present political landscape and to ensure that its freedom is not exploited for violent or unconstitutional ends.

During a press conference in Lahore, Imran Khan responded to the Prime Minister of Pakistan's announcement about creating a judicial commission to look into election rigging claims by asserting, "I will arrive in Islamabad on August 14, regardless of the circumstances." He stressed that his party intends to conduct a sit-in in the capital, adding that the nature of the protest—whether it stays peaceful—will depend on the government's behavior.

Khan pointed out that a fair investigation is impossible while Prime Minister Nawaz Sharif remains in power. He called for the immediate resignation of both the Election Commission and the Prime Minister. Having faith in Chief Justice Nasir ul Mulk, he requested the establishment of a commission under his oversight and the formation of a caretaker government. Khan noted that the Pakistan Tehreek-e-Insaf has pursued all legal channels in search of justice but has faced obstacles.

Khan cautioned that the government cannot halt the influx of individuals, insisting that if law enforcement targets PTI members, the government will be held responsible. He spoke directly to the authorities, stating, "You must choose whether to let us proceed peacefully or to create your downfall by obstructing us with containers." He ended with a fervent declaration: "I am willing to sacrifice my life for this cause. I will lead the march, and if anything happens to me during this protest, the youth will hold Nawaz Sharif accountable."

Protests, sit-ins, demonstrations, and marches have been a significant part of the political landscape in Pakistan for many years. During these activities, both politicians and religious figures frequently unite to challenge the ruling government. Some of these actions have successfully met their political aims, while others have fallen short. The primary intention behind these sit-ins is to apply pressure on the government, which various power centers have sometimes exploited.

The first significant protest in Islamabad took place on July 4 and 5, 1980, organized by the Tehreek-e-Nifaz-e-Fiqh-e-Jafria. They held a sit-in in front of Parliament House to express their discontent with the Zakat and Ushr Ordinance, which former President Zia-ul-Haq had introduced and refused to accept. Thousands joined the protest, claiming that the ordinance neglected the needs of the Shia community. During this two-day event, the police refrained from blocking roads with containers or using batons and tear gas. In the end, the government was forced to agree to their demand to exempt the Shia school of thought from the ordinance.

The phrase "long march" was first introduced in Pakistani politics by Benazir Bhutto. She announced a long march on November 16, 1992, beginning in Lahore, accusing former Prime Minister Nawaz Sharif of rigging the 1990 general elections. Benazir intended to encircle the Presidency and Parliament on November 18, believing that if 400,000 people gathered in the capital, the government would have to step down.

In response, the government implemented drastic measures to control the situation. Police leave was canceled, and military control was established in Islamabad. Although Benazir Bhutto's home in Islamabad was cordoned off, she managed to reach Liaquat Bagh in Rawalpindi. Nonetheless, the march could not proceed and ultimately concluded without achieving its goals.

On April 18, 1993, President Ghulam Ishaq Khan disbanded the National Assembly and removed Prime Minister Nawaz Sharif from office. However, on May 26, 1993, the Supreme Court mandated the reinstatement of Nawaz Sharif's administration. On July 16, 1993, Benazir Bhutto launched another long march but faced obstacles as Islamabad was barricaded with barbed wire. In this situation, Army Chief General Waheed Kakar forced both President Ghulam Ishaq Khan and Prime Minister Nawaz Sharif to resign.

In September 1996, Jamaat-e-Islami held its long march, called the 'Million March,' led by Qazi Hussain Ahmed, aimed at toppling Benazir Bhutto's administration. The Islamabad police arrested participants near Aabpara for three days, leading to confrontations between members of Jamaat-e-Islami and the police. On the third day of the sit-in, protestors were allowed to march to the current D-Chowk in front of the Parliament House, where they offered prayers, but were soon met with tear gas. After succeeding in reaching the Parliament House, the Jamaat-e-Islami workers dispersed by evening. A month later, in response to the public outcry, then-President Farooq Leghari dismissed Benazir Bhutto's government.

On March 9, 2007, former President General Pervez Musharraf dismissed Chief Justice Iftikhar Muhammad Chaudhry from his role. This decision triggered a movement led by lawyers to restore the independence of the judiciary. The movement ignited widespread protests, culminating in the long march in June 2008. Chief Justice Iftikhar Muhammad Chaudhry, along with prominent lawyers' leaders Aitzaz Ahsan, Munir A. Malik, and Ali Ahmed Kurd, spearheaded the march, which successfully arrived at the Parliament House. During the event, Nawaz Sharif, along with the leaders of the lawyers' movement, addressed the crowd, urging Aitzaz Ahsan not to escalate the protest into a sit-in. This request led to the dispersal of the crowd, leaving many lawyers who had come to Islamabad for a sit-in feeling greatly disappointed.

The movement continued beyond that point. In March 2009, the long march was renewed, starting from Lahore under the leadership of Nawaz Sharif. To stop the march, Islamabad and Rawalpindi were filled with containers. The march only reached Gujranwala when, on March 16, 2009, Prime Minister Yousaf Raza Gilani announced that all the ousted judges, including Chief Justice Iftikhar Muhammad Chaudhry, would be reinstated. Consequently, the Long March achieved its goals. It has been claimed that Army Chief General Ashfaq Pervez Kayani played a role in the reinstatement of the judiciary and affected Nawaz Sharif's decision to cancel the long march.

In January 2013, Dr. Allama Tahir-ul-Qadri, the leader of Pakistan Awami Tehreek, orchestrated a march from Lahore to Islamabad during the tenure of the Pakistan People's Party. His party conducted a sit-in in Islamabad right before the general elections, advocating the slogan "Save the state, not politics," and claimed that five million individuals participated. In reality, however, the sit-in attracted only a few thousand people and concluded without achieving its intended goals.

To restore their reputation, the PPP government engaged in negotiations with Tahir-ul-Qadri, facilitated by the Muslim League-Q leadership. On January 17, after four days of braving the cold in Islamabad, the sit-in ended with a successful agreement between the government and the protesters. Hundreds of participants were informed of their 'victory,' and it was announced that their demands would be addressed, leading to a peaceful dispersal. Despite Tahir-ul-Qadri's intentions to thwart the 2013 elections through this protest, his efforts ultimately failed.

Following the Model Town incident, Allama Tahir-ul-Qadri decided to march toward Islamabad once more, this time in collaboration with Pakistan Tehreek-e-Insaf. Preparations were ramping up for the Azadi March, organized by Pakistan Tehreek-e-Insaf, alongside the Inqilab March led by Pakistan Awami Tehreek. In response, the government implemented roadblocks and police checkpoints at the entry and exit points of major cities in Punjab to thwart the marches. In Lahore, the police increased the deployment of containers and personnel on routes leading to the Minhaj-ul-Quran central office in Model Town. Meanwhile, in Islamabad, the red zone was secured with containers, and additional containers were deployed on the Kashmir Highway and other roads throughout the city.

Lahore was locked down four days ago to thwart Allama Tahir-ul-Qadri's Martyrs' Day event. The streets, particularly in the Model Town area, looked like a battleground. Barricades and checkpoints were set up, motorbikes were targeted in crackdowns, and the city's entry and exit points were blocked. There was a petrol shortage, prices for essential goods surged, and a significant police presence was noted. Mobile phone services were partially suspended, contributing to the chaos. The citywide closure resulted in processions being turned away, wedding events being postponed, and patients struggling for survival in ambulances. Rescue operations were also heavily affected.

The government's panic and measures have greatly impacted those who depend on daily wages to support their families. This includes individuals who must travel outside the city for work and farmers whose fruits and vegetables rotted on the highways due to the city lockdown. Many have had to purchase essential goods at inflated prices, plunging the country into uncertainty. If the ruling party had effective planners and advisors, they could have disregarded the marches and protests, as those demonstrating would have likely dispersed within a few days. However, the government chose a policy of revenge and confrontation, which further escalated the situation.

Pakistan Tehreek-e-Insaf announced that 400,000 workers from Khyber Pakhtunkhwa will travel to Islamabad for the Azadi March. The PTI urged participants to come fully prepared, bringing food and other essential items. Many people and PTI workers from various parts of Pakistan joined the march in delegations and processions. The biggest group arrived from Lahore, and many participants came from multiple regions of Khyber Pakhtunkhwa. Moreover, people from Karachi, the United States, the Arab, and several European countries also joined the march and sit-in.

On August 14, 2014, the Azadi March, led by Imran Khan, departed from Zaman Park in Lahore and headed towards Islamabad. The convoy received a warm welcome as it passed through various locations in the city, with enthusiastic public participation, passionate slogans from supporters, and the singing of PTI anthems. Speeches by Imran Khan and other leaders, delivered from containers, not only energized the atmosphere but also captured the attention of both national and international media.

The PML-N administration was taken aback by the enthusiastic and successful commencement of the Azadi March from Lahore. In reaction to this unexpected turnout, PML-N supporters launched attacks on the peaceful march participants and Imran Khan's vehicle in Gujranwala, heightening the situation. Imran Khan has urged his followers to maintain peace. Despite ongoing stone-throwing incidents by PML-N supporters in several areas of the city, the government has not ensured adequate protection for the marchers. However, as the march progresses beyond the boundaries of Gujranwala, the situation begins to stabilize and return to normal.

The march that started in Lahore reached Islamabad within two days. The authorities allowed the participants to first go to Zero Point and then to Aabpara Chowk. Both the Pakistan Awami Tehreek and the Pakistan Tehreek-e-Insaf organized separate rallies at Aabpara Chowk, after which they expressed their intention to march together in front of the Parliament House. The government deployed thousands of police officers, as well as the Frontier Corps, along with containers to block the way. Despite these hurdles, Imran Khan and Tahir-ul-Qadri succeeded in entering the red zone on August 22, following the government's withdrawal of its forces.

On August 30, the sit-in participants announced a march towards the Parliament House and the Prime Minister's House. As members of the PTI and Pakistan Awami Tehreek reached the gates of the Parliament House and entered the PTV building, regular clashes began. The police responded by firing tear gas continuously, and thousands of shells were used. Seven workers were tragically killed due to the violence, while hundreds of both workers and police officers were injured, and many others were arrested. The army was eventually called in to secure the Red Zone. Following this, the sit-in participants retreated and continued their protest as a sit-in at D-Chowk.

Disagreeing with the decisions to attack Parliament and PTV, prominent party leader Makhdoom Javed Hashmi returned to Multan. A PTI team, including Arif Alvi and Mian Mahmood-Ur-Rasheed, attempted to persuade him but returned without success. Javed Hashmi said, "Imran Khan is a simple man. However, he alleged that the people with Imran Khan used him for wrong purposes. I am crying that our generation had only one leader; this is a big conspiracy. There was a conspiracy with Tehreek-e-Insaf and Imran Khan; this conspiracy is not only against Imran Khan but against every youth of Pakistan. The party was standing up; it could have filled the gap. Javed Hashmi said that he begged and requested his party to support him in convincing Imran Khan not to attack Parliament."

During the sit-in, Imran Khan and Allama Tahir-ul-Qadri addressed participants daily from a container, highlighting issues such as government oppression, intimidation, and electoral fraud. They specifically targeted Najam Sethi, the caretaker Chief Minister of Punjab, accusing him of being behind the controversial "35 punctures." Tensions mounted between government officials and the leaders of the sit-in. Imran Khan also alleged that former Chief Justice Iftikhar Chaudhry was involved in electoral wrongdoing, referring to him as the "Mir Jafar of democracy." He went to free his supporters who had been arrested at a police station. Protesters displayed clothes at the Supreme Court entrance, creating a lively atmosphere where attendees danced to bhangra music played by DJ Butt. Each evening, a diverse crowd, including families, gathered at the sit-in, inspired by the vision of a new Pakistan. They engaged with Imran Khan's speeches, boosted his spirits, and departed at night filled with hope for a better future.

Meanwhile, in a joint session of Parliament, political parties came together to back the government and invited Imran Khan and Tahir-ul-Qadri for talks. Nevertheless, the 16 meetings held through a political jirga led by Siraj-ul-Haq proved unproductive.

In his speech on the final day of the joint session of Parliament, Prime Minister Nawaz Sharif stated, "The government has demonstrated considerable patience. However, let it be clear that no one should misunderstand our resolve; neither long nor short marches can deter us from our mission. We will not permit a small group of individuals to surround Parliament and force the government or the Prime Minister to resign. No one will be allowed to undermine democracy."

Imran Khan and Tahir-ul-Qadri performed the Eid-ul-Adha prayer at D-Chowk with their supporters and party members. Imran Khan regularly delivers motivational speeches to inspire his supporters and the public. He launched a campaign of civil disobedience, symbolically burning his electricity bill to make a statement. In a fervent address, he confidently gestured towards the Chief of Army Staff (known as the Umpire's finger), claiming victory. Amidst the protests, a meeting involving Army Chief General Raheel Sharif, Imran Khan, and Tahir-ul-Qadri proved ineffective.

Eventually, after 70 days of protest, Allama Tahir-ul-Qadri announced the conclusion of the sit-in. In the aftermath, the strength of PTI's sit-in diminished further, but Imran Khan remained steadfast, asserting that the sit-in would carry on.

Imran Khan addresses the sit-in participants from a container two to three times a day. In every speech, he reiterates his commitment to building a new Pakistan. He shares insights about citizens' rights, the government's responsibilities, and the benefits of the Madina state model. He motivates individuals to participate in politics and advocate for their rights. The plan for achieving a new Pakistan is based on three key actions: taxing the wealthy, cutting unnecessary expenditures, and addressing corruption, alongside reforming the justice system to ensure fairness.

He boldly asserts that he will capture the "big crocodiles" involved in corruption and will not hesitate to imprison anyone corrupt, labeling Nawaz Sharif as the ruler of the outdated system. Imran Khan firmly believes he can outsmart the leaders of the two parties that have dominated power for the past thirty years, relying on the support of the people. He recognizes the circulating theories regarding a potential signal or a London plan, as well as the rumors that such a signal might have originated from GHQ (General Headquarters of the Army). However, he stresses the importance of public support in overcoming these corrupt figures. He believes that if the people trust the government, Pakistan could collect 7 trillion rupees in taxes.

In response to Imran Khan's call for his resignation, Prime Minister Nawaz Sharif addressed the Pakistani diaspora in New York, saying, "I am not responsible for conducting the election, nor was I the Chief Election Commissioner, nor the caretaker Prime Minister or Chief Minister of any province. So why should I be blamed for the alleged election rigging?" He sarcastically noted that if PML-N candidates received 150,000 votes while those alleging rigging only got 40,000, it raises a question about how rigging could have occurred with such a disparity of 110,000 votes.

In response to Nawaz Sharif, Imran Khan remarked, "I have no desire to become the Prime Minister. Nawaz Sharif and Asif Ali Zardari are partners. I will remain here until he steps down, not because I seek the role of Prime Minister, but because Nawaz Sharif is defending an oppressive regime allied with Asif Ali Zardari." Khan rejected the notion of a so-called "London Plan," which was reportedly discussed during a meeting between Tahir-ul-Qadri in London, and argued that the actual "London Plan" is the 2007 Charter of Democracy between the PPP and PML-N. He stated that his own plan is 18 years old and stressed that the main objective is to bring the people together and overcome these two parties through popular support. He made it clear that his plan did not originate in London, but was conceived by him nearly two decades ago. Khan concluded by stating, "Our aim is not 'Go Nawaz Go,' but 'Go Nizam Go (system should change completely).'"

During a ceremony in Attock, Nawaz Sharif remarked, "Clearing roads and streets isn't a challenging endeavor. Nevertheless, the government has encountered numerous obstacles with dignity, patience, and tolerance. The long march is demanding my resignation. But why should I resign? The people of Pakistan, numbering 180 million, have chosen me as their Prime Minister, so I will not step down for the demands of merely 5,000 individuals."

In light of rising tensions due to police actions and the detention of supporters, Imran Khan addressed the crowd, stating, "I wish to speak directly to the Chief Justice today: it is your responsibility to protect Pakistan's democracy. I must stress that the nation is on the brink of civil war. It is becoming increasingly difficult for me to keep my supporters calm, as they are ready to confront law enforcement. If you obstruct peaceful protests, it could ignite a violent uprising.

I urge you to take action to prevent this country from falling into civil strife and bloodshed. The aggression directed at our police is unjustified, as they are simply being utilized to maintain the current power dynamics."

On December 16, 2014, a horrific act of terrorism struck Pakistan when six terrorists, armed with modern weaponry and associated with the banned Tehreek-e-Taliban Pakistan (TTP), launched an attack on the Army Public School (APS) in Peshawar in broad daylight. This dreadful assault led to the loss of 132 innocent students, along with teachers and 17 staff members. Eyewitnesses recounted the scene, where the blood and bodies of children stained the school's walls, plunging the entire nation into mourning and shock. In response to this tragedy, the government organized an all-party conference in Peshawar to tackle the escalating threat of terrorism.

Following the conference, Imran Khan spoke at the D-Chowk sit-in, expressing, "We have assured Prime Minister Nawaz Sharif of our complete support for the conference focused on combating terrorism. Although I was initially reluctant to attend due to the government's stance, I ultimately joined for the sake of the country. The Corps Commander of Peshawar provided us with valuable insights into the situation, highlighting the role of external forces in the terrorism we face. We deliberated on necessary actions, as the nation requires unity in these challenging times. Given the current circumstances in Pakistan, we must conclude the sit-in.

On December 17, 2014, Imran Khan declared the end of the sit-in, reaffirming his demand for an investigation into the alleged rigging of the 2013 elections. He cautioned that should Nawaz Sharif not fulfill his promise for an inquiry, protests would resume. Khan urged the prompt establishment of a judicial commission to probe the alleged election fraud and stressed the importance of immediate discussions on the issue."

Consequently, the sit-in organized by Pakistan Tehreek-e-Insaf, lasting 126 days, ended without achieving its objectives, amidst considerable turmoil, the expenditure of millions, the loss of seven workers' lives, and the injury and arrest of hundreds. This sit-in was unprecedented, as no political party in Pakistan had ever held such an extended demonstration. While the level of attendance and support fluctuated, the sit-in's remarkable duration of over four months stands out as a significant event in the country's political history.

After the APS tragedy, the PTI concluded its sit-in. Still, it conditioned its participation in the National and Provincial Assembly sessions on the formation of a judicial commission to investigate alleged election rigging from 2013. On April 3, 2015, successful talks between the government and the PTI resulted in the issuance of a presidential ordinance establishing a judicial commission. This led the PTI to end its nearly eight-month boycott of the assemblies and re-engage in the National and Provincial Assemblies.

The agreement stipulated that if the judicial commission uncovered evidence of systematic election rigging, the Prime Minister would dissolve the National Assembly. Conversely, if no evidence were found, PTI would commit to being a constructive presence in the Electoral Reforms Committee.

The three-member Judicial Commission of the Supreme Court, chaired by Chief Justice Nasir-ul-Mulk and comprising Justices Amir Hani Muslim and Ijaz Afzal Khan, began its proceedings on April 16. The investigation concluded on July 3, 2015, after the commission held 80 hearings and gathered testimonies from 70 witnesses. They produced a detailed 300-page report outlining their findings. Imran Khan, the PTI Chairman, was present for most sessions of the commission, and PTI leadership publicly declared their respect for whatever decision the commission would make.

Before the formation of the judicial commission, Imran Khan accused former Supreme Court Chief Justice Iftikhar Muhammad Chaudhry and Punjab's caretaker Chief Minister Najam Sethi of orchestrating systematic rigging, alluding to the "35 punctures" claim. However, PTI did not include Iftikhar Muhammad Chaudhry on their witness list for the judicial commission, while Najam Sethi was listed but not questioned about the "35 punctures." In a private TV interview, the PTI leader characterized the "35 punctures" allegation as a political remark.

The Pakistan Tehreek-e-Insaf (PTI) raised three primary accusations concerning the 2013 elections: systematic rigging, insufficient transparency in the electoral process, and the usurpation of the people's mandate. However, a comprehensive investigation by the Judicial Commission ultimately dismissed all of PTI's claims. The report acknowledged some mismanagement during the elections but determined that it did not reveal systematic rigging. It noted around 44 electoral irregularities and called for immediate reforms. The report confirmed that the elections were executed legally and stated that the current government holds a valid mandate from the populace. Ultimately, it pointed out that PTI did not present any evidence to support its allegations of systematic rigging during the 2013 general elections.

The commission's finding of 44 electoral irregularities represented a notable win for Imran Khan's position. The establishment did not seek to topple the Nawaz Sharif government but aimed to diminish its strength. By concentrating on "systematic rigging" and overlooking the 44 irregularities, the Nawaz administration essentially obtained a favorable assessment. It's crucial to recognize that, even with these 44 irregularities, conducting free and fair elections is virtually impossible.

Imran Khan's reference to the Umpire's finger during the sit-in highlighted his lack of political experience. This comment proved to be a significant mistake that negatively impacted both his political aspirations and the sit-in itself. Moreover, it suggested that he was under the influence of the military establishment, a perception that continues to be a challenge for him today.

Critics of Imran Khan argue that the sit-in resulted in significant economic losses for Pakistan, leading to a sharp drop in foreign investments. At the same time, domestic investors also hesitated, contributing to economic stagnation. The political situation intensified when the PTI chairman called on citizens to practice civil disobedience, advising them to withhold payments for electricity and gas bills. The call for non-payment of taxes further aggravated the situation. Additionally, expatriates were encouraged to disregard international laws and engage in illegal hundi practices to weaken the elected government. The sit-in also caused a delay in the execution of the China-Pakistan Economic Corridor (CPEC) project, postponing the Chinese president's visit to Pakistan in 2014 and pushing the signing of the CPEC agreement to 2015.

Former ambassador Javed Hussain has indicated that the U.S. may be attempting to diminish China's growing influence in Pakistan and the surrounding region, which contextualizes the sit-in. Therefore, an independent investigation into the reasons behind this effort to destabilize the government is warranted. Were the organizers of the sit-in knowingly or unknowingly involved in this American strategy?

Imran Khan's 2014 sit-in ultimately did not yield apparent success, but its prolonged nature and intensity significantly weakened Nawaz Sharif and his government. It also enhanced Imran Khan's standing and that of the Pakistan Tehreek-e-Insaf (PTI) by increasing political awareness, advocating for citizens' rights, and highlighting issues related to the 2013 elections. This surge in strength and popularity was pivotal in establishing PTI as Pakistan's leading political party and solidifying Imran Khan's reputation as a brave and authentic leader dedicated to public service.

Following the election rigging scandal, the persistent protests, and the unfortunate events at APS, the report from the rigging commission continued to back the beleaguered Nawaz government until March 2016. However, on April 3,

2016, the International Consortium of Investigative Journalists (ICIJ) stunned the world by releasing around 11.5 million confidential documents known as the Panama Papers. These documents revealed financial corruption involving notable figures from various sectors, including world leaders, politicians, celebrities, and business magnates, and were sourced from the Panamanian law firm Mossack Fonseca.

The documents disclosed extensive information regarding the Sharif family's offshore businesses, which they had kept concealed from the public eye. The International Consortium of Investigative Journalists (ICIJ) reported that Maryam Nawaz, the daughter of Prime Minister Nawaz Sharif, along with his sons, Hassan and Hussain Nawaz, possess ownership or the authority to manage several offshore entities. The Mossack Fonseca files indicate that Nawaz Sharif's children hold ownership in foreign companies, including Nescol Limited, Nielsen Holdings Limited, Cumber Group Inc., and Hangon Property Holdings. These businesses acquired luxury real estate in London between 2006 and 2007, and according to the Panama Papers, these properties were used as collateral for a $13.8 million loan.

In the aftermath of the Panama Papers' release, the Sharif family encountered considerable criticism from both the media and political opponents in Pakistan. Calls were made for Nawaz Sharif and his children to clarify their undisclosed companies and properties in London. Rather than dispelling the suspicions, the interviews and explanations provided by Nawaz, Maryam, Hassan, and

Hussain Nawaz only fueled further skepticism regarding the family's financial dealings and assets. During a discussion with Sana Bucha, Maryam Nawaz attempted to divert attention from her properties by stating, "I don't have any property in London or Pakistan." Additionally, remarks from PML-N leaders, such as Khawaja Asif's comment, "Mian Sahib, don't worry, this nation will forget the Panama Papers," further deepened the controversy. This series of events provided Imran Khan, who had previously been discouraged by his unsuccessful sit-in, with both legal and moral justification to revitalize his campaign against the Nawaz government.

Imran Khan posed substantial challenges for Prime Minister Nawaz Sharif by threatening a nationwide protest if the government did not produce the financial trail and receipts concerning the London property. In response to mounting criticism, Nawaz Sharif announced the creation of a judicial commission, led by a former Supreme Court judge, in a public speech on April 5, 2016. However, the establishment of this commission encountered obstacles as former judges Tassaduq Hussain Jilani, Nasir-ul-Mulk, Amir-ul-Mulk Mengal, Sahir Ali, and Tanveer Ahmed Khan chose not to participate. Despite these challenges, the government continued efforts to form the commission and engaged in discussions with opposition parties, including the Pakistan People's Party and Pakistan Tehreek-e-Insaf, about the guidelines for its setup.

Facing mounting pressure from the opposition, the public, and the media, Nawaz Sharif declared in his second national address on April 22, 2016, that he would step down if he were found guilty. However, efforts to form a commission were thwarted when Chief Justice Anwar Zaheer Jamali deemed the proposal "innocuous" due to unclear rules and regulations.

In a subsequent address to the National Assembly on May 16, 2016, Prime Minister Nawaz Sharif proposed the establishment of a joint committee to create a mechanism for the judicial commission. He asserted that he welcomed accountability and criticized his opponents, who he claimed lived in luxury while leveling accusations against him. He urged them to disclose their income and tax returns to the public. During his speech, Nawaz Sharif indicated that he would clarify the matter regarding the London flats, although he did not provide further details. He insisted that the funds for purchasing these flats came from the sale of the Jeddah Steel Mill, which his father had owned. He waved some documents during his speech, stating, "Mr. Speaker, these are the sources through which we acquired the London flats."

Following Nawaz Sharif's address, Imran Khan initiated legal proceedings in the Supreme Court on August 29, 2016, represented by senior advocate Naeem Bukhari. He sought the Prime Minister's disqualification on the grounds of corruption and for allegedly hiding properties in London. The case also targeted Nawaz Sharif's son-in-law, Captain Safdar, and Home Minister Ishaq Dar. Alongside the legal confrontations, Imran Khan called for widespread public protests and rallies, popularizing the slogan "Go Nawaz Go." This phrase, accompanied by various catchy songs, energized gatherings and demonstrations organized by the Pakistan Tehreek-e-Insaf (PTI). Imran Khan's fervent speeches and countrywide protests exerted considerable pressure on Nawaz Sharif and his administration. Rather than presenting a transparent money trail and documentation for their offshore properties and businesses, the Sharif family attempted to sidestep the situation using vague explanations, interpretations, and typical political maneuvers. In retaliation, Imran Khan announced a lockdown. On September 30, 2016, PTI supporters held a sit-in outside Nawaz Sharif's home in Raiwind, where Imran Khan urged his followers to continue blocking Islamabad until Nawaz Sharif resigned and agreed to accountability.

In light of public demand, the Supreme Court has instructed both the government and the Pakistan Tehreek-e-Insaf to outline their specific needs, which will guide the court in setting up inquiries. A five-member bench led by Chief Justice Anwar Zaheer Jamali, alongside Justices Asif Saeed Khan Khosa, Amir Hani Muslim, Sheikh Azmat Saeed, and Ijaz-ul-Ahsan, commenced daily hearings for the case starting November 1, 2016. Imran Khan was represented by lawyers Naeem Bukhari and Hamid Khan, while Salman Aslam Butt and Akram Sheikh represented the Sharif family as their legal counsel. The court also took into account additional petitions from other opposition leaders, including Sirajul Haq from Jamaat-e-Islami and Sheikh Rashid Ahmed. The representatives for the Sharif family argued that their clients own properties overseas and that Hassan and Hussain Nawaz have been conducting legitimate business abroad for many years. They further asserted that Maryam Nawaz is no longer under the care of her father and should not benefit from the Nielsen and Nescol companies, claiming she only has a supervisory role. However, Justice Khosa remarked that the defendants need to prove that the funds used for these businesses were legitimately earned and legally transferred outside the country.

On November 14, 2016, Akram Sheikh, representing the Sharif family, notably introduced a confidential letter from Hamid bin Jassim bin Jaber Al Thani of Qatar. Justice Khosa remarked that this letter significantly altered the Prime Minister's public position. When questioned about its absence in the Prime Minister's May 16 speech, Sheikh stated that it was not legal evidence but simply a political remark. He also noted the difficulty in providing documentation for transactions dating back 40 years, as they were conducted using business slips.

Following the retirement of Chief Justice Anwar Zaheer Jamali in December, a new bench, led by Chief Justice Asif Saeed Khosa, was established to restart the hearings. Justices Sheikh Azmat Saeed and Ijaz-ul-Ahsan were already part of this bench, with Justices Ijaz Afzal Khan and Gulzar Ahmed joining later. The Sharif family overhauled its legal representation, replacing Akram Sheikh and Salman Butt with Makhdoom Ali Khan, Shahid Hamid, and Salman Akram Raja due to dissatisfaction with the inclusion of the Qatari letter and the case strategy. Hamid Khan expressed regret for taking on the case, stating he could engage in legal battles but not in a media conflict. The new hearings began on January 4, 2017.

Naeem Bukhari pointed out inconsistencies in the Sharif family's statements regarding the London property, highlighting contradictory and false information, as well as the absence of transaction receipts. Furthermore, the Qatari investor failed to provide the necessary agreements related to these deals. Bukhari noted that official tax records showed Maryam Nawaz reported zero taxable income and relied on her father's financial support. He also mentioned that Hussain Nawaz had gifted his father Rs. 81 crores without any taxes being paid on that sum. Additionally, Bukhari expressed concerns about the National Accountability Bureau's (NAB) inaction in prosecuting the Hudaibiya Paper Mills case from 2000, where Ishaq Dar and the Sharif family were accused of money laundering.

During the hearing, the court raised several concerns about the ineffectiveness of the country's institutions in dealing with the Panama Papers controversy. Chairman Qamar Zaman Chaudhry and Prosecutor General Waqas Qadir Dar represented the National Accountability Bureau (NAB). As they laid out their arguments, the conversation turned to the Hudaibiya Paper Mill case, for which NAB had submitted a reference back in 2000 based on Ishaq Dar's confession that he laundered $14.86 million for the Sharif family. At that time, Dar was under house arrest during Musharraf's regime and claimed his confession was coerced. In 2014, after Ishaq Dar became the finance minister, the Lahore High Court dismissed this case. The bench expressed its disappointment, stating, "The court is concerned about NAB's lack of an appeal. Typically, when an accused is on bail for theft, NAB files an appeal. However, in this case involving substantial amounts of money, NAB did not even attempt to appeal." In defense, the NAB Chairman explained their decision not to pursue an appeal. Justice Azmat Saeed warned the NAB team to prepare for serious repercussions, stressing that "today, NAB has essentially ceased to exist before us."

On February 23, 2017, plaintiffs Imran Khan, Sirajul Haq, and Sheikh Rashid Ahmed appeared before the court, which deferred its ruling on that day. On April 20, 2017, at 2 p.m., the Supreme Court reached a narrow three-to-two decision, determining that there was insufficient evidence to remove Nawaz Sharif from his position. The court also called for the establishment of a joint investigation team to probe allegations of bribery and corruption against the Prime Minister.

The verdict in the Panama Papers case opened with a quote from a French novelist, suggesting that behind every significant unknown success lies an unproven crime committed with great care. The Joint Investigation Team was given full authority to question all related individuals, including the Prime Minister. They were instructed to finish the investigation in sixty days and provide progress updates to the court every fifteen days. The 540-page ruling, written by Justice Ijaz Afzal Khan, was released on the same day and sharply criticized the National Accountability Bureau (NAB) and the Federal Investigation Agency (FIA) for their handling of the investigation, while also holding the government accountable for its inaction. The Sharif family faced criticism for their insufficient cooperation with the court. Two judges, Justice Asif Saeed Khosa and Justice Gulzar Ahmed, dissented, noting that the Prime Minister had not been truthful with the public and should be disqualified.

On May 6, 2017, the Supreme Court formed a six-member investigation committee headed by Wajid Zia, the

Additional Director General of the FIA. This group included representatives from the State Bank of Pakistan, the Securities and Exchange Commission of Pakistan, the NAB, the ISI, and Military Intelligence. They were empowered to enlist both local and international experts to probe into the foreign assets of the Sharif family. The Supreme Court made it clear that the committee should receive full support from all Pakistani institutions, given its mandate under the court's orders. A portion of the Federal Judicial Academy building was allocated for the committee's operations, along with a budget of Rs 20 million. The committee was tasked with reporting progress to the Supreme Court every two weeks and completing the investigation within sixty days.

Throughout the investigation, Nawaz Sharif, Maryam Nawaz, Captain Safdar, Hassan, and Hussain Nawaz were summoned by the Joint Investigation Team (JIT) on multiple occasions. However, their answers and the documents they provided did not establish their innocence; instead, they sparked more doubts and made the Sharif family a subject of mockery. The Pakistan Tehreek-e-Insaf, along with various opposition parties and the media, vehemently criticized the inconsistent statements made by the Sharif family, as well as the dubious use of the Calibri font, trust deed, and Qatari letter presented in court. Indecent slogans, anthems, and songs played a significant role in tarnishing the reputation of the Sharif family.

Despite various claims and promises, the Sharif family failed to provide adequate money trails and receipts to the JIT and the court. Even amid the laughter directed at them, they did not convincingly demonstrate their innocence to the nation. Furthermore, during the investigation, the JIT discovered undeniable evidence of Nawaz Sharif's resident card in the United Arab Emirates during his time as Prime Minister and his employment in his son's company without receiving a salary.

On July 28, 2017, as a result of an investigation by the Joint Investigation Team (JIT), the Supreme Court ordered the dismissal of Nawaz Sharif from his role as Prime Minister. The court also ordered the initiation of legal proceedings against him for failing to disclose his employment and the salary he received from his son's company in his tax filings. Following this decision, Nawaz Sharif stepped down from his position. Subsequently, Shahid Khaqan Abbasi of the PML-N assumed the role of Prime Minister on August 1, 2017.

What began as a democratic demand for an audit of four electoral districts due to alleged rigging quickly escalated into widespread protests nationwide. This unrest involved assaults on Pakistan Television (PTV) and Parliament, violent clashes that led to injuries and deaths among political activists, large-scale demonstrations, and a prolonged sit-in that lasted 126 days, coupled with extensive lockdown measures. The situation worsened due to the repercussions of the Panama Papers leak and ongoing legal troubles, which ultimately compelled Nawaz Sharif to resign. As a result, he ended his third term as Prime Minister following a court ruling, having been outmaneuvered by Imran Khan's powerful protests on July 28, 2017, and unable to reclaim his political or legal standing.

Had democratic principles and the rule of law been genuinely upheld in the country, Nawaz Sharif could have spared the public emotional distress, loss of life, and economic hardship by swiftly initiating a transparent investigation into the allegations of electoral fraud and accepting accountability following the revelations from the Panama Papers.

While it's understandable that the Sharif family would seek to defend their interests in light of corruption and rigging charges, it is regrettable that citizens have had to rely on protests, long marches, lockdowns, and sit-ins to prompt our judicial system to take action. Imran Khan felt the need to protest when his legitimate demands for audits of four electoral constituencies and a clear financial explanation regarding properties in London went unaddressed.

In Pakistan, it has become apparent that public or political protests are unlikely to succeed without military support, especially from the Army Chief. During the sit-in, General Raheel Sharif did not seek to completely remove Nawaz Sharif from power; instead, he aimed to weaken his position to keep him under pressure. This helps explain why Nawaz Sharif managed to stay in office despite the fervent emotions and turmoil surrounding the 126-day sit-in protest. However, after the Panama Papers were revealed, General Bajwa decided to remove Nawaz Sharif from office. The ISI and Military Intelligence, under Wajid Zia's leadership, gathered strong evidence against the Sharif family, leading to Nawaz Sharif's disqualification from the Prime Minister's role and a significant loss of dignity for the family.

Thus, it is neither a perfectly straight nor a bent finger; it's the umpire's finger, symbolizing the Army Chief, that is vital in responding to valid demands in Pakistan. As long as the military's influence remains in the system, the country will continue to face challenges and instability.

The 22nd Prime Minister

Following Nawaz Sharif's removal from the role of Prime Minister due to a substantial legal and public movement, Imran Khan became the most popular leader in Pakistan. The Pakistan Tehreek-e-Insaf (PTI) grew into the leading political party. Various surveys, expert analyses, and on-the-ground insights suggested that PTI was poised for success in the 2018 national elections, enabling Imran Khan to assume the position of Prime Minister of Pakistan.

On May 28, 2018, the National Assembly, along with the provincial assemblies of Sindh and Khyber Pakhtunkhwa, was disbanded as the five-year term of the PML-N government came to an end. The assemblies of Punjab and Balochistan were also dissolved on May 31, 2018. These events took place during the holy month of Ramadan, and political parties formally launched their election campaigns after Eid al-Fitr at the end of June.

The Pakistan People's Party (PPP) unveiled its manifesto on June 28, 2018, marking the start of its election campaign on June 30. Meanwhile, the Pakistan Muslim League-Nawaz (PML-N) launched its campaign in Karachi on June 25, 2018, and published its election manifesto on July 5, 2018. The Pakistan Tehreek-e-Insaf (PTI) began its campaign earlier on June 24, 2018, in Mianwali, and Imran Khan presented the PTI manifesto on July 9, 2018. PTI's ambitious vision for a reformed and flourishing Pakistan encompassed the following initiatives:

1. **Provincial Realignment:** Creating a separate province for southern Punjab.

2. **Engagement with Balochistan:** Reassessing dialogues with dissatisfied Baloch groups and implementing a job quota specifically for Balochistan.

3. **Development of FATA:** Formulating a detailed plan for the advancement of the Federally Administered Tribal Areas (FATA).

4. **Karachi Development Program:** Launching an initiative aimed at improving the city of Karachi.

5. **Economic Revitalization:** Initiatives focused on reducing poverty and rejuvenating the economy.

6. **Transparency Initiatives:** Prioritizing accountability and recovering corrupt funds held abroad.

7. **Debt Reduction Strategies:** Approaches for lowering external financial obligations.

8. **Institutional Reforms:** Targeted improvements for key institutions, particularly law enforcement.

9. **Educational Advancement:** Plans to set up a university on the premises of the Prime Minister's House.

10. **Housing and Infrastructure Development:** Projects aimed at housing solutions and revamping public transport systems.

11. **Industrial Reforms:** Efforts to stimulate the industrial sector and support small and medium enterprises.

12. Job Creation Commitment: Promise to build five million homes and generate ten million job opportunities.

13. Tax System Overhaul: Efforts to reform the taxation framework.

14. Tourism Growth: Initiatives designed to enhance the tourism sector.

15. Reform of State-Owned Enterprises: Adjustments to the regulations governing state-run businesses.

16. Energy Solutions: Strategies to address energy-related issues.

17. Agricultural Support: Improvements in agriculture and financial support for farmers.

During the 2018 election campaign, more than 150 people, including three candidates, were killed in attacks on rallies and meetings across the country. On July 25, a suicide bombing in Quetta during polling killed 31 civilians and injured 35.

General elections were held in Pakistan on July 25, 2018, to elect members for the 15th National Assembly and the four provincial assemblies. Voting was conducted for 270 of the 272 National Assembly seats, with elections for two constituencies, NA-60 and NA-103, postponed. NA-60 was delayed because the PML-N candidate, Hanif Abbasi, was disqualified, and NA-103 was affected by the death of a candidate.

The Election Commission of Pakistan reported that there were 105.96 million registered voters during the 2018 general elections, with an overall voter turnout of 51.82%, translating to roughly 50.5 million voters participating nationwide. The Pakistan Tehreek-e-Insaf (PTI) won 116 seats in the National Assembly, while the Pakistan Muslim League-Nawaz (PML-N) secured 64 seats. Consequently, PTI was able to establish governments both at the federal level and in Khyber Pakhtunkhwa and Punjab. Despite the elections being overseen by the judiciary, military, and intelligence agencies, allegations of rigging were made by the losing parties. The Election Commission denied these allegations, stating that there was no evidence of rigging.

All significant political parties in Pakistan, except the PTI, expressed concerns about the 2018 elections. Nevertheless, PTI emerged as the most popular party, having received approximately 3,953,485 more votes for the National Assembly than the total votes received by the PML-N. This result solidified PTI's position as the leading party among voters in Pakistan at the national level.

According to the Election Commission of Pakistan, following the general elections, the Pakistan Tehreek-e-Insaf (PTI) emerged as the largest political party in the country. PTI nominated 242 candidates for National Assembly seats, the highest number among all parties, excluding around 1,600 independent candidates nationwide. Out of these 242 candidates, 116 PTI candidates were successful, resulting in a win rate of 47.93% for PTI. The party garnered 16.86 million votes nationwide, making it the most favored choice among voters, which constituted 30.70 percent of the total votes cast for the National Assembly. In the 2013 elections, PTI had only won 29 seats, but this number surged to 116 in 2018, reflecting an increase of 87 seats.

The former ruling party, the Pakistan Muslim League-Nawaz (PML-N), saw a drop in its national popularity during the 2018 elections. The PML-N received 12.935 million votes for National Assembly positions and fielded 212 candidates, with only 64 winning, leading to a success rate of 30.18%. The PML-N's share of the total votes was 23.50%. Compared to the 2013 elections, where they secured 126 seats, this represented a loss of nearly half (62 seats). Nevertheless, the PML-N maintained its status as the second most popular party among voters nationwide.

The Pakistan People's Party (PPP) ranked third in national popularity during the 2018 elections, receiving 6.913 million votes, which resulted in 43 seats. This translated to a victory percentage of only 17% in the National Assembly, with the PPP capturing 12.59% of the overall votes. They lagged behind PTI by 9.95 million votes and were 5.95 million votes short of the PML-N.

The victory of Pakistan Tehreek-e-Insaf was celebrated throughout the country. Imran Khan's friends, cricketers, and celebrities congratulated him on his success and the formation of the government via Twitter. In celebration of PTI's victory, Imran Khan's ex-wife, Jemima, tweeted on July 26, 2018, "Despite the obstacles and problems, the father of my children achieved success after twenty-two years of hard work."

On July 26, 2018, Imran Khan delivered a 29-minute live victory speech from his residence in Bani Gala, which was broadcast across all media channels. He addressed the allegations of election rigging by various political parties in his address. He stated, "The PTI did not form the Election Commission. The caretaker government was established in consultation with political parties. We are prepared to investigate the constituencies where allegations of rigging have surfaced. I am confident that this has been the most transparent and fair election in Pakistan's history, and we are willing to investigate any concerns about rigging, together with the opposition.

In his speech, Imran Khan announced, "I will be the first to face accountability. We will uphold the rule of law." He recognized the country's current economic struggles, linking them to institutional failures.

Khan expressed his desire to reshape Pakistan into a welfare state akin to Madina, referencing the system established during the time of the Prophet Muhammad (peace be upon him), from which he draws great inspiration. Additionally, he urged his political opponents to come together for the country's progress, emphasizing, "My goals go well beyond personal interests. Our government will not seek political revenge."

In his vision for the future administration, Imran Khan emphasized, "Previous leaders have misused resources for personal pleasures like extravagant houses and international travel. Our government will prioritize simplicity. Safeguarding taxpayer money will be my foremost concern." Additionally, he shared his discomfort with living in the Prime Minister's House, stating, "We aim to redefine the function of the Prime Minister's House by converting it into an educational facility and turning the Governor's Houses into community spaces."

Imran Khan stated that foreign policy is the country's most significant challenge. He expressed a desire to establish improved relations with neighboring countries. He highlighted the China-Pakistan Economic Corridor (CPEC) and emphasized the need to learn from China's experience lifting 700 million people out of poverty. Additionally, Khan discussed the importance of fostering good relations with Iran and Saudi Arabia. He expressed Pakistan's willingness to mediate the differences between various countries in the Middle East, particularly with Saudi Arabia. On Afghanistan, Khan remarked that the Afghan people need peace and that his government would try to promote stability in Afghanistan by any means necessary. He expressed a wish for Pakistan and Afghanistan to have an open border, similar to the arrangements in European countries.

Imran Khan discussed India's role in regional relations by stating, "We want to trade with India." He noted that recent portrayals of him in the Indian media made him feel like a villain from Bollywood. Khan addressed the Indian government directly, suggesting that poverty reduction could be achieved through trade between the two nations. He pointed out that the core issue affecting their relationship is Kashmir, where he cited ongoing human rights violations. He emphasized the importance of dialogue, encouraging both countries to come together to find a mutually beneficial resolution. Khan warned that without addressing ongoing accusations, the Kashmir situation would remain unresolved. He concluded with a message of goodwill, saying, "If you take one step, we will take two steps in response."

Imran Khan stated, "My government will strengthen accountability institutions. The accountability process will begin with me and then extend to others." He emphasized his commitment to strengthening anti-corruption institutions, such as the National Accountability Bureau (NAB). He noted that previously, accountability efforts had been primarily directed at the opposition, but his government would demonstrate that the law would be enforced fairly for all. He declared that establishing such institutions would be a fundamental principle aimed at improving the country's governance system. "I will initiate the accountability process with my ministers and members of parliament," he added.

Imran Khan's speech garnered significant praise from various segments of society across the country, including some of his staunchest critics and opponents, as well as political analysts, all of whom also extended their best wishes for his success.

In the 2018 elections, the Pakistan Tehreek-e-Insaf (PTI) emerged as the largest party in Parliament, securing 116 general seats, along with 26 reserved seats, for a total of 142 seats. However, PTI did not achieve the simple majority required to form a government. This shortfall may have been influenced by delays in the Results Transmission System (RTS) on election night, which hindered PTI's chances of securing a majority.

To form a coalition government with a simple majority, the PTI allied with several other parties, including the Muttahida Qaumi Movement (MQM), the Grand Democratic Alliance (GDA), the Balochistan Awami Party (BAP), the Q-League, the Mengal Group, and independent parliamentarians. Together, the ruling coalition held a total of 183 seats, comprised of 142 from PTI, 14 from MQM, five from BAP, four from GDA, four from the Q-League, four from the Mengal Group, and three independents. Additionally, seven members from the Federally Administered Tribal Areas (FATA) also joined the government.

On the other hand, the opposition had a total of 158 seats in the National Assembly, which included 83 from the Pakistan Muslim League-Nawaz (PML-N), 58 from the Pakistan People's Party (PPP), 16 from the Muttahida Majlis-e-Amal (MMA), and one from the Awami National Party (ANP).

According to the Election Commission of Pakistan, in the 2018 general elections, the ruling party, Tehreek-e-Insaf, received 33.858 million votes. The coalition parties received the following vote counts: GDA 2.520 million, MQM 1.466 million, PML-Q 1.034 million, Balochistan National Party (Mengal Group) 0.435 million, Balochistan Awami Party (BAP) 0.541 million, Awami Muslim League 0.238 million, and Functional League 0.145 million. The combined votes for the government and coalition parties amounted to 41.833 million. Additionally, three independent members—Fakhar Imam (Khanewal), Aslam Bhutani

(Gwadar), and Ali Nawaz (Mirpurkhas)—received separate votes and later joined the government.

On the other hand, the PML-N received the highest number of votes among the opposition parties in the 2018 general elections. According to the Election Commission of Pakistan's records, the PML-N secured 25,868,889 votes, while the PPP garnered 13,848,380 votes. The Muttahida Majlis-e-Amal (MMA) opposition alliance obtained 5,141,494 votes. The Awami National Party received 1,631,996 votes. However, the parties led by Mahmood Khan Achakzai, Hasil Bizenjo, and Aftab Sherpao did not secure any seats in the National Assembly. Specifically, Achakzai's party received 29,692 votes, Bizenjo's party earned 66,000 votes, and the Qaumi Watan Party received 144,000 votes. The united opposition parties collectively received approximately 46.6 million votes, about 6.6 million more than the votes obtained by the government and its coalition parties.

August 18, 2018, was a pivotal day for Imran Khan. After 22 years of challenges and difficulties, he finally reached this milestone. Sworn in as the 22nd Prime Minister of Pakistan, he experienced great joy along with a profound sense of duty. This was his opportunity to realize his long-held aspiration of creating a state similar to Madina, which he referred to as New Pakistan.

Imran Khan's outstanding achievements in cricket, health, and education have generated a sense of happiness and optimism among PTI voters, supporters, and a large segment of the population. Since assuming the role of Prime

Minister, they are confident that he will honor his promises and meet his obligations.

Imran Khan's position was strengthened by his statements on December 3, 2018, in which he informed reporters about the support of the Pakistani military for the PTI manifesto. He mentioned three significant eras of military rule: one under General Zia, another under General Musharraf, and a third during General Bajwa's tenure. Khan noted that only General Bajwa had worked in harmony with the elected government. When questioned about whether he had made decisions independently, Khan confirmed that he had indeed been responsible for all the decisions, emphasizing his personal involvement in each one. This indicated that he enjoyed the full support of General Bajwa and the military in executing his plans and decisions. However, following his ouster as Prime Minister due to a regime change operation and a no-confidence vote, Khan later revealed the reality of the situation to the public.

Imran Khan shared this insight during a meeting with journalists at his home in Lahore, stating, "While I was in government, I was accountable for all actions and outcomes, but the true authority lay with someone else. Although the responsibility fell on me, the actual control was not in my hands. He expressed that if he had been granted even a fraction of the powers during his three and a half years in office, he could have competed with Sher Shah Suri. He also mentioned that there were cases prepared against Shahbaz Sharif and Asif Zardari, but he faced pressure not to pursue them."

Critics have pushed back against Imran Khan's recent comments by referencing his earlier statements. They are asking why the former Prime Minister, who once advocated for a cohesive stance ('one page'), only acknowledged his powerlessness after leaving office. On the other hand, Khan's supporters argue that no serving prime minister has ever dared to confront the powerful military establishment for the country's benefit. This time, a former prime minister has publicly addressed these issues following his removal from office.

What matters more than analyzing his inconsistent statements is looking into Imran Khan's governance as Prime Minister, which reveals his weaknesses, diminished authority, and contradictory comments.

In Pakistan, it is a common observation that when a child comes home in tears after being bullied and assaulted by a rogue, ill-mannered person on the streets. Typically, mothers react in one of four ways:

The first type of mother immediately leaves home to confront the bully. The second type picks up a shoe and scolds her child, saying, "Why did you go in front of that bully again, despite my warnings?" The third type begins to curse that loud and rude boy. The fourth type, a wise mother, takes an entirely different and wise approach than the other three types, sitting beside her child, wiping his tears, and listening attentively. With great love, she explains, "My son, I know you are completely innocent. Even if we wanted to, we could not fight against this tyrant. However, that does not mean we should spend our lives enduring the oppression of such people and living in misery. There is only one solution:

you must work hard and strive to achieve a high status and position in society so that these oppressors will appear small and insignificant compared to you." By educating and nurturing her child, this wise mother protects him from feelings of deprivation and helps him become a successful person.

The government protects its citizens as a nurturing mother would. The leadership of the head of state guides the populace through challenging periods, alleviates their hardships, and supports them in achieving their aspirations, enabling them to stand alongside respected and thriving nations.

In the second volume of our book series titled "The Dreamer," we will thoroughly analyze Imran Khan's governance style. This examination will encompass his decisions regarding administration, politics, social issues, welfare, the economy, and foreign policy during his tenure as Prime Minister, along with the results of those decisions. We will also delve into the various situations and events that led Imran Khan to create difficulties for himself and his administration by behaving like the first three mothers, rather than assuming the role of the wise fourth mother. Additionally, we will investigate the factors that contributed to the end of his rule, which represented a significant moment in Pakistan's political history, as he was the first Prime Minister to be ousted from office through a successful no-confidence vote.

Addressing the small audience during the initial days of PTI

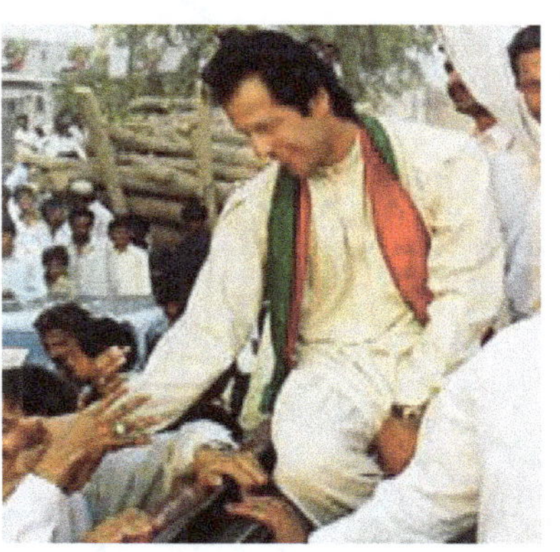

Election Campaign in 2002

In support of Parvaiz Musharraf along with MMA

Leading Islamabad Sit-In

Addressing the Sit-In participants

Addressing the public rally in Lahore

Nation expressing their support and solidarity

Leading the Azadi March

Welcome by students at Punjab University, Lahore

Torture by Jamiat students at Punjab University

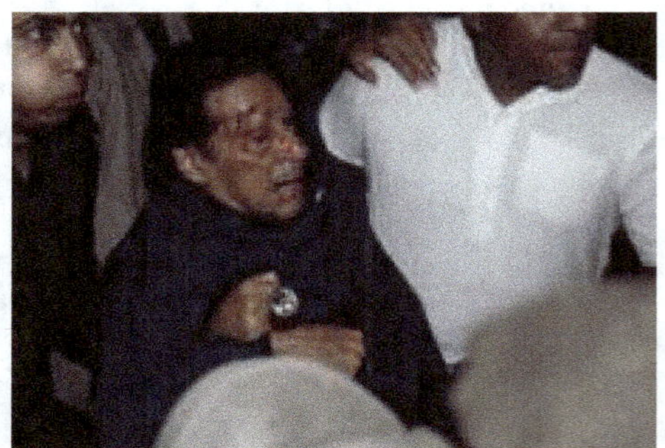

People shifting Imran Khan to ambulance after fall from lifter during election campaign

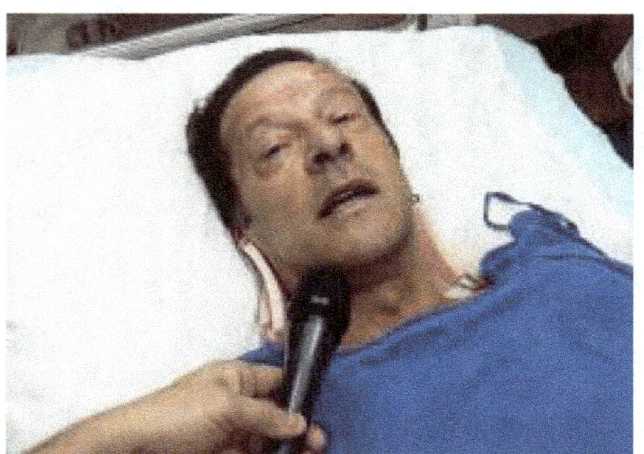

Addressing from hospital bed during 2013 election campaign

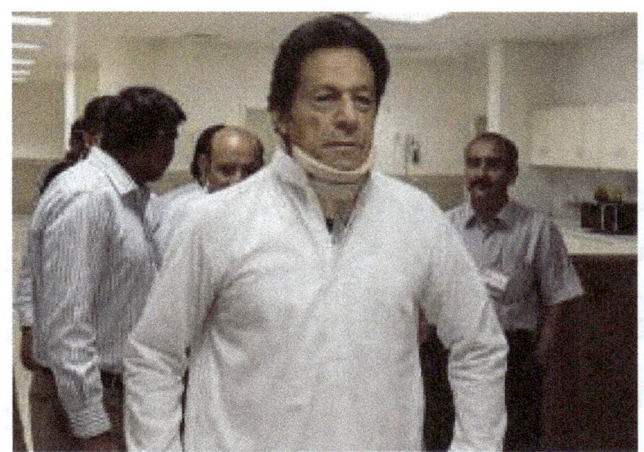

Getting discharged from hospital with cervical collar

Showing courage after a bullet injury and a narrow escape from an assassination attempt

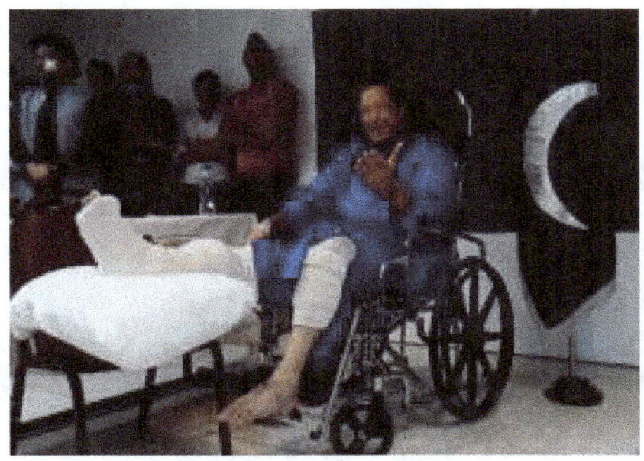

Recovering from bullet injury

Illegal arrest by rangers from Islamabad High Court premises

Parvaiz Musharraf welcoming Imran Khan at President House

Meeting and Supporting Parvaiz Musharraf Referendum

Imran Khan taking Oath as 22nd PM of Pakistan

Receiving Guard of Honor as PM Pakistan

With General Bajwa in early days of his government

Founder and chairman of Namal University

Captain of Cricket world champion team 1992

Inauguration of Shaukat Khanum Memorial Cancer Hospital Lahore

Imran Khan, the Chancellor of Bradford University

The 22nd Prime Minister of Pakistan.

Prime Minister Imran Khan representing the whole Muslim world during his address at UNO

Trust in God

Following the establishment of Pakistan Tehreek-e-Insaf on April 25, 1996, there were high hopes that Imran Khan would quickly dominate the political landscape. His charismatic persona, international fame, World Cup victory, and the establishment of a cancer hospital sparked these aspirations, particularly in light of the unimpressive performances of the PML-N and PPP. However, Khan's journey turned out to be much longer and more challenging than expected.

After 15 years of dedicated efforts, Imran Khan's landmark rally at Minar-e-Pakistan on October 30, 2011, marked a pivotal moment in his political career. This event brought Pakistan Tehreek-e-Insaf into the national and international limelight. Taking place at the iconic Minar-e-Pakistan, the rally drew a significant crowd. The vibrant energy of the youth, combined with widespread public support and compelling speeches advocating for change, caught many by surprise and ignited unrest within the political arena.

A standout moment was when Imran Khan opened his speech with the Quranic Verse "إِيَّاكَ نَعْبُدُ وَ إِيَّاكَ نَسْتَعِينُ" (O Allah, we worship You and only seek Your help). His supporters lauded him, while critics claimed he was invoking religious references to distance himself from his previous Playboy persona and win over the Pakistani populace. However, a look at Imran Khan's past speeches reveals that he often started with "إِيَّاكَ نَعْبُدُ وَ إِيَّاكَ نَسْتَعِينُ" well before this event.

Khan's rivals were likely unaware that he had chosen to leave his former way of life behind and pursue a journey centered on truth, preparing himself for the challenges ahead. As time passed, it became increasingly evident that the global recognition he received early in his career, along with the luxurious lifestyle associated with cricket and Western culture, had somewhat estranged him from his faith and his connection with God. However, his strong character, commitment to family values, the impact of his mother's upbringing, and his deep affection for her helped preserve his noble spirit.

That is why, following his mother's death, Imran Khan chose not to succumb to grief. Instead, he sought to earn God's grace by understanding and addressing the difficulties that every Pakistani endures, striving to reduce their pain. The teachings of the Holy Quran, the wisdom of Rumi, the philosophy of Iqbal, and the guidance of Mian Bashir played a crucial role in helping this former Playboy regain his connection with God.

Humans, among the roughly 8.7 million species on our planet, possess intellect, understanding, and wisdom that set us apart. This cognitive ability and self-awareness allow relatively frail humans to overcome much mightier beings, including strong animals, high-flying birds, marine creatures, and those who delve into the cosmos and the unseen forces surrounding us. This combination of intellect, awareness, and wisdom propels humans to seek out the most rewarding experiences in life. Such a quest not only enriches those in search of truth but also draws them closer to their

Creator, Master, and true God, as they seek His guidance and approval.

Trusting in God means placing complete reliance on Allah Almighty for the success of our endeavors, while also taking the necessary actions to achieve our goals. It involves surrendering the results of our efforts to Him. This deep trust in Allah is a unique and significant feeling, with the notion of "trust" directly associated with Him. A firm reliance strengthens the connection between Allah and the believer. For those who truly believe in Allah, He meets all their needs.

The Holy Quran repeatedly emphasizes trust in Allah:

1. "Put your trust in the Ever-Living One, Who will never die." (Al-Furqan: 58)

2. "When you decide to undertake a matter, place your trust in Allah." (Al Imran: 159)

3. "Whoever puts their trust in Allah, then Allah is sufficient for them." (At-Talaq: 3)

4. "If Allah supports you, no one can defeat you; and if He abandons you, who can assist you? Believers should place their trust in Allah." (Al-Imran: 160)

From the inception of his political party to the rally on October 30, 2011, he faced numerous challenges over 15 years. He navigated a demanding environment, confronted aggressive tactics from rivals, endured personal attacks, and faced mockery from his opponents. Throughout this journey, he made considerable personal sacrifices, jeopardizing his marital and family relationships while spending a significant amount of time away from his children. His commitment to his goals was deeply rooted in a strong faith and trust in God. By starting his speech with the verse "إِيَّاكَ نَعْبُدُ وَ إِيَّاكَ نَسْتَعِينُ", Khan highlighted the foundation of his strength. Since that crucial moment, he has consistently demonstrated through his actions that his true power stems from the prayers of the people and his unwavering trust in God.

On May 7, 2013, he had a fall from the stage but astonishingly emerged without any long-term disabilities. While dealing with severe injuries and great pain, he spoke to the nation from his hospital room, sending messages of encouragement. He openly opposed drone strikes and U.S. military tactics in Afghanistan, engaging with global leaders, including Donald Trump, as equals. In response to the Pulwama incident, he took swift action by ordering the downing of Indian planes. At the United Nations, he advocated for "righteousness" and firmly dismissed Jonathan Swan's inquiry about the U.S. establishing a base in Pakistan with a strong "Absolutely not." He tenaciously fought against attempts to destabilize his government and survived numerous assassination attempts, both overt and covert. Following a murder attempt by sharpshooters in Wazirabad, he boldly raised his fists in defiance. He faced unlawful detentions by the Rangers at the Islamabad High Court and endured attacks by the Punjab Police at his home in Zaman Park, Lahore. Despite experiencing tear gas assaults and feeling betrayed by certain party members, he showed remarkable strength. He bravely contended with 200 unjust and illegal cases filed against him, confronting the hardships of imprisonment alongside his principled, non-political wife.

Despite the numerous challenges and obstacles he encountered in his life, he remained steadfast in his dedication to his principles and goals, showcasing his unwavering faith and courage. This reality has led to global recognition of his ability to not only express his beliefs " إِيَّاكَ نَعْبُدُ وَ إِيَّاكَ نَسْتَعِينُ"—but also to embody them in his actions. His deep conviction has enabled Imran Khan to achieve success in all endeavors. Even now, amid physical constraints and various adversities, this faith continues to give him the strength to confront political, governmental, military, and judicial challenges with unwavering resolve.

The influential individuals behind the regime change operation to oust Prime Minister Imran Khan mistakenly believed that imprisoning him would weaken his determination. They underestimated this 72-year-old patriot, assuming that his privileged upbringing and successful life would make him susceptible to the pressures from influential local and global powers. They believed he would, like many politicians, become compliant and frail both physically and mentally, instead of confronting the trials of incarceration.

However, Imran Khan chose to resist these malevolent forces. Instead of yielding to hopelessness or stepping back from his principles, he stood firm against his oppressors and refused to negotiate for his freedom. With remarkable confidence, steadfast faith, and decisive actions, he has consistently challenged his adversaries, leaving them, along with political commentators, the global media, and even his supporters, astonished by his resilience and determination.

The oppressors subjected Khan, who is also the most beloved leader of the Pakistani nation, to harsh physical torture. He is confined in a small, dark cell, forced to lie on a cold floor in the freezing winter, left without a fan during the sweltering heat, and served poor-quality food. Instead of giving in to despair, Khan surprised and disturbed his power-hungry tormentors by smiling, increasing the duration of his exercises, reading a variety of religious, historical, and spiritual books, and audibly reciting "إِيَّاكَ نَعْبُدُ وَ إِيَّاكَ نَسْتَعِينُ" in front of the cameras placed in his cell.

When the oppressors aimed to break Khan by placing him in solitary confinement, capturing his daily life in jail on camera around the clock, pressuring his party leaders to hold press conferences against him, prohibiting his image and voice on media, imprisoning his beloved and loyal wife, and testing his moral and mental resilience through an un-Islamic, immoral, and illegal "Iddat case," Khan chose not to yield to these false forces or beg for mercy. Instead, he sought guidance from the Book of Allah, finding strength in his daily prayers and Tahajud prostrations. This showed his remarkable steadfastness and thwarted the plans of those who wanted to break his spirit.

The illegitimate PDM government, backed by a powerful military establishment and obedient judges, made numerous attempts to intimidate Khan and his wife through biased trials based on various unlawful charges while in jail. They later imposed arbitrary sentences. Nonetheless, Khan chose to maintain his composure and fought back legally within the bounds of the Constitution and the law. Ultimately, he was vindicated in every unjust case, successfully overcoming the unlawful authorities and the judges who had acted unlawfully.

Instead of giving in to despair over the numerous injustices and the immoral, inhumane, and illegal actions surrounding him, Khan chose to uphold his beliefs. He did not beg for mercy or compromise his values, turning away from the idea of yielding to the tyrants of his time. By proclaiming "لا الہ الا اللہ (There is no one worthy of worship except ALLAH)" and "إِيّاكَ نَعْبُدُ وَ إِيّاكَ نَسْتَعِينُ", he demonstrated his commitment to achieving true freedom for his oppressed and vulnerable nation. He aimed to transform his cherished homeland into an Islamic welfare state akin to the State of Madina. Throughout this journey, he remains resolute, fueled by sincere dedication, trust, and a strong sense of commitment.

It is worth noting that all of Khan's decisions, which were based on hopes linked to vested interests rather than genuine faith in God or sound principles, ultimately proved wrong, resulting in significant consequences for him. For instance, in the 2013 and 2018 elections, Imran Khan opted to rely on wealthy politicians and electable candidates rather than dedicated party workers. His dependence on external influences was particularly evident during the sit-in, as was his reliance on General Bajwa's extension and the misplaced loyalty he placed in many of his morally questionable ministers and advisors. He faced blackmail from his allies to maintain his government and remained silent about undue interference from the military establishment. Imran Khan has openly acknowledged these facts and is currently focused on rectifying his past mistakes and wrong decisions.

Currently, he is undergoing a significant challenge, yet he continues to enjoy immense public support and blessings. His oppressors, who have incarcerated Khan, thought that physical and mental torment would break his spirit; however, he has only grown stronger. Although his presence and voice may seem absent, he remains a beloved figure in the hearts of the people as their hero. Rather than feeling powerless or disconnected from decision-making due to his forced isolation from the outside world and his party, Khan finds comfort in his relationship with his Creator through solitary worship and ascetic practices. This connection has empowered him to make wise decisions and thwart the schemes of those intent on undermining him.

Khan has gained significant respect, status, and recognition during his imprisonment, arguably more than he ever had before. This was reflected in the general elections on February 8, 2024, where the patriotic citizens of Pakistan granted the PTI a resounding two-thirds majority, despite the various injustices and illegal actions imposed by the establishment, the PDM, and the judiciary. This level of support stems from his unwavering commitment, trust, and selfless love for his nation, as well as the prayers of his supporters. Despite facing numerous challenges and conspiracies, his opponents have been unsuccessful in defeating him, the hypocrites have been unable to sway him, the conspirators have not been able to displace him, and his enemies have not succeeded in removing him. This steadfast trust will undoubtedly pave the way for Khan's eventual freedom and the realization of his vision for a state inspired by Madina. God willing.

Passionate Devotion

The words we use mirror our innermost thoughts. As we consistently articulate these phrases, they evolve into symbols of our resolve and dedication. When our beliefs resonate with our genuine values, they motivate us to act and pursue our aspirations. When someone truly commits to the challenging path of reaching their goals, that dedication evolves into a passion that brings both comfort and meaning to life. Focusing this passion toward the Prophet Muhammad (peace and blessings be upon him) lays the groundwork for a fulfilling and significant existence.

In his autobiography, "Pakistan, A Personal History," Imran Khan reflects on how his early understanding of religion and his connection with God were primarily shallow. However, the illness and subsequent passing of his dearest mother had a significant impact on his outlook, lifestyle, and plans. It was during this challenging time that he began to delve into the Holy Quran, the life of the Prophet Muhammad (PBUH), and Islamic teachings, seeking peace and deeper insight. Through this journey, Imran Khan uncovered the profound significance of the Prophet's (PBUH) legacy.

Imran Khan often urges the public, especially the youth, to study the biography of the Prophet Muhammad (PBUH). He believes that this understanding is essential for recognizing that, despite our flaws, we are guided by an extraordinary prophet who has illuminated humanity's path.

The Prophet (PBUH) played a crucial role in guiding individuals toward God, revealing divine wisdom, purifying their hearts, enlightening their spirits, shaping their thoughts, and refining their characters. He led humanity through all circumstances—whether in times of difficulty or prosperity, youth or old age, calm or chaos, hope or despair, wealth or poverty, indulgence or devotion, joy or sorrow. He embarked on a journey of divine insight, soaring to great heights and delving into profound depths, illuminating darkness with light, and embodying the brilliance of the sun, the warmth of fire, the speed of particles, and the freshness of a single drop of water.

The Prophet (PBUH) transformed desolate areas into thriving centers of knowledge, enabling wisdom to emerge even from the most challenging circumstances. He prompted individuals to recite the Quran joyfully, reshaping those who relied on flattery and begging into skilled navigators of vast spiritual waters. In difficult moments, he provided solace to those who had faced hardships, uplifting a nation from despair to extraordinary achievement. His teachings and leadership transformed formerly enslaved people into influential figures worldwide.

On September 27, 2019, Imran Khan, the Prime Minister of Pakistan, addressed the United Nations General Assembly, conveying the sentiments of over 1.8 billion Muslims who hold a deep affection for the Prophet Muhammad (PBUH). He stated, "The Prophet Muhammad (PBUH) holds a special place in our hearts, and when he is attacked, it brings us immense sorrow. The anguish of the heart surpasses any other form of suffering, making it unbearable for anyone. Billions of Muslims worldwide cannot accept any disrespect towards the Prophet

Muhammad (PBUH)." The Prime Minister also dismissed European notions of Islamophobia and Radical Islam, affirming that the only version of Islam we acknowledge is the one that is aligned with the teachings of our beloved Prophet (PBUH).

Imran Khan frequently refers to Pakistan as a "state of Madina" in his interviews, articles, and speeches, highlighting his intense dedication to this vision. It is a natural human inclination to prioritize something in life only when there is genuine passion for it. When the objective is to please God and His Messenger (PBUH), while also promoting the well-being of humanity, this passion transforms into a noble and commendable purpose. The concept of the state of Madina emphasizes human welfare and carries significant importance. Islam encourages us to actively help the poor, needy, ill, destitute, and vulnerable during their times of struggle.

To revitalize the values of the state of Madina, the Imran Khan government established the National Rahmatul-Ul-Alameen Authority on October 14, 2021. This organization focuses on nurturing the character of the young generation by drawing on the wisdom of international scholars, promoting good behavior, and preventing misdeeds. It engages in research related to the life of the Prophet Muhammad (peace be upon him) and the hadiths, aiming to foster a fair and welfare-oriented society. Additionally, it intends to convey the genuine essence of Islam to the global audience.

To bring this vision to life, the government set up Al-Qadir University in the Sohawa region of Jhelum. The primary objective of the university is to explore the Quran, the Sunnah, the lives and teachings of scholars, and Sufism, while integrating these disciplines with modern science and research. The educational philosophy emphasizes imparting contemporary sciences through the lens of the Quran and Sunnah, preparing students to implement these principles in their original contexts. Furthermore, the government initiated various programs, including shelter homes, free meal services, Ehsaas programs, health cards, and other innovative projects, aimed at supporting those in need. These initiatives mark the initial tangible steps toward creating a welfare state akin to that of Madina.

In his article titled "The Spirit of the State of Madina: Reshaping Pakistani Society," published in national newspapers on January 17, 2022, Imran Khan expressed his thoughts on the importance of the State of Madina. He mentioned that "The great Prophet (PBUH) established the foundation of the greatest civilization in human history by creating the State of Madina and provided guiding principles for governance. His vast and multifaceted character serves as an example for everyone. He (PBUH) delivered a message of justice, equality, and religious tolerance to humanity. Today, how many individuals are eager to see that system put into practice? We must work diligently to shape our nation according to these essential principles." Imran Khan highlighted the pressing need for Pakistan to align with the values of the State of Madina, claiming that "our survival and prosperity depend on it."

Imran Khan has demonstrated a profound and sincere affection for the Prophet Muhammad (PBUH) through his writings, speeches, and actions. As a devoted follower, he is reported to have walked barefoot in Madina to honor the Prophet's Holy Shrine. In March 2012, he took a stand by refusing to attend a conference in Delhi due to his objections regarding the presence of Salman Rushdie, who was embroiled in blasphemy controversies. As a result of Imran Khan's advocacy, the United Nations acknowledged Islamophobia as a significant concern, leading to the establishment of March 15 as the International Day Against Islamophobia.

Imran Khan was probably the sole leader among the heads of 55 Islamic nations who openly advocated for the universal principles of Islam on both national and global stages. He highlighted the significance of the Madina State ideology. He took tangible actions to put it into practice, including the establishment of the Rahmatul-ul-Alameen Authority and Al-Qadir University.

Regrettably, the unconstitutional and illegal government of the PDM, which rose to power through a regime change operation, not only disbanded the Rahmatul-ul-Alameen Authority but also unjustly imprisoned Imran Khan by accusing him of his involvement in establishing Al-Qadir University. Additionally, the closure of welfare initiatives, such as Langar Khana (free meal kitchens), shelter homes, the health card program, and the Ehsaas Program, has caused significant and lasting harm to the foundational efforts aimed at creating the State of Madina, making it difficult to comprehend the extent of the damage inflicted fully.

Despite the challenges presented by opponents and the hurdles established by the PDM government and its powerful allies, it is evident that Pakistan will eventually transform into a state akin to Madina. Whether this transformation occurs during Imran Khan's lifetime or afterward, the credit for it will ultimately be attributed to him. God willing.

Patriotism

Patriotism, or the love for one's homeland, is a pure, unique, and inherent sentiment. Regardless of a person's family, ethnicity, race, religion, or cultural background, their primary identity is tied to their country. A homeland is not merely where one is born or lives; it includes the landscapes, gardens, streets, markets, fields, valleys, rivers, seas, and deserts, along with the friends, family, and community members who inhabit those spaces. These elements foster a sense of belonging and provide deep satisfaction to one's spirit. Therefore, the affection for one's homeland is a fundamental part of human nature.

As a young boy, he was captivated by tales of the courage exhibited by Tipu Sultan and the Muslim conquerors, which his cherished mother shared with him. At the age of thirteen, he picked up a gun during the Indo-Pakistan war, driven by a desire to protect his homeland. His faith serves as his foundation, while his patriotism fuels his passion. He faced life's challenges and difficulties with optimism, confronting adversaries and overcoming obstacles, achieving success in various areas, and ultimately impressing the world.

What accusations have been left unspoken against him? What defamation has he not faced? What obstacles has he not overcome? What pain has he not experienced? What grief has he not felt? What false claims has he not encountered? What hardships has he not battled? What intense attacks has he not survived? on his challenging journey, which he undertook for the greater good, progress, and the upliftment of his country and nation

Despite the obstacles he faces, this extraordinary patriot, driven by a deep affection for his country and a commitment to helping others, has continuously placed the well-being of his fellow citizens above his own and that of his family. His steadfast loyalty, honesty, and pride in his nation inspired him to pursue the ambitious vision of "New Pakistan", reminiscent of the State of Madina, all on his own. Currently, he enjoys the support of over 80% of the Pakistani population.

Imran Khan has demonstrated a deep devotion to his nation, viewing his endeavors as both a responsibility and a form of reverence. This intense dedication has enabled him to excel in multiple fields and establish a benchmark for merit, excellence, and success that is recognized by both the citizens of Pakistan and the global community.

In the 1992 World Cup, despite facing numerous challenges, including a struggling team, an injured shoulder, and a series of defeats, Imran Khan remained resolute. He made a consistent vow to secure the World Cup victory during interviews and team discussions. Against all expectations, he guided the team to triumph over the unbeaten New Zealand in both the quarter-finals and semi-finals. During the final match, his confident and victorious attitude during the toss put pressure on the England captain. Batting at number three during a difficult phase, Imran significantly uplifted the team's score, boosted their confidence, and raised the spirits of the nation. He clinched the World Champion trophy for Pakistan by taking the last wicket of the England team on the final ball of his career. Imran Khan's remarkable leadership shone brightly in this achievement, deserving high commendation. His unwavering belief and patriotism turned the seemingly impossible into reality. Even in the face of challenging and frustrating circumstances, he maintained his optimism and determination. This remarkable victory not only brought immense joy to the troubled nation of Pakistan but also inspired its people to dream big and pursue their ambitions with courage and determination.

Following a grand and honorable retirement from cricket as a triumphant captain, Imran Khan dedicated himself to serving his nation, with a special focus on healthcare. The experience of watching his beloved mother suffer during her illness profoundly affected him, sparking a desire to relieve the suffering of everyday Pakistanis. This empathy evolved into a vision of creating a top-tier, free cancer hospital.

To achieve his vision, Imran Khan was ready to make sacrifices he never imagined he would have to endure, leaving behind his once luxurious lifestyle. He departed from a life of comfort, filled with extravagant beds and opulent homes, and embarked on a strenuous and unwavering mission across the country to establish the free cancer hospital. Breaking away from his typical demeanor, he ventured into streets, markets, schools, and various locations to solicit donations. Despite receiving discouraging advice from experts, Imran Khan, motivated by his love for his country and the nation's support, accomplished what many thought was impossible. On

December 29, 1994, he inaugurated the Shaukat Khanum Hospital in Lahore, followed by the launch of the second-largest cancer facility in Peshawar on the same date in 2015, which offers treatment to 75% of its patients free of charge.

Next year, the largest cancer hospital in Asia is set to be inaugurated in Karachi, God willing. In a developing and financially challenged country like Pakistan, Khan has managed to establish and run top-notch cancer hospitals, relying solely on the generous contributions from its citizens rather than on government funds or foreign assistance. It is nothing short of a miracle that Imran Khan has demonstrated his selfless love for his homeland. The Pakistani nation has consistently supported him, helping to complete every project he has undertaken.

Imran Khan has demonstrated remarkable patriotism through various initiatives.

He established Namal University to provide world-class education and degrees to underprivileged students in a backward area of his native land. He also initiated the Billion Tree Tsunami Project, planting billions of trees to combat climate change and protect his country. Khan has successfully raised billions of rupees to support those affected by floods and earthquakes.

Over the course of his 22-year political career, he has played a significant role in the decline of family-oriented political parties and has launched public welfare projects upon assuming power. He has established shelters and safe spaces for poor travelers in major urban areas and introduced health cards to ensure access to quality medical services for low-income individuals. During the COVID-19 pandemic, he implemented adequate measures to combat hunger among at-risk communities. In the aftermath of the Pulwama attack, he took bold actions to protect his nation's dignity and security, showing a willingness to face possible repercussions. His strong opposition to the establishment of a U.S. military base in the country further highlights his commitment to national interests and leadership. These efforts demonstrate his commitment to the well-being of the populace and his country.

Imran Khan, the cherished son of Shaukat Khanum, has consistently shown extraordinary dedication and affection for Pakistan. His words and actions in various situations reveal his steadfast commitment to the nation. His past and ongoing efforts illustrate that every decision he has made has been focused on serving his country and its citizens. He has chosen to prioritize the welfare, dignity, and international standing of his nation over personal fame or wealth.

He had the choice to live a relaxed and luxurious life in England with his family, but he decided to go back to his homeland, leaving his loved ones behind. Unlike many other cricket players who took advantage of their renown through commentary and international travels, he chose to tackle the challenges facing Pakistan, raise awareness among his fellow citizens, and fight for their rights. Instead of purchasing properties abroad, he channeled all his earnings into Pakistan, financing welfare initiatives that went beyond his personal needs, and ultimately bequeathed all his assets to the Shaukat Khanum Hospital in his will.

He had the option to make a deal in response to the unethical and illegal attacks from his opponents aimed at him, his family, the hospital, and his party (PTI), or he could choose to escape. Rather than succumbing to despair, he demonstrated his steadfast dedication and patriotism by confronting and overcoming various challenges across different fields. Even now, instead of renouncing his principles, he faces the trials of imprisonment with unwavering passion and resolve.

Historically, only a few individuals have significantly impacted their country's development and prosperity without wielding power. Imran Khan has not only raised awareness among his fellow citizens but has also motivated them to unite and advocate for their rights. His incredible patience, unparalleled bravery, perseverance, and patriotism have inspired both overseas Pakistanis and those living in various regions of Pakistan, from the mountains to the plains, coastal areas, deserts, and fertile valleys. They hold a deep affection for him and are dedicated to creating a new Pakistan under his leadership.

Regardless of the actions taken by his adversaries—be it intensifying repression or raising fraudulent and unlawful accusations against him—Khan will remain undefeated. His lifelong struggle and the remarkable achievements that have come from it demonstrate that he is destined for victory and will always hold a special place in the hearts and prayers of the people of Pakistan. God willing.

Valuable Capital

Young people are an essential resource for their nation, serving as the architects of the future and reflecting the essence of their homeland. They carry the aspirations and dreams of their families and mentors, who find happiness, solace, and reassurance in their presence. Energized by their youth, they navigate a dynamic world filled with endless possibilities, crafting new ambitions daily. They aim to achieve significant accomplishments, explore space, delve into the depths of the oceans, set new records, establish new standards, innovate groundbreaking ideas, excel in their fields, and inspire others as role models. Young individuals often demonstrate bravery, resolve, and vitality that exceed those of middle and older age groups.

Pakistan is fortunate to have a youth demographic that represents 60 % of its total population. However, for several decades, the lack of security, combined with insufficient education, training, and guidance, as well as limited job opportunities and career counseling, has resulted in economic and social decline. This scenario has rendered the youth susceptible to mental stress. Despite the immense potential among young people, many are dissatisfied. The despair caused by poverty, unemployment, and social injustice has driven many capable individuals to leave Pakistan. At the same time, those who remain feel disheartened by the system and discouraged about their future.

Twenty-eight years ago, Imran Khan recognized a harsh truth and decided to enter the world of politics. His goal was not to pursue wealth, fame, or authority, but to transform Pakistan into an actual Islamic welfare state, reminiscent of the State of Madina. He committed himself to the people's welfare, championing the rights of the youth, fostering tolerance, and advocating for social, economic, and societal justice. This dedication inspired him to establish his political party, Pakistan Tehreek-e-Insaf. Before his political journey, Khan was already regarded as a national hero, having achieved significant global recognition as a distinguished cricketer and as the founder of Pakistan's first world-class cancer hospital. He had won the affection of the Pakistani populace, especially the younger generation, long before he entered politics. During the development of the cancer hospital, schoolchildren actively participated, becoming vital to its mission.

After the hospital was constructed, Imran Khan founded the Pakistan Tehreek-e-Insaf and presented his manifesto to the public. A significant number of young people, dissatisfied with traditional political parties and dynasties, were attracted to Khan and became essential members of his team. Although he faced many obstacles and setbacks due to his inexperience, along with strategic tactics and allegations from opponents, the youth remained steadfastly supportive of Khan.

On one side, Khan would advocate for his party and share his viewpoints through the media. On the other hand, it was the youth, despite facing ongoing challenges within the political and electoral arena, who actively promoted Khan's ideology and conveyed his message at the grassroots level. The passion of the youth for Imran Khan's vision, combined with their faith in his leadership, has transformed the Pakistan Tehreek-e-Insaf into the largest political party in the country, effectively pushing opposing parties to the sidelines, as they now exist primarily at the provincial, regional, and factional levels. Due to PTI's strong resonance with the youth, critics have derisively dubbed PTI supporters "Youthia," a term also used to describe middle-aged or older supporters.

It is essential to grasp the factors contributing to the impressive resilience displayed by the youth in Pakistan. Even in the face of significant challenges and intense state repression and violence, they steadfastly support Imran Khan, boldly opposing fascism, brutality, and oppression. They are crafting stories of perseverance and bravery. This is the result of an unwavering spirit of awareness instilled in the Pakistani populace, particularly among the younger generation, by Imran Khan.

In today's world, characterized by scientific progress and an abundance of online information, the young generation is cautious about embracing any perspective or assertion without substantial evidence and credible sources. This creates difficulties in uniting them under a particular ideology. However, Imran Khan has managed to overcome this obstacle through years of dedication and persistence.

Imran Khan has long been a source of inspiration for the youth, thanks to his remarkable achievements in cricket. During his efforts to establish a cancer hospital in the 1990s, the children involved in fundraising saw firsthand his deep dedication and the successes that resulted. They regarded him as an exceptional figure: an alumnus of Oxford, former cricket team captain, ex-chancellor of Bradford University, and the 1992 World Cup champion at Melbourne Stadium. He built and now manages a leading cancer hospital and university, both of which are sustained by public contributions. Additionally, he has left a significant impact on the political scene, addressing challenges posed by the Pakistan Democratic Movement (PDM) parties. He is a notable representative of Pakistan and Islam at international venues such as the OIC and the UN. Imran Khan stands out as the only leader in Pakistan who has committed his life to serving the nation, embodying hope and faith since his youth.

The younger generation believes that "Imran Khan will not rest until he fulfills his goals and dreams. He tirelessly promotes meritocracy and stands against corruption. His vision includes a society founded on equality and justice. He wants the green crescent flag and passport to gain global respect and recognition. Imran encourages the youth to think big, draw inspiration from the life of the Prophet (PBUH), and have trust in God alone. He consistently overcomes challenges with sincerity and determination, aiming for the glory of his country and the prosperity of its people. In contrast, previous and current military rulers and their elected officials do not embody these qualities."

Realizing this, the youth and children chose to rally behind Khan in his political pursuits. As time passed, their bond with Khan and his ideals grew stronger. Today, due to their unwavering commitment and effort, Pakistan Tehreek-e-Insaf has risen to become the most powerful political party, with Imran Khan as its most beloved leader.

Khan not only roused his nation from apathy but also educated them about their rights and duties as citizens of Pakistan. He demonstrated how to advocate for their rightful claims in a peaceful manner. Khan emphasized the persistent issues of corruption, favoritism, mismanagement, lawlessness, and injustice that have plagued Pakistan for decades. He identified those responsible for these problems and worked to raise awareness among the public. As a result, he has achieved a significant milestone, and the positive outcomes of his efforts will surely begin to benefit our beloved country and its people in time, God willing.

Despite the attempted regime change and an unprecedented increase in state repression, the Pakistan Tehreek-e-Insaf has become more robust and popular than ever. This revival is primarily due to Imran Khan's remarkable bravery and resolve. By cultivating a strong sense of awareness, Khan has sparked a movement that resonates throughout the country, particularly among youth. This wave has gained momentum, challenging the ruling elite, their supporters, and their obsolete system.

A shared spirit brought the nation together on April 10, 2022, in support of Imran Khan after he left the Prime Minister's House with just a diary on the night of April 9, following a regime change. This collective emotion empowered educated women like Tayyaba Raja, Aaliya Hamza, Khadija Shah, Sanam Javed, and Falak Javed, turning them into a potent force. It also inspired the innocent Zil-e Shah to give his life for a noble cause and enabled

Ibtisam to thwart an assassination attempt against Khan in Wazirabad successfully. Furthermore, this movement boosted the morale of countless young workers who are unjustly imprisoned and sparked enthusiasm among millions of overseas Pakistanis for Khan. It rendered the illegitimate PDM government ineffective and weakened the repressive tactics of the powerful establishment, finally lifting the veil that had obscured the vision of the Pakistani nation for the last seventy-eight years.

This awareness empowers the youth to effectively defend Khan and the PTI on social media, countering government propaganda with compelling arguments in a rapid and effective manner. Regardless of the narrative spun by the ISPR, government ministers, or advisors about Imran Khan and the PTI, the youth on social media swiftly prove it false with solid evidence.

The power of awareness galvanized the youth, enabling them to rally and unify the entire nation, successfully navigating the challenges faced by the PTI during the national elections on February 8, 2024. By effectively and swiftly utilizing social media, they sparked a conscious revolution in Pakistan, resulting in the PTI securing a two-thirds majority on election night. Despite support from the military establishment, the Supreme Court, the Election Commission, and various government institutions, the defeat of the Sharif and Zardari families, along with other parties in the PDM, seemed almost miraculous. Under Khan's leadership, the enthusiastic youth and determined populace triumphed in this difficult election.

The danger of unchecked power lies in its ability to foster arrogance in individuals in powerful positions while undermining their ability to think critically, empathize, engage in active listening, and perceive reality accurately. This situation is evident in the current PDM government and its influential military supporters in Pakistan. Instead of viewing PTI workers merely as adversaries, it would have been more prudent for the PDM government and its allies, who seem overly focused on Imran Khan, to see them as patriotic citizens. They should have opened channels for dialogue rather than resorting to oppression and tyranny. By considering their viewpoints, providing reasoned arguments, and recognizing their valid demands, they could have gained respect and built trust in both the government and its institutions.

Regrettably, the current leadership has chosen to impose fear, repression, and state power as tools against PTI supporters and patriotic youth, rather than pursuing constructive dialogue. As a result, thousands of young individuals are facing unlawful detention in jails and military custody across the nation. Despite these repressive actions, the state has failed to silence young activists, even with tactics such as imprisoning them, abducting their family members, ruining their businesses, dismissing them from their jobs, branding them as digital terrorists, prohibiting them from traveling internationally, subjecting them to physical abuse, and abusing state authority and resources.

The military establishment and the illegitimate administration of the PDM must realize that a system founded on dishonesty and oppression might operate for a while, but it is ultimately bound to collapse. The brutal methods of oppression, intimidation, and lawlessness aimed at undermining Imran Khan and dismantling the PTI have not only failed to achieve their harmful goals but have also revealed the true nature of the illegitimate PDM government and its influential supporters to both the people of Pakistan and the global community. As a result, they have lost their credibility, dignity, and respect.

In this conflict, fueled by personal vendettas among the powerful military elite and their quest for unchecked authority, Pakistan is left as the primary loser. The current illegitimate leaders still have a chance to move beyond their pride and obstinacy by relinquishing power to those who genuinely deserve it, as stipulated by the constitution, legal frameworks, and the will of the Pakistani populace. By making this choice, they could help guide the nation out of its current turmoil. Ultimately, no matter how formidable the military becomes, it cannot prevail against the will and awareness of its nation.

Endurance

Everyone dreams of achieving fame, immense wealth, and power. However, it's entirely possible to live a dignified and tranquil life without these accomplishments. Basic needs, such as food, clothing, and a house, are essential for all individuals. However, in the face of poverty, hardships, and obstacles, a self-sufficient person can overcome adversity through patience, gratitude, hard work, and bravery. They can even withstand the trials of homelessness and hunger. Nonetheless, criticism, accusations, and slander are unacceptable forms of social behavior for anyone.

Every famous, wealthy, and influential person in the world encounters criticism, accusations, and slander to varying degrees. While most people can tolerate some level of criticism, there comes a point when the words and actions of critics cross a line. When this happens, those who spread accusations and slander may face consequences, whether through legal action or illegal means.

Pakistan is a developing nation where even minor criticisms of the powerful establishment can be viewed as acts of treason or threats to national security. Those who challenge religious parties and leaders may face charges of desecration of religion, while questioning the performance of judges can lead to contempt of court notices. Individuals who speak out against landlords, bureaucrats, or prominent politicians, including the Zardari and Sharif families, often endure severe consequences. In stark contrast, it is considered acceptable in Pakistan for critics and opponents to repeatedly attack, accuse, and malign Imran Khan, who has gained global recognition and raised Pakistan's profile on the international stage over the last fifty years.

Before he entered politics, Imran Khan was widely revered by the people of Pakistan, celebrated as a national hero, and the subject of countless well-wishes. However, once he ventured into the political landscape, he encountered a relentless barrage of unjust criticism, accusations, and defamation from his rivals, all aimed at undermining and defeating him. What allegations haven't been thrown at him? What types of criticism haven't been aimed his way? What insults haven't been directed toward him? Despite this onslaught, Imran Khan has chosen not to respond with bitterness or vengeance. Instead, he remains committed to his vision of a 'New Pakistan,' demonstrating remarkable resilience and grace in the face of adversity.

Imran Khan is not perfect; he is human and prone to making mistakes like everyone else. Throughout his life, he has likely committed numerous overt and covert sins. In his political career, Khan has also made several significant blunders. However, just like his contemporaries and fellow citizens, he has the opportunity for reform and repentance. He can seek forgiveness for both minor and major sins, whether committed knowingly or unknowingly. He holds onto the hope and firm belief in being forgiven and pardoned by his Merciful and Forgiving God.

The harsh reality is that dishonest and cowardly politicians, along with certain religious and non-political opponents, make sweeping accusations and issue hurtful statements to portray Imran Khan's mistakes as unforgivable offenses. Despite their own shortcomings, they try to present him as an immoral individual. They scrutinize his past, present, character, speech, ethics, and private life excessively and unfairly, holding him to standards appropriate only for angels and ridiculing every word and action he takes.

Can those who accuse Imran Khan of wrongdoing substantiate their own virtue?

Can the self-righteous rivals who have labeled Imran Khan as an unforgivable sinner ensure their own salvation and forgiveness on Judgment Day?

Can those who criticize Khan's youth withstand examination of their own past?

Can those who maliciously target Khan's personal life accept public scrutiny of their own deeds?

Can those who claim Khan is a thief defend their financial practices?

Can those who label Khan as ill-mannered seek public opinions about themselves?

Can those who mock Khan as a drug user and a Playboy allow others to peek into their private social events?

Can those who brand Khan a traitor, terrorist, and Jewish agent outshine him in patriotism, service to the community, or affection for the Prophet (PBUH)?

Can those who impose a red line on Khan and demand "an end" to him venture into public spaces without security protocols?

The answer to all these questions is a resounding no.

It is evident that in the political arena, all those who have faced humiliating defeats at the hands of Imran Khan—whether rivals in politics or not—are driven to resort to oppressive measures, authoritarian tactics, criminal actions, personal attacks, and negative propaganda. This response arises from their desire to conceal their own disgrace and maintain their long-standing, illegitimate grip on power.

Now, let's take a closer look at the allegations, criticisms, slanders, and negative propaganda that have been directed at Imran Khan over the past 28 years.

1. Playboy

Imran Khan, a graduate of Oxford and fluent in English, is recognized for his tall, slender physique, fair complexion, long, beautiful hair, and charismatic personality. His technical prowess in cricket, coupled with his captivating bowling style and a streak of impressive achievements, launched him to significant fame early in his life—a dream for every young athlete.

Experiencing such immense fame and respect at a young age often leads to admiration and popularity, particularly among women. Maintaining self-discipline during this period is challenging within the traditional eastern cultural context of Pakistan and even more so in the free-spirited atmosphere of the West. In these situations, it can feel nearly impossible to resist forming connections with attractive women.

Imran Khan found himself in a similar predicament. With his engaging personality, masculine appeal, and cricket fame, he attracted considerable attention from women worldwide, particularly in Western nations. Notable figures such as Sita White, Emma Sargent, Stephanie Beacham, Goldie Hawn, Caroline Kellett, and Christina Baker were known to be close to him. As a result, he was dubbed the "Playboy of Cricket" by the Western media.

A playboy is an individual who projects an image of sophistication while indulging in worldly delights and surrounding himself with attractive, affluent, and renowned women.

In his book "Imran Khan: The Cricketer, the Celebrity, the Politician," Christopher Sandford mentions that Imran Khan often visited well-known nightclubs in Britain and Australia. He enjoyed socializing and dating women, and even though he abstained from alcohol, he had no problem enjoying nights out with his teammates.

British author Ivo Tennant references artist Emma Sargent, who noted that she had a four-year relationship with Imran Khan from 1982 to 1986, describing him as "the perfect blend of East and West."

During his cricket career, President General Zia-ul-Haq offered him a position in the government. Following the World Cup victory, Nawaz Sharif invited Imran Khan to join his party, but Khan declined the offer gratefully. Instead, he ventured into regular politics by founding the Pakistan Tehreek-e-Insaf party. However, the PML-N leaders, who had initially invited Imran Khan to join their ranks, launched a nationwide campaign to undermine him by accusing him of being a playboy. Additionally, journalists, analysts, and other opponents, motivated by financial incentives, joined the effort to discredit him. Imran Khan was caught off guard, as he never anticipated that his opponents, particularly the Sharif brothers, would attack his personal life rather than engage him in political competition.

Rather than engaging in character attacks against the Sharif family and other opponents in an attempt to present himself as morally superior, Imran Khan opted to concentrate on his political endeavors. As the Sharif family began to feel threatened by Khan's increasing popularity and the youth's growing enthusiasm for the Pakistan Tehreek-e-Insaf, they orchestrated a campaign to damage Khan's reputation. This effort was primarily based on an American court ruling that linked Khan to his former girlfriend, Sita White, and her daughter, Tyrian, resulting in significant damage to Khan's political image.

Whenever Imran Khan was questioned about Sita White, Tyrian Khan, and his image as a Playboy, he would recount how, in his youth, he indulged in a lavish lifestyle in the West and considered himself a nominal Muslim. However, after experiencing his mother's illness and gaining a deeper understanding of his faith, he regretted his past choices and chose to change his path. Now, he strives to live as a dedicated Muslim, actively seeking forgiveness and guidance through his daily prayers.

Despite facing numerous allegations, character attacks, and setbacks in the early elections, Khan managed to maintain his patience and hope. In contrast, his opponents have consistently resorted to personal attacks rather than following Islamic principles that discourage accusations and slander. Notably, Imran Khan's ex-wife, Reham Khan, has been a central figure in this negative campaign, having released a 900-page book containing inappropriate content. Additionally, former Chief Justice Iftikhar Chaudhry has made significant contributions to these assaults by filing a legal case related to Tyrian. During an August 2022 meeting, former Army Chief General Bajwa mocked Khan by calling him a former "Playboy," to which Imran Khan replied, "I never claimed to be an angel."

In Pakistan, every politician, military official, civil servant, and elite individual has their own shortcomings and mistakes. The stories and disputes involving many of these people are well-known. Imran Khan, if he had chosen to, could have attacked the personal lives of his opponents and tarnished their reputations. Nonetheless, Khan decided to uphold his integrity by refraining from discussing anyone's private matters publicly.

Oscar Wilde famously remarked, "Every saint has a past, and every sinner has a future." This suggests that those who are presently regarded as "holy" have once sinned, and those seen as sinners can aspire to holiness. It highlights that everyone has the chance for redemption and change at any stage of life.

Each person makes mistakes, commits sins, and may stray from the right path. When someone commits a grave sin, Allah Almighty has provided a way to repent and seek forgiveness. The teachings in the Holy Quran emphasize the importance of seeking forgiveness and repentance.

Additionally, various hadiths underscore the significance of turning to Allah, offering assurance that individuals should not feel disheartened or anxious after committing sins.

The Holy Quran addresses wrongdoers:

"O My servants who have wronged themselves, do not despair of Allah's mercy. Indeed, Allah forgives all past sins. He is the Most Forgiving, the Most Merciful." (Al-Zumar: 53)

"Whoever commits a sin or wrongs themselves, then seeks forgiveness from Allah will find Him Oft-Forgiving and Most Merciful." (Al-Nisaa': 110)

"O you who believe! Turn to Allah in repentance, all of you, so that you may achieve success." (Al-Noor: 31)

"He is the One who accepts repentance from His servants and forgives their sins. He is fully aware of everything you do." (Al-Shura: 25)

"Will they not turn to Allah and seek His forgiveness? Indeed, Allah is Oft-Forgiving and Most Merciful." (Al-Maidah: 74)

The Prophet (peace and blessings of Allah be upon him) said:

"Every human being is a wrongdoer, and the best among them are those who repent." (Sunan Ibn Majah/Al-Zuhd 29 (4251))

"O people! Before you die, all of you should repent to Allah." (Sunan Ibn Majah, Barqam: 1081)

"Whoever conceals the faults of a Muslim, Allah will conceal him on the Day of Resurrection. Conversely, whoever reveals the sins of a Muslim, Allah will expose him, to the extent of humiliating him, even while he is sitting at home." (Sunan Ibn Majah: 2546)

The immense regard and love from the nation for Imran Khan clearly show that Almighty ALLAH has acknowledged his sincere regret for past actions. Rather than focusing on the criticism from his opponents, people are coming together in support of him in a way that has never been witnessed in history.

I hope the critics and adversaries who have been disparaging Imran Khan—calling him a Playboy despite his genuine remorse—would take a moment to consider their own actions. They should question whether, out of animosity towards Imran, they are risking their own well-being in this life and the hereafter by turning away from the principles outlined in the Quran and Sunnah. It's simple to claim to be virtuous, but truly following those principles is much more challenging. Everyone has imperfections, which is why we are encouraged to seek forgiveness for our wrongdoings and to hide the shortcomings of others.

For the sake of divine approval and achieving success both in this life and the hereafter, a believer's faith and character should prioritize concealing the flaws and shortcomings of others rather than exposing them. Instead, believers should concentrate on self-improvement by reflecting on their flaws. Remember, every son of Adam (peace be upon him) is fallible. Acknowledging mistakes, confessing them, and asking for forgiveness from the Almighty while striving to walk the right path is in line with the teachings of Adam (peace be upon him). Conversely, fixating on errors and repeatedly committing them while justifying those actions leads one toward the devil's path. We need to examine our hearts and determine whether we are adhering to the teachings of Adam (peace be upon him) or following the path of the devil.

2. Jewish Agent

Imran Khan married Jemima Goldsmith, the daughter of British billionaire Sir James Goldsmith, on June 20, 1995. Jemima, who comes from a Jewish background, converted to Islam before their marriage and chose to live in Pakistan permanently. During her nine years there, she faced a variety of ideological, cultural, social, familial, and environmental challenges. Nevertheless, Jemima made a significant effort to embrace Pakistani traditions, understand Islam, and learn the Urdu language, all of which were motivated by her love for Imran Khan. She was pretty successful in these endeavors. In return, Imran Khan expressed profound love and respect for her. Together, they enjoyed a rewarding life, enriched by their children, Qasim and Suleman.

Sadly, Imran Khan's seemingly perfect marriage ended in divorce in 2004. This was primarily influenced by the challenging political climate in Pakistan and the baseless allegations and smear campaigns orchestrated by his political adversaries. Much of the negativity arose from propaganda propagated by rivals, including some religious figures and intellectuals, who targeted Jemima Khan's family background and branded Imran Khan as a foreign and Jewish agent. The repercussions of these attacks were profoundly painful for Jemima, leading her to take their children back to London and pursue a divorce from Imran Khan.

In October 2021, Jemima Khan revealed in an interview that she had to leave Pakistan because of politically motivated illegal charges against her. She mentioned that she was threatened with imprisonment and asserted, "Actually, I was being targeted to harm Imran Khan."

Islam is a religion that embodies decency and transparency. It encourages its followers to reflect on these qualities and make significant contributions to a better society. The tenets of Sharia impose strict penalties for false accusations and slander, with no exceptions in this matter.

GOD commands in the Holy Quran:

"O you who have faith! If someone untrustworthy delivers news to you, be sure to verify it carefully. Otherwise, you might unintentionally hurt others and later regret your actions." (Al-Hujrat:6)

The Prophet (peace and blessings of Allah be upon him) said:

"Anyone who talks about a believer in a false manner will be put among the inhabitants of Hell by Allah until they repent for their words." (Abu Dawud Hadith No 3597, Musnad Ahmad Hadith No 5385, Silsila Sahih Hadith No 437)

Numerous narrations with a similar message can be found in Sahih Bukhari and Sahih Muslim. These narrations emphasize that labeling a Muslim as an infidel can, in itself, lead to disbelief. This is particularly concerning when a group of scholars disseminates false information and continues to spread it without verifying its accuracy. Their actions become even more reprehensible, especially if they claim to be followers of the Book and the Sunnah. In such cases, the risk posed by their misleading narratives increases significantly.

Despite the explicit guidance provided by the Quran, the teachings of the Prophet (PBUH), and the principles upheld by Islamic society, Imran Khan's political rivals—most notably Maulana Fazal-Ur-Rehman, leader of the Pakistan Jamiat Ulema-e-Islam—have consistently labeled Khan as a Jewish agent. This baseless accusation has been made for years.

In May 2024, Maulana Fazal-Ur-Rehman stated, "Calling Imran Khan a Jewish agent was merely a political statement. It is not intended as an insult, but rather as a form of protest. You should have asked me why I referred to him as a Jewish agent." However, in the past, Maulana Fazal-Ur-Rehman expressed a different viewpoint, claiming, "Imran Khan was given the government to protect and promote Israeli interests. He is a Jewish agent who received funding from Jewish and Indian agencies. The primary objective of this funding was to facilitate Israel's recognition. The purpose behind granting the PTI government in Khyber Pakhtunkhwa during the 2013 elections was to change the culture of the region."

The Jewish agent's propaganda against Khan was so intense that even the renowned Islamic scholar Dr. Israr Ahmed felt compelled to address it. Years ago, Dr. Israr Ahmed stated, "Goldsmith has targeted Imran Khan. Imran was an emerging figure, and great hopes were associated with him. Now, he will receive a payment of 50 million pounds from Goldsmith. What is the reason for this? If we examine the entire conspiratorial role of the Jews, "Everything will be revealed."

On social media, there has been a spread of misinformation claiming that Hakeem Muhammad Saeed Shaheed, the former Governor of Sindh and the founder of Hamdard University, published a book titled "The Story of Japan" in 1996. It is alleged that in this book, he wrote passages between pages 13 and 15 stating, "Foreign forces have selected a former cricketer, Imran Khan. The Jewish media has started to promote him. CNN and BBC are doing their utmost to laud him. The Pakistani press has received millions of rupees to elevate Imran Khan's status. Britain, which played a pivotal role in the establishment of a Jewish state by giving Palestine to Israel, is also supporting Imran Khan while backing the Aga Khan.

Furthermore, Imran Khan has married a Jewish woman. I question, 'Will the next government of Pakistan be under Jewish influence?'" However, it has been established that Hakeem Saeed never authored a book by that title, nor did he make any such statements or comments regarding Imran Khan.

Someone who engages in slander is generally regarded as unworthy and unwelcome in any community. In Islam, making false accusations against someone without a valid reason is considered a grave sin and is prohibited by Islamic law.

In the Quran, Allah Almighty emphasizes that:

"Verbally causing harm to innocent believing individuals, especially via slander, is a grave sin." (Al-Ahzab:58)

"Anyone who errs or sins and blames it on an innocent person bears a significant burden of slander and has committed a clear wrongdoing." (Al-Nisa:112)

The teachings of the Prophet (PBUH) concerning slander include:

"Anyone who falsely accuses a Muslim to disgrace him will be held at the edge of Hell by Allah until they either reconcile with the person they wronged or endure a punishment that fits their offense" (Abu Dawud, Hadith 4883)

"Whoever labels another person as evil or refers to him as an infidel, when he is not, that accusation will come back to harm the one making it." (Sahih al-Bukhari, Bab Ma-inhi an al-Sabab and Curse 2/893, Number: 5810; Mishkaat al-Masabih 411; Kanz al-Umal 3/802, Hadith Number: 8810)

Pakistan is a nation that has witnessed the tragic loss of countless innocent lives due to intolerance and sectarian divisions. These conflicts have significantly fractured society, with religious extremism prevalent throughout. It is highly perilous to label a national hero and highly regarded political figure like Imran Khan as a Jewish agent. Instead of yielding to the distress caused by such harmful accusations and threats, Khan has chosen to continue his political path and pursue his vision for a new Pakistan. He has confronted the propaganda aimed at him with bravery, wisdom, and patience.

The current circumstances and events indicate that Imran Khan is not a Jewish agent but rather a faithful follower of the Prophet Muhammad (PBUH) and a committed Muslim. He has stood up for oppressed Muslims in Kashmir, Palestine, and around the world through both his speeches and his actions. His deep love, dedication, and humility towards the Prophet (PBUH) are reflected in his barefoot walks in the streets of Madina. Imran Khan founded Al-Qadir University, intending to enhance the knowledge and appreciation of the Prophet's (PBUH) teachings, and he envisions transforming Pakistan into a nation that reflects the values of Madina. He has consistently refused to recognize Israel and has been outspoken on international platforms like the United Nations, playing a vital role in the establishment of Islamophobia Day on March 15 to honor the dignity of the Prophet (PBUH). Despite losing his government and facing unjust imprisonment for challenging oppressive forces, he continues to be a source of pride for both the Pakistani nation and the global Muslim community.

Had Dr. Israr Ahmed been alive today, he would not only withdraw his previous statements about Imran Khan but would also take pride in his efforts for Islam and the Muslim Ummah.

If Imran Khan were genuinely a Jewish agent, the efforts to bring down his government would have failed. His party would not have endured the extensive, unlawful, and cruel oppression enforced by the illegitimate PDM government and its powerful partners. There would have been no restriction on his speeches, image, or public appearances, and he would not have been wrongfully imprisoned, since the Jewish establishment prioritizes safeguarding its interests at all costs.

In contrast, the secret visit of a Pakistani delegation to Israel during the illegitimate PDM government, the ban on public protests against Israel in Pakistan, the repression by state institutions against those who wave the Palestinian flag in stadiums and public places, Prime Minister Shehbaz Sharif's covert meeting with the President of the American Jewish Congress during the UN session, along with both Sharif and Deputy Prime Minister Ishaq Dar offering their unwavering support for US President Donald Trump's unilateral peace plan for Gaza—without consulting the nation or Parliament—has sparked concerns. Furthermore, President Trump's commendation of both the Prime Minister of Pakistan and the Army Chief during a press conference, along with his acknowledgment of their support for the Gaza peace initiative from the beginning, raises significant questions about the PDM government's actions and the possible secret arrangement with Israel.

3. Taliban Khan

When Imran Khan's political rivals and critics found it challenging to diminish his popularity or influence in Pakistan through various accusations and insults—labeling him a Playboy and a Jewish agent—they shifted their strategy. They began portraying him to the United States and the Western world as a supporter of the Taliban and an extremist Muslim, coining the term "Taliban Khan." These so-called liberals and political opponents, who view themselves as champions of enlightenment, deem Imran Khan's religious beliefs as extremist and fundamentalist.

Is Imran Khan truly a supporter of terrorism and the Taliban?

The circumstances and events involving Imran Khan, along with his views and actions, suggest that he has never supported terrorism or the Taliban. He has always maintained that warfare is not a viable solution to conflicts, and he advocates for negotiations as the most effective means of achieving lasting peace. Even after conflicts come to an end, he believes that dialogue is crucial for tackling underlying issues. This is why Khan places such a strong emphasis on negotiations. Unfortunately, his opponents have wrongly interpreted this stance as an endorsement of extremist groups. The decision to conclude the two-decade-long Afghan war and the withdrawal of U.S. forces from Afghanistan were purely the outcomes of negotiations.

Imran Khan is a notable political figure known for his distinct and unwavering stance: he is against involvement in the American-led war on terrorism. While he initially backed Musharraf during the referendum, his support wavered when Pervez Musharraf announced Pakistan's role as a frontline ally in the U.S. war against terrorism in Afghanistan. Khan began to openly criticize him from that point on. Despite the potential advantage of maintaining his support for Musharraf in the 2002 elections, he chose to condemn Musharraf's decisions whenever possible, prioritizing national interests over his personal goals.

Imran Khan has repeatedly expressed his stance against the presence of foreign military forces in Pakistan. He has asserted, "We will confront terrorism on our own," highlighting the need to define who is considered a terrorist. Every sovereign nation has the right to shape its own future. When foreign troops are allowed to operate within a country, it can cause the local population to view their own military as a foe, alongside these foreign forces. The consequences of these choices have a significant impact on the country and its population. The tragic loss of 75,000 lives, encompassing both civilians and military members, underscores the harsh truth during the U.S.-led operations against the Taliban, which also incurred economic damages in the billions. Presently, no city or individual in Pakistan is safe from the threats of terrorism.

Khan has also frequently condemned drone strikes, organizing a two-day sit-in in April 2011 along the road in Hayatabad, Peshawar. This protest attracted thousands of participants, including students from schools and colleges as well as supporters of the PTI from various areas. Demonstrators carried banners and placards calling for an end to drone strikes. During this event, numerous trucks and containers carrying supplies for NATO were parked along the GT Road, from the Attock district to Peshawar city, effectively disrupting the logistics for NATO operations in Afghanistan for two days.

During the sit-in, Imran Khan highlighted the desire of Pakistanis to live as a sovereign nation. He remarked, "Key issues confronting Pakistan include our subservience to America and the corruption among our leadership. The people of Pakistan want their military to avoid bombarding their own citizens just to satisfy the U.S." In October 2012, under Khan's guidance, the Pakistan Tehreek-e-Insaf organized a peace march towards Waziristan to protest against drone strikes, but the march was halted at Tank city.

Between 2004 and January 1, 2018, American forces carried out 409 drone strikes in Pakistan under the leadership of PML-Q, PPP, and PML-N. These strikes led to approximately 2,000 deaths. While some of the targets were leaders of banned groups, the majority of those who lost their lives were innocent civilians from Pakistan's tribal areas. Notably, during Imran Khan's tenure as Prime Minister, there were no drone strikes, as he had stated that he would order the Air Force to intercept and shoot down any drones that entered Pakistan's airspace under his administration.

Imran Khan has never supported any terrorist incidents that have occurred in Pakistan. On December 16, 2014, when the Army Public School in Peshawar was attacked and more than 100 innocent children were killed, Imran Khan was engaged in a 126-day sit-in protest in Islamabad. Following this tragic incident, he not only condemned the cowardly act of terrorism but also announced an immediate end to the sit-in, offering his full cooperation to the government.

Most political leaders in Pakistan tend to align their views on the Taliban and Afghanistan with those of the military establishment and the United States. In contrast, Imran Khan stands out as the only political figure who has consistently held a fact-based perspective, even amidst criticism from both the U.S. and the powerful Pakistani establishment. His views have proven to be correct over time. Khan has repeatedly responded to the accusations made against Pakistan by the U.S. and Europe after their withdrawal from Afghanistan with reasoned arguments, refusing to appear submissive or apologetic.

On November 19, 2018, President Donald Trump tweeted that the United States would stop providing billions in aid to Pakistan, claiming that the country does nothing for the U.S. despite receiving financial support. He cited two significant examples, Osama bin Laden and the ongoing situation in Afghanistan.

In response, Prime Minister Imran Khan retweeted to assert that it's essential to set the record straight about Pakistan. He pointed out that no Pakistanis were involved in the 9/11 attacks, yet Pakistan supported the U.S. in its fight against terrorism. Khan highlighted that during this effort, 75,000 Pakistanis lost their lives and the country's economy faced losses of over $123 billion, while the U.S. only offered $20 billion in aid. He questioned whether Trump or his associates had made similar sacrifices. Imran Khan called on Trump to avoid using Pakistan as a scapegoat for the failures of his administration in Afghanistan. He questioned why the

Taliban had gained strength despite the presence of 14,000 NATO troops, 250,000 Afghan forces, and a war budget of one trillion dollars. Khan highlighted that the collaboration with the U.S. in the fight against terrorism led to the destruction of homes in tribal regions, forced displacements, and significantly affected the lives of ordinary people. He also pointed out that during the War on Terror, Pakistan granted free access to its land and air routes for U.S. military operations.

In this tweet, Imran Khan highlighted the devastating impact of war, particularly the loss of lives and its economic repercussions. His rational and fact-oriented message boosted his respect and standing in Donald Trump's eyes. This was apparent in the way Trump received him during his visit to the United States.

As Prime Minister of Pakistan, Imran Khan stated, "If any country other than Afghanistan has been affected by the situation in Afghanistan, it is Pakistan." This situation can be traced back to the 1980s, when Pakistan was a frontline ally against the Soviet Union's invasion of Afghanistan. The US and Pakistan collaborated to train 'Mujahideen' groups to wage jihad and liberate Afghanistan. However, after the collapse of the Soviet Union and the end of the Cold War, the US left Afghanistan, abandoning the Mujahideen. After the events of September 11, 2001, when the US invaded Afghanistan, it once again sought Pakistan's support. Ironically, the Mujahideen that had been trained to fight the Soviets were now labeled as terrorists by the US. Consequently, these former allies turned against Pakistan, declaring jihad against the country. At that time, more than

3 million Afghan Pashtun refugees were living in Pakistan, many of whom sympathized with the Afghan Taliban. This was the first time Pakistan faced the extremist Taliban, who opened a front against the Pakistani government. When the army first moved into the tribal districts, collateral damage occurred, further fueling extremism as people sought revenge for the losses they had suffered."

Imran Khan has repeatedly emphasized that "the Afghan people are an independent nation, and Afghanistan cannot be governed from outside. Therefore, the Afghan community must forge its own government within its borders. The ongoing civil conflict in Afghanistan poses a risk of spilling over into Pakistan. Pakistan's economic strategy is heavily reliant on achieving stability in Afghanistan. The turmoil will affect not just Afghanistan but also the citizens of Pakistan. A peaceful Afghanistan would enable Pakistan to benefit from connecting to Central Asia via the proposed railway from Peshawar."

Unlike many prominent political leaders and military rulers in Pakistan who have often prioritized their own interests and those of the United States, Imran Khan distinguishes himself by not aligning with the fight against terrorism merely to appease American interests. Instead, he has concentrated on humanitarian issues and national pride. He has highlighted the grim realities faced on the ground and consistently cautioned the United States and the Western world about the dire consequences of this ineffective war.

Although time and circumstances have continually affirmed Imran Khan's views and stance, his adversaries, critics, and sure progressive liberals—motivated by animosity—persist in labeling him as "Taliban Khan" to audiences in the U.S. and Europe. This hostility reached a peak when Imran Khan applied to run for chancellor at the University of Oxford, prompting members and leaders of the PML-N party to flood the University of Oxford administration and British media with numerous letters and emails. In these messages, they inaccurately portrayed Khan's comments regarding terrorism and the Taliban.

On August 28, 2024, the British newspaper "Daily Mail" expressed serious concerns regarding Imran Khan's candidacy for the Chancellorship of Oxford University, calling him a "disgraced" former prime minister. The publication highlighted a significant backlash against Khan's announcement, noting that Oxford University received numerous emails and protest petitions filled with anger about his candidacy. Many messages labeled the founder of the Pakistan Tehreek-e-Insaf (PTI) as an unsuitable candidate for the Chancellor's role. The "Daily Mail" pointed out that Khan's extremist views, particularly his prior support for the Taliban and Osama bin Laden, have posed significant challenges to his candidacy. His past advocacy for the Taliban and its extremist ideology has attracted substantial criticism.

On September 1, 2024, Catherine Bennett authored an article in the British newspaper "The Guardian," questioning whether the Chancellor of Oxford University had referred to the Taliban as a friend. It examined Khan's eligibility to run for the position and whether he would be an appropriate choice for Chancellor. The article also prompted Oxford voters to consider: "Do you want to vote for a candidate who is friendly to the Taliban?" Additionally, it compared the PTI founder to Andrew Tait, a social media personality known for making provocative comments about women.

"The Guardian" condemned Imran Khan's potential election as Chancellor, branding him a "Taliban friend." The article noted Khan's congratulations to the Afghan Taliban after the withdrawal of American, British, and allied forces, claiming they had "broken the chains of slavery." It also highlighted his controversial remarks, suggesting that women who faced sexual harassment were partly to blame, and his refusal to label Osama bin Laden as a terrorist, instead calling him a martyr. Khan has also backed the Taliban's prohibition on women's education.

Those who have disseminated negative propaganda against Imran Khan and attempted to obstruct his candidacy for the chancellorship at Oxford University appear to have overlooked an important point: the real impact of their actions was more detrimental to Pakistan than to Imran Khan personally. The respect and esteem that Imran Khan has achieved render the chancellor position somewhat less important to him. However, his selection would have certainly elevated the honor and prestige of Pakistan.

4. U-Turn Khan

Politics operates within a landscape of possibilities. Within this space, no policy, statement, decision, movement, or protest is absolute. A true leader is committed to their beliefs and objectives, but achieving success requires the ability to adapt plans and strategies to shifting circumstances. Given that these factors are constantly evolving, revising one's approach is crucial. Stubbornness can result in setbacks and failures. This capacity to pivot when needed is often described as wisdom, insight, foresight, practicality, or simply making a U-turn.

In 1996, Imran Khan founded the Pakistan Tehreek-e-Insaf, emphasizing the importance of nurturing leadership among the country's youth and middle class. His vision encompassed ensuring basic education and healthcare for all, combating corruption, promoting justice, upholding the rule of law, implementing meritocracy, and creating a welfare state. However, during his tenure as Prime Minister, his actions often contradicted these original commitments. Initially, critics described these moves as a clear shift in direction for Imran Khan. Over time, opposition parties intensified their criticism, dubbing him "U-Turn Khan."

In March 2019, during an event, Imran Khan criticized the leadership of his rival party, the Pakistan People's Party. He argued that if Bilawal Bhutto and his father had addressed corruption issues instead of ignoring them—meaning, if they had changed their approach to corruption—they would not be facing legal troubles today.

During a National Assembly session in June 2019, Khursheed Shah, a member of the PPP, highlighted various inconsistencies in Prime Minister Imran Khan's previous statements. Some notable contradictions included:

- Khan's assertion of "I will not take loans," which was contradicted when the PTI government borrowed from numerous sources, including the International Monetary Fund (IMF).

- He claimed, "I will make petrol, gas, and electricity more affordable," yet there were multiple increases in prices instead.

- His promise, "I will not allow the dollar to become more expensive," was undermined when the dollar reached record highs against the rupee during his tenure.

- Khan stated, "I will not pursue friendship with India," but the PTI government initially extended a gesture of goodwill towards India, although relations later deteriorated.

- He declared, "I will not include independent candidates," but independent candidates were indeed included to fulfill the member requirements needed for forming the government.

- Khan promised, "I will not accept excessive security and protocol," but this pledge was not upheld.

- He announced intentions to "turn the Prime Minister's House into a university and bulldoze the Governor's House," yet this plan was never realized.

-Despite saying, "I will not travel abroad," he made several international trips to countries like the US, Saudi Arabia, and Indonesia within his first year as Prime Minister.

- He claimed, "I will go on a regular commercial flight," but this promise went unfulfilled.

- Khan promised, "Instead of a helicopter, I will commute to the office on a bicycle like the Prime Minister of the Netherlands." However, this announcement was not implemented either.

- He stated, "I will form a small cabinet," but the number of ministers and advisors in his cabinet grew significantly.

- Lastly, he claimed, "I will not give office to anyone who is accused." However, several current and former PTI ministers are facing court cases.

According to the opponents, in addition to the points mentioned above, the following actions and statements also qualify as U-turns.

Imran Khan, who once referred to Chaudhry Pervez Elahi as a dacoit of Punjab, not only allied with him but also appointed him as the Chief Minister of Punjab to protect his government.

Before assuming power, Imran Khan frequently criticized the Metro bus project, calling it a "Jangla bus." However, after taking office, he was so impressed with this "Jangla bus" concept that he ultimately built a similar system in Peshawar.

Imran Khan initially referred to the amnesty scheme as a way to "cleanse black money." Nonetheless, once he assumed office, his position shifted, and he appeared convinced of the necessity for such a program.

Before becoming Prime Minister, Imran Khan frequently stated that he was not someone who would rely on the establishment to make decisions. Throughout his tenure, he consistently claimed that all government decisions were made by him, not by the establishment. However, after losing power, Khan made a surprising statement in an interview, claiming that it was actually the establishment running the government, not him. He alleged that he had to submit to the agencies to get the budget passed.

Imran Khan responded to the accusations directed at him by defending his position on the importance of making 'U-turns' in politics. He remarked, "Every great leader takes a 'U-turn.' If someone never does this, it shows they are not a true leader." To support his argument, he mentioned historical figures like Adolf Hitler and Napoleon Bonaparte, suggesting that if they had made 'U-turns,' they might not have experienced failure. Khan asserted that the ability to adapt decisions is a key trait of effective leadership. He emphasized that the choices he made were for the country's and its people's best interest and were intentional. He pointed out that as situations and events are continually changing, it's vital to modify our decisions accordingly.

The following day, PML-N leader Khawaja Asif criticized Prime Minister Imran Khan for his statement about U-turns. In a message on Twitter, he predicted that Imran Khan would eventually make a U-turn regarding his own statement about making a U-turn. This issue of U-turns doesn't stop here; members of the opposition to the PTI government even proposed that the government should establish a "Ministry of U-turns."

According to the Collins Dictionary, the term "U-turn" in politics refers to a complete reversal of a political policy. The motivation for making a U-turn typically stems from the belief that the previous political policy was ineffective or misguided.

Significant U-turns mark the history of political leaders in the Indian subcontinent. Figures such as Gandhi, Nehru, Jinnah, Bhutto, Nawaz Sharif, and Imran Khan have all made notable U-turns at various points in their political careers when necessary.

Quaid-e-Azam Muhammad Ali Jinnah began his political career in 1906 as a member of the Indian National Congress. Like Gandhi, Jinnah envisioned a united India, aspiring to free the country from British rule in alignment with the Congress philosophy. Throughout his time in Congress, he consistently advocated for Hindu-Muslim unity. He worked to promote peaceful coexistence between the two communities, as outlined in the "Lucknow Pact of 1916." he was not successful in achieving this goal.

In 1920, after serving in the Congress for 14 years, Jinnah decided to resign due to growing differences with Gandhi. Nevertheless, he continued to pursue better relations between Hindus and Muslims until the 1930s. From 1930 to 1934, he lived in Britain. It was during this time that Allama Iqbal convinced Jinnah to return from his self-imposed exile and re-enter Indian politics. Allama Iqbal's ideas had a significant impact on Jinnah's political vision.

Upon his return from London, he became a strong advocate for the two-nation theory and the Pakistan movement, serving as the leader of the All-India Muslim League. Jinnah supported Iqbal's vision in his speeches. This marked a significant political U-turn, as he departed from the belief that "Hindus and Muslims are one nation" and adopted the opposing view that "Hindus and Muslims are two separate nations." This shift ultimately led to the creation of Pakistan. Imagine if Quaid-e-Azam had not made this U-turn and had remained with the Congress; perhaps Pakistan would not exist on the world map today.

The poem "Sare Jahan Se Acha Hindustan Hamara," written by Allama Iqbal in 1905, expresses a profound love and pride for India, asserting its superiority over the rest of the world. It was first recited at Government College in Lahore and is part of Iqbal's initial poetry collection, "Bang-e-Dra." Years later, in 1930, Iqbal advocated for the idea of a separate homeland for Muslims during his famous sermon in Alla-abad, a reflection of the socio-political context of that era.

When the renowned biographer Oriana Fallaci asked Zulfikar Ali Bhutto, the founder of the Pakistan People's Party and former Prime Minister, "Someone has told me that you are not a balanced person? You say one thing one day and completely change your statement the next day. This makes it difficult to understand what is actually going on in your mind." Bhutto responded with a thought-provoking answer. He said, "The only thing I accept from philosopher John Locke is that consistency is the characteristic of small minds. He stated that while the core idea should remain strong, it is not a bad thing to change other aspects frequently. Sometimes one can go to the right and at other times to the left. Intellectuals, according to Bhutto, should not cling to a single idea; instead, they must exhibit flexibility in their thinking. Otherwise, they risk falling into self-deception and madness. Politics is dynamic, and a politician should adapt their ideas as needed. There must be room for contradictions, and one should critique the weaknesses of political rivals from every angle."

According to Zulfikar Ali Bhutto, inconsistency is a characteristic of intelligent people. In his response, he referenced the late Prime Minister of India, Indira Gandhi, stating that she did not grasp this concept and, as a result, failed to appreciate the beauty of the political profession. However, he noted that his father understood this idea well. This insight is derived from an interview with Zulfikar Ali Bhutto, conducted by Oriana Fallaci, and can be found in her renowned book, "Interview with History".

Former Malaysian Prime Minister Mahathir Mohamad stated that there is nothing inherently wrong with a leader going back on their initial promises or making a U-turn. He explained that sometimes people make mistakes and reconsider their decisions upon realizing that it is wise to do so. According to him, we may occasionally choose the wrong path, but it is important to turn back when necessary, as no one is perfect.

Imran Khan has consistently emphasized the importance of "compromise for ideology, but never on ideology." He believes that one must never waver from one's mission and vision. Imran Khan's mission is to establish a corruption-free Pakistan and to create a welfare state. To achieve this mission and realize his vision, it is sometimes necessary to take a U-turn, pause the journey, or change the approach; however, the mission and vision themselves will remain unchanged.

During his tenure as Prime Minister, Imran Khan had to reverse several of his claims and decisions due to pressures from coalition partners, the impact of the coronavirus pandemic, a struggling economy, and undue interference from General Bajwa. However, after the regime change operation, it has become evident that despite facing significant mental, physical, political, legal, and imprisonment challenges, he remained steadfast in his beliefs and refused to compromise. This resilience highlights that Imran Khan is the only political leader whose approach is driven not by personal or family interests, but by his vision for a "New Pakistan," inspired by the principles of the State of Madina.

If you take a closer look at the U-turns of the opponents who criticized Imran Khan for his U-turns, you may find it surprising and troubling. Their choices seem driven more by personal and familial interests rather than by national interest or ideology.

Maulana Fazal-Ur-Rehman's decision to label women's leadership as illegitimate while collaborating with Benazir Bhutto's administration is noteworthy. Likewise, both Benazir Bhutto and Nawaz Sharif publicly endorsed a Charter of Democracy to oppose military ruler Pervez Musharraf. However, they later made secret agreements with him, securing an NRO (National Reconciliation Ordinance). Zardari once proclaimed his intention to dismantle the military establishment "brick by brick," yet he ended up acting as a representative for the military generals. Shehbaz

Sharif had pledged to "tear Zardari apart" and drag him through the streets of Larkana, but eventually apologized and engaged in duplicitous politics. Nawaz Sharif aimed to reduce the military's power by claiming to honor the people's vote, but ultimately chose to respect military authority instead. Maryam Nawaz emphasized her intention to avoid aligning with military interests; however, she ultimately followed a similar path.

Every member of the Pakistan Democratic Movement (PDM) has committed to supporting democracy. However, their actions have, in practice, reinforced military rule and weakened constitutional governance, the rule of law, and democratic principles. This conduct suggests that Zardari, the Sharif family, and Maulana Fazal-Ur-Rehman are primarily driven by their own family and personal agendas.

5. Project Imran Khan

In the initial 15 years of his political journey, Imran Khan encountered numerous challenges. During this period, his opponents not only questioned his character but also ridiculed him, labeling him as clumsy and the PTI as a "Tanga Party". Observing Khan's persistent difficulties in the political arena, many critics and analysts suggested that he should leave politics and focus on cricket commentary or charitable work. Nevertheless, Imran Khan remained committed to realizing his vision of a "New Pakistan." After years of determination, he finally experienced a significant breakthrough on the evening of October 30, 2011. PTI's landmark rally at the historic Minar-e-Pakistan represented a moment of joy and optimism that Khan had long sought.

Paradoxically, although the rally on October 30, 2011, was deemed successful and sparked public excitement, critics credited its achievement to the military establishment rather than acknowledging Imran Khan's dedicated efforts, struggles, and the awareness he fostered among the public. They specifically pointed to former ISI chief General Pasha as the architect of "Project Imran Khan," overlooking Khan's extensive political journey and accomplishments. In Pakistan, it's widely believed that achieving political success and forming a political party typically requires military backing. Military leaders have historically nurtured notable figures like Zulfiqar Ali Bhutto and Nawaz Sharif politically. As a result, many analysts and critics have unfairly grouped Imran Khan with Bhutto and Nawaz Sharif, ignoring the distinct elements of his political journey.

Zulfiqar Ali Bhutto's political ascent did not start with a political party or grassroots initiatives; instead, it was shaped by his alliances with Sikandar Mirza and General Ayub Khan. As noted by Justice Dr. Javed Iqbal in his book "Apna Gireban Chaak," Bhutto gained access to Mirza during his presidency through considerable efforts. In a feudal style, he arranged for chickens to be sent to the Presidency's kitchens, with the help of the late Sardar Abdul Rashid, over several weeks. This gesture culminated in Bhutto hosting an extravagant champagne celebration in honor of Sikandar Mirza at his opulent residence in Karachi. When Mirza later abolished the 1956 Constitution, he appointed Bhutto to his cabinet. After General Ayub Khan ousted Sikandar Mirza, Bhutto remained in Ayub's cabinet, thus establishing him as his new mentor while distancing himself from Mirza. When asked about this transition, Bhutto remarked, "So that General Ayub would not get angry."

It is often mentioned that Bhutto referred to Ayub Khan as "Daddy." Following the imposition of martial law by Ayub Khan on October 27, 1958, the then 30-year-old lawyer Bhutto became the Minister of Commerce. He soon held multiple ministries. On January 24, 1963, he took on the role of Foreign Minister of Pakistan. As Ayub Khan's power began to wane, Qudrat-Ullah Shahab observed in his book "Shahab Nama" that Bhutto was eagerly awaiting the right moment to challenge him. Capitalizing on this opportunity, Bhutto launched his campaign against Ayub Khan. The two ultimately parted ways on June 17, 1966, and later, on November 30, 1967, Bhutto founded the Pakistan People's Party in Lahore.

Mian Nawaz Sharif embarked on his political journey in the 1980s, backed by Governor Ghulam Jilani, driven by his ambition to safeguard and expand his family's business, as suggested by his father. He received his political training under the regime of military ruler General Zia-ul-Haq. During this period, Nawaz Sharif served on the Punjab Provincial Council before being appointed as the Finance Minister of Punjab in 1981.

In the 1985 non-party elections, he secured a substantial number of seats in both the national and provincial assemblies, leading to his swearing-in as the

Chief Minister of Punjab on April 9, 1985. After the dismissal of the Junejo government by Zia-ul-Haq on May 29, 1988, Nawaz Sharif opted to support the military dictator rather than his party leader, Muhammad Khan Junejo. His loyalty was rewarded with his continuation as the caretaker Chief Minister of Punjab, highlighting the close ties he had with General Zia-ul-Haq.

In the aftermath of the Bahawalpur incident, the name of the late Zia-ul-Haq was echoed by many people, including Mian Nawaz Sharif. On the anniversary of Zia-ul-Haq, during a gathering at Faisal Mosque, Nawaz Sharif boldly declared that the Bhutto ideology had been buried and that the Zia ideology had been revived. He also announced his commitment to continuing Zia-ul-Haq's mission.

Benazir Bhutto also acted out of political convenience; her decision to grant General Aslam Beg the Medal of Democracy was primarily aimed at securing her hold on power.

Chaudhry Pervaiz Elahi, the leader of the Muslim League-Q, who emerged from Pervez Musharraf's regime, often voiced his support for Musharraf's presidency during his speeches while still in uniform.

Asif Ali Zardari is often referred to as the "king of reconciliation." Following Benazir Bhutto's death, he renamed the Q-League as the "Killer League." Subsequently, he appointed the leader of this very "Killer League," Chaudhry Pervaiz Elahi, as Deputy Prime Minister. Zardari also extended General Kayani's tenure, claiming that General Kayani was a pro-democracy military leader, which made his extension necessary.

Over its 77-year history, Imran Khan has distinguished himself as the sole Pakistani politician who emerged into the political arena by establishing his own party, "Pakistan Tehreek-e-Insaf," rather than having military backing. He showcased his leadership and dedication not through serving under a dictator as a foreign or finance minister, nor by building relationships with military leaders, but by confronting the various challenges and obstacles that come with politics and ultimately triumphing. Unlike many traditional politicians, Khan could have easily chosen the safer route of aligning himself with military regimes and engaging in opportunistic politics, accepting offers from figures such as military ruler Zia-ul-Haq in 1987 and Nawaz Sharif in 1992. Instead, he chose a more difficult yet rewarding path.

Various political and non-political critics of Imran Khan assert that the ISI chief, General Ahmed Shuja Pasha, initiated Project Imran Khan in 2011. Following his retirement in 2012, Zaheer-ul-Islam took charge of the project and employed Imran Khan to oust Nawaz Sharif from power. Imran Khan's march toward Islamabad in 2014, along with the ensuing sit-in at D-Chowk, was part of a plan created by the ISI, which ultimately did not succeed. After Zaheer-ul-Islam retired, the Project Imran Khan file was put on hold. Still, it was revived after General Qamar Javed Bajwa assumed the role of army chief, who is alleged to have influenced Khan's rise to the prime minister's office in 2018 through electoral manipulation.

According to analysts, as well as Imran Khan's opponents and critics, "Project Imran Khan" had several aims and objectives. For instance:

1. One of the primary goals of Project Imran Khan was to implement various constitutional and political reforms in Pakistan, including the shift from a parliamentary system to a presidential system.

2. To regain its declining influence and power, the military establishment started to support and promote Imran Khan and his party. This effort aimed to disrupt the entrenched political dominance of the PPP and the PML-N. This dominance was particularly evident during the first peaceful transfer of power between civilian governments in 2013, a transition made possible by the Charter of Democracy signed between the PPP and PML-N during Pervez Musharraf's dictatorship.

3. Another key objective was to liberate the Pakistani people from the political monopoly, corruption, and family dynasties of the Sharif and Zardari families. By positioning Imran Khan—a charismatic, honest, and internationally recognized figure—as Prime Minister, the aim was to improve Pakistan's image globally and establish a "hybrid government" within the country.

The lengthy sit-in held in 2014, Imran Khan's mention of the umpire's finger during the protest, the surprising entrance of prominent political figures into PTI, the unforeseen establishment of a coalition government in 2018 with traditional parties like the MQM, the unwarranted praise and extension of General Bajwa's tenure through alliances with opposition groups, the ongoing difficulties posed by corrupt coalition partners, and the failure to enact reforms within state institutions all point to concerns raised by critics. Additionally, the passage of government legislation and budgets with military and ISI backing, the management of government activities under the leadership of General Bajwa and General Faiz Hameed, and Khan's claim of being an ineffective prime minister after his ousting, further highlight the criticisms labeling him as the "Project Imran."

It is generally acknowledged that establishing and effectively managing a government in Pakistan requires the backing and endorsement of the influential military establishment. Nevertheless, Imran Khan has many attributes that differentiate him from politicians such as Zulfiqar Ali Bhutto, Nawaz Sharif, Benazir Bhutto, and Asif Ali Zardari. For example, Khan began his political journey as an independent figure, not depending on military support or family connections. He secured his position as Prime Minister through widespread public support and acceptance, following a remarkable 22-year journey filled with challenges and adversity. After being removed from power, instead of succumbing to fear and fleeing like many politicians do, he chose to address the nation honestly and advocate for genuine freedom. These actions illustrate that Khan is not tied to the establishment; instead, he is a born leader.

The aftermath of the regime change operation on April 9, 2022, illustrates that General Pasha, the ISI, and the military did not support the popularity or successful protests of Imran Khan and the Pakistan Tehreek-e-Insaf. Instead, these demonstrations were fueled by Khan's principles, increasing public awareness, and widespread discontent with the political actions of the Sharifs and Zardari.

Following the regime change that ousted Khan's government, which had the backing of the military establishment, there were expectations that the PTI would fade from the political landscape. However, despite facing oppression from both the establishment and the Pakistan Democratic Movement (PDM) government, as well as rampant lawlessness and breaches of moral, cultural, and religious values, Imran Khan and the PTI have demonstrated remarkable resilience. Their capacity to confront the illegitimate PDM government and its powerful allies resulted in a significant victory, securing a three-fourths majority in the general elections on February 8, 2024. This clearly illustrates that Imran Khan is capable of achieving success and recognition independently, without the support of the powerful military establishment.

Every Pakistani now views the decision to halt the election results by disabling the RTS (Result Transmission System) on the night of the 2018 general elections as a tactic to limit the number of seats PTI could secure. This approach was intended to pressure Imran Khan into forming a coalition government rather than permitting him to lead with a clear majority.

Khan considers his decisions to form a coalition government and extend General Bajwa's term in 2018—made under the pressure of the establishment—as his most significant blunders. While he admits these mistakes, he is now working to reshape his political persona by rejecting offers from the establishment and taking a more defiant approach. If Imran Khan had genuinely aligned himself with the establishment, he wouldn't be facing unjust imprisonment and hardship. Instead, he would have agreed to their offers and continued to hold his position, similar to the heirs of the Sharif brothers and the Bhutto family.

6. The Ill-Mannered One

For many years, leaders from the PML-N, PPP, and various other political parties, along with their chosen journalists, intellectuals, and media outlets, have propagated the idea that "Imran Khan and his party are responsible for bringing disrespect and indecency into politics, reaching new heights." However, our 77-year history tells a different tale and contradicts this standard view. The issue stems from the fact that a large portion of our population shows little interest in reading and often forgets, combined with a recurring disregard for history, research, and critical thinking. What does our history encompass? It covers a mere 77 years—an amount of time easily counted on one hand.

Let's delve into our more complex history by examining the statements made by military dictators and political leaders. This analysis will enable us to understand the true nature of rudeness, disrespect, and ill-mannered one. We can trace its origins, identify those responsible for disrespectful acts, outline when these events occurred, and assess the extent of such behaviors. Additionally, it's crucial to consider who has escalated this behavior to its highest level.

The "Shahab Nama" recounts an incident where Liaquat Ali Khan likened Hussain Shaheed Suhrawardy to an animal. Ghulam Muhammad, the Governor General, was infamous for verbally attacking his rivals. During the 1965 presidential election, General Ayub Khan's son in Karachi and Khurram Dastgir's father in Gujranwala mockingly adorned a dog with a white dupatta, suspending the election symbol—a "lantern" that represented Fatima Jinnah—from its neck, which unfortunately drew comparisons to Quaid's sister. Moreover, in his book "Friends Not Masters," Ayub Khan made an inappropriate comment, saying, "We, being the sister of Quaid-e-Azam, cared for Fatima Jinnah; otherwise, we could have said much more." In Karachi, retired Air Marshal Asghar Khan openly expressed a desire to execute Bhutto on the Kohala bridge. Additionally, the Pakistan National Alliance (PNA) insulted Bhutto with slogans like "The plow will run on his bald head," demonstrating that the culture of rudeness and disrespect in politics did not originate with Imran Khan; rather, it has been a persistent issue in national politics and the elite since the early days of Pakistan.

Zulfiqar Ali Bhutto frequently ridiculed his political rivals during his speeches. He insulted Nawabzada Nasrullah Khan by calling him a "Huqqah Topi," Mumtaz Daulatana a "Rat," Asghar Khan "Aloo Khan," Chaudhry Zahoor Elahi "Foot Constable," Khan Abdul Qayyum Khan "Double Barrel Khan," and Maulana Maududi the "Pope of Ichhra." To gain favor with Ayub Khan, he used highly disrespectful language toward the esteemed Fatima Jinnah and demeaned Bengali Muslims by saying, "Go to hell, you piglets." In response to Jamaat-e-Islami's attacks against him, Bhutto's supporter, Maulana Kausar Niazi, released a magazine that featured an image of a prostitute's torso with Maulana Abu Ala Maududi's face edited onto it. These instances clearly illustrate that Zulfiqar Ali Bhutto's harsh language had a profound impact on all those involved.

Asif Ali Zardari labeled former President Rafiq Tarar as a "briefcase cleric" and issued a warning to the military establishment, saying, "We will hit you brick by brick." In the meantime, Benazir Bhutto organized a protest in Parliament, chanting "Go Baba Go," directed at President Ghulam Ishaq Khan. Additionally, Sharmila Farooqui from the PPP took a jab at Maryam Nawaz, insinuating that she has never run away with her father's ADC. Bilawal Zardari's characterization of his opponents as "Begharit (shameless)" in the assembly, coupled with his threats of a "brute majority" and "lathi wali (stick) democracy," highlights a concerning truth: the grandson of Bhutto and his party display language and conduct that are equally rude and aggressive as those of their adversaries today.

General Zia-ul-Haq once stated about his political opponents, "They will come to me like obedient pets whenever I wish." In 2005, former military leader Pervez Musharraf accused Dr. Shazia, a gang rape victim from Balochistan, of being "a malicious woman staging a drama to secure visas for Europe and America." Altaf Hussain, founder of the MQM, threatened his rivals with the ominous phrase "Thok den ge (we will kill)" during his speeches.

Sheikh Rasheed referred to Bilawal as "Biloo Rani (Queen)" while Maulana Fazal-Ur-Rehman threatened to escalate the heat for the PTI and mocked PTI's female supporters by calling them butterflies. These instances demonstrate that military dictators, alongside leaders from diverse religious, linguistic, and regional backgrounds, all contribute to the promotion of harsh language and indecency in politics.

In 1988, Nawaz Sharif initiated a smear campaign against Benazir Bhutto and her mother, Nusrat Bhutto, by allegedly releasing fake nude photographs from a helicopter. Members of the PML-N, including Sheikh Rasheed, shouted slogans like "yellow taxi" at Benazir in the National Assembly, while Nawaz Sharif seemed to revel in the chaos. He also mocked former President Farooq Leghari, derisively stating that he bathes British dogs, and made disrespectful comments about women during PTI rallies. Khawaja Asif resorted to crude language in Parliament, derogatorily labeling Shireen Mazari as a "tractor trolley" and Firdous Ashiq Awan as a "dumper," while also making veiled references to "diesel" regarding Maulana Fazal-ur-Rehman. Former Prime Minister Shahid Khaqan Abbasi made an inappropriate comment, stating, "I am a mountaineer. Instead of one, I abuse ten." I will hit the Speaker of the National Assembly with a shoe." Maryam Nawaz used indecent language to humiliate Imran Khan, labeling him as "bad character," "stinker," "disgusting," "anarchist", and "jackal" during her speeches. PML-N members branded Asif Ali Zardari as "Mr. Ten Percent," while Shehbaz Sharif vowed to "rip Asif Zardari's stomach and drag him through the streets of Larkana." This behavior exemplifies how Nawaz Sharif and his party leaders, including his brother and daughter, have cultivated and perpetuated a culture of rudeness and abusive language in politics.

The comments, jokes, and segments from speeches mentioned earlier indicate that the responsibility for abuse, slander, defamation, character attacks, and negative campaigning does not rest solely with Imran Khan. Instead, it is a shared issue among all military dictators and politicians.

Although Imran Khan condemns the politics of corruption, deceit, and hypocrisy—referring to Zardari as king of corruption, Nawaz Sharif as a thief and fugitive, Shehbaz Sharif as a bootlicker, and Maulana Fazal-Ur-Rehman as "diesel"—he has never criticized their private lives, family matters, or religious beliefs.

When Imran Khan and his party, Tehreek-e-Insaf, emerged on the chaotic political landscape, many expected him to rise above the indecent and offensive strategies employed by his opponents and focus on promoting his vision. It was hoped to cultivate a more respectful and civilized political climate across the nation. His rivals are mainly recognized for their corruption, deceitfulness, hypocrisy, hostility, accusations, and slander. In contrast, Imran Khan aims to create a "New Pakistan," inspired by the principles of the "State of Madina." Regrettably, rather than transforming or eradicating this negative political culture, he found himself drawn into it.

7. Drug Addict

Holding onto grudges and fostering hatred can cloud one's perspective and decision-making, potentially leading to self-destruction. In these cases, individuals become their own worst enemies, with their resentment serving as the real threat rather than any external foes. This situation is clearly observable today among those who are critical of Imran Khan, motivated by jealousy and hostility towards him.

Maryam Nawaz, Hanif Abbasi, Abdul Qadir Patel, and many other political and non-political opponents have ridiculed Imran Khan by labeling him a drug addict. They have made unfounded allegations regarding his use of substances such as alcohol, cocaine, hashish, and opium. They even went as far as to dare him to undergo blood and urine tests and threatened to have him tested while in jail, while also presenting manipulated results.

By enduring unjust imprisonment with resilience and unwavering determination, Imran Khan has not only refuted the false allegations made against him but has also demonstrated to the world that, even at 72 years old, he remains both mentally and physically strong in the face of oppression. In a country of 250 million people like Pakistan, Khan stands out as a symbol of strength and resilience. The level of solitary confinement and the hardships he has faced in prison are challenges that neither Nawaz Sharif nor Asif Zardari could have managed, even in the slightest. This illustrates why the Sharif and Zardari families chose to forge deals and compromises with military rulers instead of pursuing a genuine democratic struggle that requires steadfast perseverance and dedication.

For athletes, maintaining physical fitness and strength is frequently prioritized over honing technique and skill. Regardless of a player's natural talent, insufficient physical fitness can result in their dismissal from the team. Many well-known athletes, both in Pakistan and worldwide, have faced health and fitness challenges that have forced them to leave their sport earlier than expected, sometimes well before their planned retirement. After they retire, many athletes may seem to have abandoned their fitness routines, often struggling with problems such as obesity or the inevitable effects of aging.

Imran Khan stands out among his peers and countrymen for his impressive fitness, even at the age of 72. He manages to maintain both his mental and physical health, along with a charming appearance and engaging personality. His exceptional strength and vitality, despite the years, can be attributed to his relentless hard work and a nutritious, balanced diet.

Can a person known for their exceptional health and fitness, admired by young people and athletes alike, whose commitment is recognized by all in Pakistan, whose strength is respected even by rivals, and whose achievements and leadership are celebrated around the world, fall into substance addiction? The answer is no.

Substance addiction significantly impacts both the mental and physical health of individuals, often leading to diminished effectiveness and various setbacks. In contrast, Imran Khan has dedicated the last 53 years to making significant strides in different fields, including sports, education, healthcare, social welfare, and politics. Now, at

72 years old and facing the difficulties of imprisonment, he is shaping a new story of resilience and leadership.

For the last two years, Imran Khan has been wrongfully and forcibly detained by the illegitimate PDM government and its military allies. Despite this, he has consistently confronted the authority and legitimacy of his opponents, exhibiting resilience and an unwillingness to retreat. If the accusations of "intoxication" directed at him were true, his rivals would have managed to prove their allegations by now.

I hope that Imran's opponents acknowledge that "no matter how quickly a falsehood spreads, the truth will eventually surface." Over time, the blatant lies of the unlawful PDM government and its influential supporters have been exposed. In contrast, Imran Khan has remained committed to the truth, even while enduring solitary confinement, and has come to embody it.

In light of these facts, if Khan's adversaries persist in branding him as addict, we kindly urge the PDM government to designate the substance linked to Imran Khan as a mandatory national necessity. This would ensure that everyone in the country— including Army generals, political figures, workers, and the general populace, who frequently experience illness, weakness, and premature aging despite having a healthy diet and drinking pure milk—can remain youthful and physically fit throughout their lives by using Imran Khan's substance.

8. **Superstitious, Polytheist, Witchcraft**

In addition to his success in sports, Imran Khan has made significant strides in the political arena. He has confronted the established political families by promoting a message of change. By firmly opposing corruption and injustice, he has exposed the dishonest practices that have plagued the country's politics, revealing their true nature to the public.

Imran Khan's political rivals, whom he has previously outperformed, should have accepted their defeat and demonstrated their integrity and transparency by challenging him in the political arena. Rather than engaging in meaningful political discussions based on ideology and narrative, they opted for negative propaganda aimed at mocking Khan and tarnishing his public image through baseless accusations and derogatory language. When these tactics failed, his opponents began to undermine Islamic and Eastern traditions by labeling him as superstitious and polytheistic. They also referred to his wife, "Bushra Bibi," in a derogatory manner, calling her "Pinky Peerni" and a "sorceress."

Sufis and saints have played a crucial role in spreading and nurturing Islam across the Indian subcontinent. Their unwavering devotion to Allah has significantly contributed to the well-being and happiness of ordinary people through their commendable deeds and moral conduct. In Pakistan, millions pay their respects at the shrines of Sufis and saints, engaging in prayers, sharing food, performing voluntary prayers (Nawafil), and seeking the blessings of Almighty Allah. The visit of Bushra Bibi and Imran Khan to Hazrat Baba Farid's shrine in Pakpattan exemplifies this deep reverence and love. However, dismissing these practices as superstition or polytheism is an overstatement. Only Allah knows the true intentions and sincerity of one's heart, and He alone will decide on the Day of Judgment who deserves to enter Paradise. Therefore, who are we to pass judgment on others?

Unfortunately, the ineffective political rivals, who lack the bravery to engage in genuine political competition on democratic principles, have created a questionable government backed by the powerful military establishment. They have mocked Bushra Bibi's religious attire and her dedication to Sufism, presenting these traits as her main shortcomings, while also unjustly criticizing Imran Khan.

These political opponents, along with the journalists and media channels they have chosen, have been spreading misinformation, claiming that during a police raid at Imran Khan's home in Zaman Park, various suspicious items related to witchcraft and talismans were discovered. It is alleged that these items included charred bones, thought to be human, as well as ashes and cloth dolls with needles inserted in multiple places, among other objects connected to sorcery.

Had Imran Khan engaged in similar propaganda against his opponents, it would probably have sparked considerable criticism and backlash. Instead, he and his wife responded to the unfounded claims and misinformation with poise and composure. Rather than reacting with anger, they demonstrated patience, highlighting the negative tactics and petty behaviors of their rivals in politics and other areas, thereby exposing their true character to the public.

Interestingly, neither political nor non-political adversaries have credited the World Cup win, the establishment of the free Cancer Hospital, Namal University, or the international recognition and prestige to witchcraft or amulets. The so-called PDM government, which has disregarded ethical and legal norms and exhibited significant animosity towards Imran, along with its self-serving allies, could have easily made such allegations with the backing of their preferred judges and corrupt media if that had been their goal.

9. Thief

Imran Khan ventured into politics not for personal gain, fame, wealth, or power, but to combat the rampant injustice and corruption plaguing the nation. Already celebrated internationally for his cricket achievements—particularly his World Cup triumph and the establishment of a cancer hospital—he had won the admiration of the entire Pakistani populace. This level of respect was something both military and political leaders aspired to, and Khan had earned it even before his political career began. However, once he entered the political arena, intending to free the country and its people from corruption and injustice, all corrupt political and non-political factions rallied against him.

Despite the long-standing dominance of the Zardari and Sharif families in Pakistan's political arena, Imran Khan's Pakistan Tehreek-e-Insaf has gained significant traction and support. Khan's strong opposition to the corruption linked to these political dynasties resonated with many marginalized Pakistanis facing poverty, deprivation, and injustice. His reputation for honesty and integrity is recognized worldwide, even by those who oppose him. At the same time, the corruption tied to the Zardari and Sharif families is well-documented and widely acknowledged.

The nickname "Mr. Ten Percent" refers to Asif Zardari, who has been embroiled in various controversies, including the "Surrey Palace" and the "Omni Group" scandals, as well as a smuggling case linked to Ayyan Ali. An article from The Daily Mail discusses the "Penthouse Pirates," highlighting corruption allegations against the Sharif family. Additionally, Raymond Baker's book, "Capitalism's Achilles Heel," provides substantial evidence of such misconduct. The "Panama Papers" also reveal the illegal activities of the Sharif family, and Ishaq Dar, a financial advisor and relative of Nawaz Sharif, acknowledged his involvement in the "Hudaibiya Papers Mill" case.

Historically, both the governments of Benazir Bhutto and Nawaz Sharif have been dismissed due to allegations of corruption. Each family has accused the other of engaging in corrupt activities. Rather than clearing their names in court, they have attempted to escape legal repercussions through National Reconciliation Ordinances (NROs), changes in regime, modifications to NAB laws, and alliances with favorable judges. These actions underscore a longstanding connection between the Zardari and Sharif families, particularly in relation to corruption and dishonesty.

Rather than pursuing a National Reconciliation Ordinance (NRO), modifying laws concerning the National Accountability Bureau (NAB), or attempting to influence the judicial system, both Zardari and the Sharif family should have presented credible evidence of their income and assets. This would have helped them gain legitimacy in the public and legal spheres, effectively countering Imran Khan's corruption claims. Rather than proving their innocence, they chose to present Imran Khan as a symbol of corruption.

When Khawaja Asif and various officials from the PML-N openly accused Imran Khan of misusing zakat funds meant for Shaukat Khanum Hospital. In response, the hospital's administration quickly refuted these claims by releasing an audit report and providing an online record of all donations. Rather than supporting the PML-N's unfounded accusations, the people of Pakistan chose to increase their donations to Shaukat Khanum Hospital, reinforcing their trust in Imran Khan's honesty and integrity. The successful establishment of hospitals in Lahore and Peshawar, along with the construction of Asia's largest free cancer hospital in Karachi—all funded entirely by public donations—stands as clear evidence of Imran Khan's commitment to honesty, integrity, and transparency.

Following the humiliation and scorn caused by the Zakat thief's unfounded claims, the PML-N had an opportunity to demonstrate true integrity by acknowledging its error and apologizing to Imran Khan. Instead, they opted not to change their approach. To respond to the Panama case, they filed a lawsuit in the Supreme Court, spearheaded by Hanif Abbasi, accusing Imran Khan of corruption related to the purchase and development of land for the "Bani Gala House."

When the Supreme Court sought evidence, Imran Khan took a different approach from the Sharif family, who were unable to substantiate their ownership of properties in London. Khan provided four decades of bank statements, records of his cricket earnings, and documentation related to the acquisition of a flat in London in 1983. He also presented proof of the flat's sale, the transfer of funds to Pakistan, and the paperwork for purchasing land in Bani Gala and constructing a house there. As a result of this evidence, the Supreme Court deemed Imran Khan honest and trustworthy, which led to his acquittal from corruption charges, ultimately undermining the assertions and negative narratives put forth by the PML-N.

When their initial attempts to discredit him failed, the illegitimate PDM government sought help from NAB, FIA, Judge Humayun Dilawar, Muhammad Bashir, and the military to frame Imran Khan as corrupt. They created a false case regarding a watch that was lawfully acquired from the Toshakhana (state gift repository). Selective judges were appointed to expedite an unlawful trial that took place in jail. On August 5, 2023, and January 31, 2024, verdicts that aligned with their agenda were announced, sentencing him to three and fourteen years of rigorous imprisonment, respectively. However, the Islamabad High Court swiftly overturned this ruling and suspended the sentences on April 1, 2024, after just a few hearings, thereby dismantling the fabricated claims surrounding the Tosha Khana.

The PDM government and its powerful backers have decided that Imran Khan will not be released from jail under any circumstances, leading them to fabricate as many cases as necessary. On January 17, 2025, Accountability Court Judge Nasir Javed Rana sentenced Imran Khan to 14 years in prison and his wife to 7 years, along with a fine of 1 million rupees, in a fabricated corruption case involving £190 million related to the Al-Qadir Trust. It is essential to note that the £ 190 million was directly transferred from London to the account of the Supreme Court, not to Imran Khan. The PDM government has already utilized these funds. Since the judiciary is entirely under the control of the PDM, they have implemented a plan to keep Imran Khan in jail for an extended period by imposing this wrongful sentence in an illegal case. However, when this case is eventually heard on its merits, Khan will honorably be acquitted immediately.

The failure of the illegitimate PDM government and its influential supporters to successfully portray Imran Khan as a thief or corrupt—despite numerous fabricated accusations, collaborations with the NAB and judges from the Accountability Court, and a spread of misleading media narratives through various unscrupulous tactics—reinforces Khan's reputation for honesty and integrity.

10. Traitor, Terrorist, Anarchist

Despite attacking Imran Khan's past, present, character, private life, religious beliefs, financial affairs, political ideologies and social concepts through derogatory slander, accusations, epithets, and terms such as playboy,

Jewish agent, Taliban Khan, U-turn Khan, project Imran Khan, Disrespectful, drug addict, thief, polytheist, and witchcraft, his opponents, critics, and envious individuals were unable to defeat him in the political arena. Consequently, these cowardly opponents resorted to a dirty tactic of inciting innocent Pakistanis against Khan by making provocative allegations of being a terrorist, a traitor, and an anarchist. This turned political opposition into a matter of deep personal enmity.

Allegations such as terrorist, traitor, and anarchist demonstrate the utter failure of Imran Khan's political rivals to participate in constructive discussions, maintain democratic principles, or offer a cohesive narrative and ideology. Consequently, these opponents, along with their supporters and non-political adversaries, resort to using this harmful propaganda in an attempt to eliminate Imran Khan instead of competing with him fairly.

The entire world recognizes and appreciates Imran Khan's nobility, commitment to the constitution and the law, patriotism, and philanthropic achievements. Unfortunately, his opponents, disregarding these qualities, are engaged in a futile effort to satisfy their egos by filing numerous false charges of terrorism and treason against him. They have subjected him to unjust sentences from arbitrary courts and judges and have wrongfully imprisoned him.

Imran Khan has represented his country throughout his life, making Pakistan known to the world. He has raised the green crescent flag on countless cricket fields and chanted "Pakistan Zindabad." Despite facing challenging conditions with a weak team, he led his nation to its only one-day cricket World Cup victory. He has built three world-class free cancer hospitals for his fellow countrymen and established Namal and Al-Qadir Universities in underprivileged areas, providing free higher education to talented yet poor students. Moreover, he has raised and invested billions of rupees to aid victims of floods and earthquakes. He has also sacrificed his peaceful and comfortable family life in pursuit of true freedom and prosperity for his country and its people. Additionally, he has bravely exposed the political and non-political mafias that have been undermining the nation. Is it fair to label someone like him a traitor?

Khan has devoted his life to humanitarian causes and achieved notable accomplishments in sports, education, and healthcare. He has denounced terrorism at all levels, both domestically and internationally. He has highlighted the tragic loss of innocent lives due to the American-led war on terror and stressed the necessity of addressing the underlying issues to prevent further violence. He has actively taken part in marches and sit-ins to protect his homeland and citizens from the repercussions of drone strikes. Additionally, he has been a vocal advocate for Kashmir, Palestine, and other underrepresented groups on various global platforms, including dialogues with world leaders, the Organization of Islamic Cooperation (OIC), and the United Nations (UN). He has declined to permit the U.S. to use a Pakistani airbase, putting himself at risk as a result. As Pakistan's Prime Minister, he has played a crucial role in advocating for the resolution of the Afghan conflict through negotiations, ensuring the safe withdrawal of NATO forces and foreign nationals from Afghanistan. Can someone with such a profile truly be considered a terrorist?

He managed to unite a nation divided by linguistic, regional, provincial, caste, and sectarian disparities under the concept of the State of Madina. He instilled hope in the youth, who feel disillusioned by Pakistan's current state and uncertain about its future, by sharing a vision of a new Pakistan. He mobilized the middle and educated classes, who had become disenchanted with politics, and encouraged their participation. In the face of fear, intimidation, and injustice, he displayed remarkable courage by advocating for genuine freedom. He greatly aided those in need by providing health card services, constructing shelter homes for the vulnerable, and offering assistance to the hungry. His Ehsaas program has supported low-income families, while the Billion Tree Tsunami initiative seeks to address environmental challenges. His genuine dedication, tireless work, and commitment to serving the public have earned him immense love, respect, and admiration from diverse groups, provinces, and ethnicities. He has resonated with the hearts of every Sindhi, Balochi, Punjabi, Kashmiri, Gilgiti, and Pathan, whether rich or poor, young or old, residing in Pakistan or abroad. Additionally, he has stood up for the honor of the Holy Prophet (peace and blessings be upon him) and embodied what it means to be a true devotee and servant of the Prophet (PBUH). Is it justifiable to label this type of patriot an anarchist?

Calling Khan a traitor, terrorist, or anarchist is not only extreme but also illogical, considering the evidence of his patriotism, dedication to peace, and humanitarian efforts.

Regrettably, his adversaries—both in politics and beyond—who have repeatedly lost to Khan in moral, democratic, constitutional, legal, and political arenas, exhibit a considerable degree of arrogance. Rather than acknowledging their failures and working on self-improvement, they have chosen to resort to insults, revealing their incompetence.

A prevalent belief is that the greatest weakness in the world lies in nobility, which can be exploited by individuals lacking ethical standards. Imran Khan's adversaries, both in politics and beyond, sought to exploit this vulnerability through intimidation, threats, manipulation, and blackmail. However, every attempt they made ended in their own humiliation, ridicule, and failure.

Despite wielding immense power to perpetuate oppression and fascism, disregarding the constitution and the law, violating Eastern and Islamic values, and imprisoning PTI women, children, the elderly, and youth, the PDM government and its powerful allies have utterly failed to defeat Imran Khan and dismantle his party. They have created an atmosphere of nerve-wracking fear and drawn a red line around Khan, yet their efforts have proven completely ineffectual. What is the explanation for this?

The main factor behind this situation is the lasting strength of Imran Khan, a quality that his rivals have frequently underestimated. Had they recognized the extent of Khan's resilience, they might have refrained from antagonizing him to such an extreme degree. This extraordinary trait of Khan is his ability to endure. It is this endurance that provides him with the solid reliability of a rock, the boundless nature of the ocean, and the infinite expanse of the sky, rendering him genuinely unbeatable.

The ability to endure hardships is an accurate indicator of an individual's strength. Those who can effectively manage challenges and suffering develop remarkable resilience. This endurance is essential for coping with feelings like anger and disappointment, helping us maintain our energy and avoid impatience. Intolerance often reflects a lack of this ability. The more we can handle, the better our endurance becomes, which in turn enhances our strength even further. Patience is one of the most powerful qualities a person can possess. A person who embodies both patience and endurance is truly unbeatable.

Hazrat Wasif Ali Wasif said that "when Allah Almighty shows mercy to an individual, He enhances their courage and broadens their capacity for endurance." We often claim that we cannot tolerate wrongdoing. However, the ability to tolerate wrongdoing is frequently seen as a sign of perfection. Right doing is not merely tolerated; it is accepted. If you learn to tolerate, you will find that depression will fade away. Tolerance fosters further tolerance and imparts the blessing of patience. Indeed, "Allah Almighty is with those who have patience". The truth is that Allah grants some individuals the ability to endure. Tolerance should not be mistaken for weakness; it is a vital principle for a meaningful life. A person with a great capacity for endurance cannot be truly defeated.

Imran Khan is among the fortunate few who have an extraordinary ability to endure challenges. This trait cultivates vital qualities such as dignity, stability, strength, and patience. An individual possessing these qualities thoughtfully considers each circumstance, acts purposefully, seeks advice, evaluates possible consequences and their importance, and then decides on the most effective approach to address the matter at hand.

Consider this:

Could someone like him feel powerless in tough times?

Might he find himself caught in a cycle of difficulties?

Is it possible for weaker adversaries to overcome him?

Furthermore, could he fall short of reaching his objectives?

Absolutely not.

Imran Khan's endurance has allowed him to make history by resisting the intense, defamatory, and dangerous propaganda from his opponents. Instead of succumbing to fear or abandoning the democratic struggle for a New Pakistan, he has demonstrated that he is a genuine leader of the Pakistani nation, especially in times of crisis.

For the past 77 years, the powerful military establishment has been ruling Pakistan, either under the guise of a fake democracy or by imposing direct martial law. This establishment has maintained its control by coercing and manipulating corrupt political and religious leaders, often exploiting their vulnerabilities through fear, intimidation, and greed. For the first time in its history, when Imran Khan posed a threat to their power, instead of embracing reforms and democratic principles, the establishment and its corrupt allies banded together to tarnish Khan's reputation and eliminate him from the political scene.

In response to every injustice, act of oppression, accusation, slander, and character assassination by his opponents, Imran Khan chose not to be heartbroken or intimidated. Instead of being afraid or giving up, he acted with patience and forbearance. He exposed the connections and ambitions of the establishment and the Pakistan Democratic Movement (PDM) to the public. Through this, he raised awareness about the various problems facing Pakistan and their underlying causes, striving for true freedom and a path to salvation from these issues.

The growing awareness among the public has led to the downfall of all the tactics employed by the deceitful PDM government and its influential allies to incite hatred, rally support, or intimidate individuals against Imran Khan. The citizens of Pakistan, recognizing Khan's honesty, integrity, competence, hard work, courage, patriotism, and dedication to service, have observed a concerning trend. Rather than engaging in fair competition, military leaders have ignored their oaths; political clerics have prioritized their own interests over their religious beliefs; the PML-N has shown a lack of respect for the importance of votes; the PPP has abandoned its democratic principles; the ANP has deviated from Bacha Khan's philosophy; the MQM has overlooked human rights; journalists have compromised their ethical standards; judges have failed to deliver justice; and various institutions have neglected their responsibilities, all with the singular aim of ousting Khan.

The citizens of Pakistan chose to disregard the ridiculous accusations, insults, and personal attacks aimed at Imran Khan. Rather than staying passive or yielding to tyranny, fascism, and chaos, they showed their determination to support Khan. This choice represented a pivotal moment in the nation's democratic development, showcasing its strength against the influential establishment and surprising both the establishment and the global community.

Currently, Imran Khan maintains a strong public image, supported by a growing awareness among the public. Despite facing opposition and intense propaganda, his integrity and reputation remain intact, and he continues to grow in popularity with each passing day. This reinforces his position as one of the most respected leaders in Pakistan, second only to Quaid-e-Azam Muhammad Ali Jinnah.

Bibliography

Kelly, F. (August 2016). "Schoolboy Imran

https://www.thecricketmonthly.com/story/1032793/schoolboy-imran

"1st ODI, Pakistan tour of England at Leeds, Aug 31, 1974". ESPNcricinfo. ESPN.

"CRICKETERS OF THE YEAR: Imran Khan". ESPNcricinfo. 15 April 1983

https://www.espncricinfo.com/story/imran-khan-154467

Imran Khan, http://cricketarchive.com/Archive/Players/1/1383/1383.html

Imran Khan retired from Test cricket on this day: See his top records here, https://www.geo.tv/latest/392043

https://www.foxsports.com.au/the-sideline/the-packer-revolution/news-story/18ef12781ed1cd7c5f93f43b64e5061c

https://www.espncricinfo.com/story/stats-analysis-imran-khan-484478

https://www.espncricinfo.com/cricketers/imran-khan-40560

http://news.bbc.co.uk/sport2/hi/in_depth/2001/england_v_pakistan/1295868.stm

https://www.guinnessworldrecords.com/world-records/382476-first-player-to-score-a-century-and-take-10-wickets-in-a-test-match

Oborne, Peter (9 April 2015). Wounded Tiger: A History of Cricket in Pakistan. Simon & Schuster UK. ISBN 978-1-84983-248-9.

https://www.espncricinfo.com/story/cricket-s-turning-points-neutral-umpires-511175

https://www.dawn.com/news/777764

Paracha, Nadeem F. (10 January 2013). "Cross-batted: Cricketers as politicians".
https://www.dawn.com/news/777764

"A giant among all-rounders",
https://africa.espn.com/cricket/story/_/id/22507448/imran-khan

"PM Imran Khan shares story of winning International Cricketer of the Year prize in 1989".
https://www.geo.tv/latest/335291

https://www.spiegel.de/politik/ausland/pakistan-musharraf-laesst-cricket-legende-imran-khan-festnehmen-a-517256.html

Memon, Ayaz (28 July 2018),
https://www.deccanchronicle.com/sports/cricket/290718/imran-khan-is-the-epitome-of-excellence.html

https://bleacherreport.com/articles/1017237-the-top-10-all-rounders-of-all-time

Ramis, Mohammad (2002).
https://www.espncricinfo.com/story/the-1992-world-cup-an-ambition-fulfilled-for-pakistan-119141

https://www.smh.com.au/sport/cricket/from-the-archives-1992-pakistan-on-top-of-the-world-20220317-p5a5fa.html

https://www.icc-cricket.com/hall-of-fame/hall-of-famers/hall-of-famer-imran-khan

DNA India. 26 July 2018, https://www.dnaindia.com/cricket/report-imran-khan-the-kaptaan-who-was-changed-pakistan-cricket-2642079

https://shaukatkhanum.org.pk/about-us/our-story/

https://www.cancercontrol.info/2019-4/establishing-a-tertiary-care-cancer-hospital-in-a-developing-country-the-story-of-the-shaukat-khanum-memorial-cancer-hospital-and-research-

Badar F, Mahmood S. Cancer Statistics from the Shaukat Khanum Memorial Trust's Hospital-based Cancer Registry, Pakistan, 1994-2022: An Observational Study. J Cancer Allied Spec. 2024 Aug 16;10(2):615. doi: 10.37029/jcas.v10i2.615. PMID: 39156948; PMCID: PMC11326659.

Ali, Mukarram, and Syed Sohaib Zubair. "Training and Development: A Review of Shaukat Khanum Memorial Cancer Hospital and Research Centre." 2015 International Business Conference June 7-11, 2015. The Clute Institute, 217-224., 2015, pp. 217–224.

https://shaukatkhanum.org.pk/about-us/publications/research-publications/

https://en.wikipedia.org/wiki/Shaukat_Khanum_Memorial_Cancer_Hospital_and_Research_Centre

Bibliography

https://namal.edu.pk/the-namal-story

https://namal.edu.pk/

https://namalknowledgecity.com/namal-knowledge-city-splash

https://en.wikipedia.org/wiki/Namal_Institute

Yasir Riaz, Namal Institute: A Mission for Rural Uplift, Sustainable Development, and Social Impact, Journal of Sustainability Perspectives: Special Issue, 2021, 319-325

Imran Khan appointed Bradford chancellor. https://www.theguardian.com/education/2005/nov/23/highe reducation.news

Jonathan Brown, Tuesday 25 February 2014, https://www.independent.co.uk/student/news/bradford-university-defends-former-pakistan-cricket-captain-imran-khan-after-students-demand-he-steps-down-as-chancellor-as-he-fails-to-attend-a-graduation-since-2010-9152144.html

Imran made to quit as chancellor of UK University, December 01, 2014, https://www.thenews.com.pk/archive/print/641977

"Imran Khan resigns as University of Bradford chancellor". BBC News. 2 June 2014, https://www.bbc.com/news/uk-england-leeds-27664806

"University delegation goes east to establish new College". University of Bradford. 22 February 2006, https://www.brad.ac.uk/admin/pr/pressreleases/2006/delegation.php

https://www.thetelegraphandargus.co.uk/news/846369.lege
nd-imrans-dream-for-his-school/

"TI chief plans Knowledge City". Dawn. 18 October 2009,
https://www.dawn.com/news/497161/

https://ora.ox.ac.uk/objects/uuid:9b666e3c-0018-4505-
b27f-c650c626c016/files/dbv73c068k

Adams, Tim (2 July 2006). "The path of Khan". The
Guardian. UK.

https://www.theguardian.com/sport/2006/jul/02/cricket.feat
ures3

"A   Pakistani   Cricket   Star's   Political   Move",
https://www.washingtonpost.com/wp-
dyn/content/article/2005/07/03/AR2005070301078.html

https://www.thetimes.com/article/fe87d649-aa3c-4cac-
aa0f-8b933432801e, Kervin, Alison (6 August 2006).
"Imran Khan: 'What I do now fulfils me like never before'"

https://reuters.screenocean.com/record/178959,   "Pakistan:
Cricket bat used by Imran Khan in Pakistan's victorious 1992
World Cup campaign raises 20,000 US dollars for flood
victims at auction". Reuters. 4 August 2001

Imran Khan Foundation provides relief for ignored
Waziristan   IDPs,
http://www.dailytimes.com.pk/default.asp?page=2013%5C
01%5C17%5Cstory_17-1-2013_pg7_20.

Undaunted, Imran returns to the stump, "Imran Khan
Standing for Election Again". The Guardian. UK. 26
September 2002

https://www.theguardian.com/sport/2005/aug/31/cricket.pakistan, Walsh, Declan (31 August 2005). "When you speak out, people react". The Guardian. UK

https://www.dawn.com/news/27176. "Opposition parties may boycott referendum". Dawn. 22 March 2002

"Khan 'optimistic' about Pakistan elections". BBC News. 21 June 2002, http://news.bbc.co.uk/2/hi/south_asia/2056431.stm

http://www.newyorker.com/archive/2005/05/30/050530ta_talk_hertzberg, (30 May 2005). "Big News Week

https://www.abc.net.au/news/2006-03-04/imran-khan-detained-amid-anti-bush-protests/811460

http://timesofindia.indiatimes.com/World/Imran_Khan_escapes_from_house_arrest/articleshow/2517638.cms, The Times of India. India. 5 November 2007

Page, Jeremy (14 November 2007). "Imran Khan comes out of hiding to lead students in street protests". The Times. UK. hp://www.timesonline.co.uk/tol/news/world/asia/article2866163.ece

https://www.dawn.com/news/275959/ji-students-wing-hands-over-imran-to-police

https://www.dawn.com/news/275889/manhandling-of-imran-condemned

https://womensactionforumlahore.org/wp-content/uploads/2023/02/Statement-on-the-attack-on-Imran-Khan-in-Punjab-University-English.pdf

https://www.dawn.com/news/276082/imran-shifted-to-dera-jail

https://www.reuters.com/article/world/imran-khan-released-from-jail-idUSCOL104844/

https://www.theguardian.com/world/2007/nov/15/pakistan. declanwalsh, Walsh, Declan (14 November 2007). "Khan arrested under terror laws as Musharraf defends crackdown"

Wilkinson, Isambard; Moore, Matthew (21 November 2007). "Imran Khan released from prison in Pakistan" https://www.telegraph.co.uk/news/worldnews/1570106/Imran-Khan-released-from-prison-in-Pakistan.html

"Imran Khan's 'tsunami' sweeps Lahore". The Express Tribune. Pakistan. 30 October 2011, https://tribune.com.pk/story/285058/pti-rally-in-lahore-live-updates

https://www.dawn.com/news/670096/thousands-gather-at-the-minar-e-pakistan-ground-for-pti-rally

https://frontline.thehindu.com/the-nation/article30177832.ece. Political test for Imran

Published : Dec 02, 2011

https://www.theguardian.com/world/2011/oct/31/imran-khan-acclaim-pakistan

"IRI survey shows PTI on top of popularity list". The News. Pakistan. 7 May 2012, https://web.archive.org/web/20120510000701/http://www.thenews.com.pk/Todays-News-13-14418-IRI-survey-shows-PTI-on-top-of-popularity-list

https://www.washingtonpost.com/world/asia-pacific/pakistani-cricket-hero-imran-khan-becomes-a-political-player/2011/08/31/gIQAVYYBxJ_story.html

https://caravanmagazine.in/reportage/ill-be-your-mirror, What Pakistan sees in Imran Khan

https://www.files.ethz.ch/isn/135577/ISAS_Insights_149_-Imran_Khans_Political_Rise_27122011175801.pdf

https://tribune.com.pk/article/70445/my-journey-with-imran-khan-from-the-tanga-party-to-a-one-man-show

https://english.aaj.tv/news/30316068/history-of-ptis-power-shows-at-minar-e-pakistan

https://www.latimes.com/archives/blogs/world-now/story/2012-10-06/imran-khan-leads-drone-protesters-into-volatile-pakistan-region

https://www.nation.com.pk/21-Apr-2013/imran-opens-lahore-poll-war-front

https://www.nation.com.pk/22-Apr-2013/imran-khan-vows-to-release-pakistan-from-us-slavery

https://tribune.com.pk/story/546938/imran-khan-gains-in-pakistan-vote-haggling-over-government-expected

Imran Khan falls from rally stage in Pakistan. https://www.youtube.com/watch?v=qH_ouzFyg1k

Imran Khan injured in Pakistan campaign rally fall, 7 May 2013, https://www.bbc.com/news/world-asia-22440518

https://www.dawn.com/news/812515/imran-falls-off-stage-at-lahore-rally-sustains-serious-injuries

https://www.dawn.com/2013/05/07/imran-injured-after-rally-stage-fall/

http://www.ndtv.com/article/world/imran-khan-s-emotional-appeal-from-hospital-bed-364970

https://www.newyorker.com/magazine/2012/08/13/sporting-chance

https://edition.cnn.com/2013/05/12/world/asia/pakistan-election/index.html, Laura Smith-Spark; Saima Mohsin; Aliza Kassim (12 May 2013). "Amid violence and vote-rigging complaints, Pakistan elects new leaders". CNN.

https://www.theguardian.com/world/2013/may/13/pakistan-elections-nawaz-sharif-imran-khan

https://tribune.com.pk/story/548459/imrans-tsunami-khyber-pakhtunkhwa-lives-up-to-tradition

https://tribune.com.pk/story/555048/pti-received-second-most-votes-in-general-election?amp=1

https://tribune.com.pk/story/547893/pti-concedes-defeat-in-pakistan-elections

https://www.abc.net.au/news/2013-05-12/imran-khan-welcomes-pakistan-vote-but-alleges-rigging/4684760

https://www.dawn.com/news/1811006,

 Khan, Ismail (4 February 2024). "Pervez Khattak — a 'candidate' for all seasons". Dawn.

https://noria-research.com/south-asia/south-asia-5-pakistan-tehrik-e-insaaf/

http://www.thenews.com.pk/Todays-News-13-30285-Imran-demands-new-ECP-resignation-of-its-members

https://tribune.com.pk/story/748978/destination-islamabad-azadi-march-takes-off

https://www.aljazeera.com/news/2014/8/28/pakistan-set-for-decisive-day-of-protests

https://www.nytimes.com/2014/09/01/world/asia/pakistani-unrest.html, Masood, Salman; Walsh, Declan (31 August 2014). "Pakistani Army Calls for Calm After Protest Turns Deadly". The New York Times

https://www.dw.com/en/analyst-pakistans-military-seeking-to-destabilize-government/a-17893659, "Army 'destabilizing' government – DW – 09/01/2014". dw.com

https://www.dawn.com/news/1305784/hashmi-says-imran-conspired-with-disgruntled-elements-in-the-army-during-2014-sit-in

https://www.dawn.com/news/1129011, "Islamabad stand-off: Army not backing PTI or PAT, says ISPR". Dawn. 31 August 2014

https://www.aljazeera.com/news/2014/9/1/anti-pm-protesters-storm-pakistan-broadcaster

Qamar Zaman (17 December 2014). https://tribune.com.pk/story/808784/for-a-national-cause-pti-calls-off-dharna-after-126-days

https://web.archive.org/web/20160106095135/http://www.pakistantoday.com.pk/2015/03/23/national/pti-pml-n-come-together-in-national-interest/

https://www.dawn.com/news/1195875, Haider, Irfan (23 July 2015). "JC finds 2013 elections 'fair and in accordance with law'"

Haider, Irfan (23 July 2015). "Imran Khan accepts findings of judicial commission report", https://www.dawn.com/news/1195870

https://www.aljazeera.com/news/2016/11/1/pakistan-supreme-court-hears-panama-leaks-case

https://www.geo.tv/latest/137187, "Want to become prime minister: Imran Khan". Geo. Jang Group. 7 April 2017

http://time.com/5349389/pakistan-election-imran-khan-lead-fraud/, Gannon, Kathy (26 July 2018). "Unofficial Results in Pakistan's Election Show Lead For Imran Khan, But Opponents Allege Fraud"

https://www.geo.tv/latest/205011, "ECP declares results of 251 of 270 NA seats; Imran Khan's PTI leads with 110". Geo News. 27 July 2018

Morrison, Sean (27 July 2018). "Imran Khan wins Pakistan general election but needs to form coalition". London Evening Standard. https://www.standard.co.uk/news/world/imran-khan-wins-pakistan-general-election-but-needs-to-form-coalition-government-a3897541.html

"Imran makes history by winning 5 NA seats". Business Recorder. 27 July 2018, https://epaper.brecorder.com/2018/07/27/1-page/729916-news.html

Wasim, Amir (21 May 2018). "Imran unveils ambitious agenda for first 100 days of govt", https://www.dawn.com/news/1409003

Wilkinson, Bard; Saifi, Sophia; Westcott, Ben (26 July 2018). "Imran Khan claims victory in disputed Pakistan election" https://edition.cnn.com/2018/07/26/asia/pakistan-polls-close-intl/index.html

"ECP rejects political parties' claim of 'rigging' on election day". The Express Tribune. 25 July 2018, https://tribune.com.pk/story/1766411/ecp-rejects-political-parties-claim-rigging-election-day

"Pakistan election: Party of Ex-PM Nawaz Sharif concedes to Imran Khan". BBC News. 27 July 2018, https://www.bbc.com/news/world-asia-44980344

"EU mission terms election satisfactory, calls it better than 2013". Dawn. 26 July 2018, https://www.dawn.com/news/1422911

https://www.aljazeera.com/news/2018/7/26/imran-khans-speech-in-full

"PTI formally nominates Imran Khan as prime minister candidate". Geo.tv. 6 August 2018, https://www.geo.tv/latest/206277

https://www.aljazeera.com/news/2019/2/21/pakistans-imran-khan-approves-military-response-if-india-attacks

https://www.vanityfair.com/news/2019/09/the-once-and-future-imran-khan?srsltid=AfmBOoonrGBRg6AY-SvD7ZTTHBrvx5wuh3-9io0buhrzjovJSSvQL1rw

https://news.un.org/en/story/2020/09/1073782, "Prime Minister Imran Khan of Pakistan warns of rising Islamophobia". un.news.org. UN News. 25 September 2020.

https://www.aljazeera.com/news/2021/4/19/pakistan-pm-calls-for-west-to-criminalise-blasphemy-against-islam

"UN declares March 15 International Day to Combat Islamophobia". TRT World. 2022, https://www.trtworld.com/life/un-declares-march-15-international-day-to-combat-islamophobia-55542

https://www.reuters.com/world/asia-pacific/pakistani-opposition-rallies-press-pm-khan-resign-2022-03-08/

https://www.dawn.com/news/1682104, "PM Imran says 'foreign-funded conspiracy' out to topple his govt, claims to have evidence in writing". Dawn. 27 March 2022

"US sought to punish 'disobedient' Imran Khan, says Russia". Dawn. 5 April 2022. https://www.dawn.com/news/1683565

Chaudhry, Fahad (9 April 2022). "Imran Khan loses no-trust vote, prime ministerial term set for unceremonious end". Dawn. https://www.dawn.com/news/1684168

"Imran Khan ousted as Pakistan's PM after key vote". BBC News. 9 April 2022, https://www.bbc.com/news/world-asia-61055210

https://www.aljazeera.com/news/2022/4/11/imran-khan-removal-as-pm-triggers-protests-across-pakistan

Rasool, Danyal (31 January 2024). "Imran Khan sentenced to 14 years in prison in 'Toshakhana' case", https://www.espncricinfo.com/story/imran-khan-sentenced-to-14-years-in-prison-in-toshakhana-case-1419023

"Pakistan's former PM Imran Khan 'shot in the leg' in assassination attempt". LBC. 3 November 2022, https://www.lbc.co.uk/news/imran-khan-shot-in-leg-suspected-assassination-attempt/

Shah, Saeed (3 November 2022). "Former Pakistan Prime Minister Imran Khan Shot in Leg at Protest Rally". The Wall Street Journal. https://www.wsj.com/articles/shots-fired-at-pakistan-protest-rally-held-by-ex-prime-minister-imran-khan-11667478021

Saifi, Sophia; Taylor, Jerome (9 May 2023). "Former Pakistan Prime Minister Imran Khan arrested by paramilitary police" https://edition.cnn.com/2023/05/09/asia/imran-khan-arrest-intl/index.html

https://profit.pakistantoday.com.pk/2023/05/09/what-is-the-story-behind-the-al-qadir-trust-case-that-imran-khan-has-been-arrested-for/

"Pakistan's ex-PM Imran Khan, wife get seven-year jail term for unlawful marriage". France 24. 3 February 2024, https://www.france24.com/en/asia-pacific/20240203-pakistan-s-ex-pm-imran-khan-wife-get-seven-year-jail-term-for-unlawful-marriage

https://www.aljazeera.com/news/2024/7/13/pakistan-court-acquits-former-pm-imran-khan-wife-in-unlawful-marriage-case

Ahmed, Munir (1 July 2024). "UN group demands release of ex-Pakistan PM Imran Khan; says his detention violates international law". AP News, https://apnews.com/article/pakistan-un-group-demands-rekaese-imran-khan-4394c5f87d072dc03c68435f6469a7b3

"Pakistan: Authorities Must Immediately Release Imran Khan From Arbitrary Detention". Amnesty International.https://www.amnesty.org/en/documents/asa33/8507/2024/en/

"'Locked in death cell for terrorists,' claims Imran in rare interview with UK publication". Dawn. 21 July 2024. https://www.dawn.com/news/1847067

"Bushra Bibi alleges life threats and inhumane conditions for Imran Khan". The Times of India. 20 July 2024, https://timesofindia.indiatimes.com/world/pakistan/bushra-bibi-alleges-life-threats-and-inhumane-conditions-for-imran-khan/articleshow/111890559.cms

"How many cases is Imran Khan facing?". The Express Tribune. 6 December 2024, https://tribune.com.pk/story/2514206/how-many-cases-is-imran-khan-facing

"'Won't cut any deal' come what may, reiterates Imran Khan". The News International. 18 February 2025, https://www.thenews.com.pk/latest/1284131

"Imran Khan's popularity soars ahead of vote, Pakistan survey shows". The Straits Times. 7 March 2023.

https://www.straitstimes.com/asia/south-asia/imran-khan-popularity-soars-ahead-of-vote-pakistan-survey-shows

Baloch, Shah Meer; Ellis-Petersen, Hannah (24 May 2023). "'He's fighting for our future': Pakistan's young voters rally behind Imran Khan". The Guardian. https://www.theguardian.com/world/2023/may/24/future-pakistan-young-voters-imran-khan-cricketer-politician

Khan, Azizullah (8 August 2023). "Pakistan: Imran Khan's supporters are silenced but determined". BBC News. https://www.bbc.com/news/world-asia-66436731

Baloch, Shah Meer; Ellis-Petersen, Hannah (14 May 2023). "Imran Khan accuses Pakistan's military of ordering his arrest". The Guardian. https://www.theguardian.com/world/2023/may/14/imran-khan-arrest-pakistan-military

Fazl-e-Haider, Syed. "Why is Imran Khan running for chancellor of University of Oxford? Lowy Institute. https://www.lowyinstitute.org/the-interpreter/why-imran-khan-running-chancellor-university-oxford

Gul, Ayaz (18 August 2024). "Pakistan's jailed ex-PM Khan seeks Oxford University chancellor role". Voice of America. https://www.voanews.com/a/pakistan-s-jailed-ex-pm-khan-seeks-oxford-university-chancellor-role-/7747135.html

Ethan Gudge; Shahzad Malik (16 October 2024). "Imran Khan uni chancellor bid rejected, says adviser". BBC. https://www.bbc.com/news/articles/cglk74dwg0ro

https://tribune.com.pk/story/2492023/disgraced-ex-pm-oxford-urged-to-bar-imran-khan-from-chancellor-election

https://www.dailymail.co.uk/news/article-13787409/oxford-university-angry-protests-ex-pakistan-prime-minister-imran-khan-chancellor-plans-prison.html

https://www.theguardian.com/commentisfree/article/2024/sep/01/imran-khan-oxford-university-chancellor

https://www.dawn.com/news/754413, "Americans gather crowds for Imran Khan's Waziristan march". Dawn. 5 October 2012

https://www.rferl.org/a/pakistan-drone-imran-khan/24730742.html,

"Antidrone Rally Stopped By Pakistani Army". Radio Free Europe. 6 October 2012.

https://www.theguardian.com/global/2011/sep/18/imran-khan-america-destroying-pakistan

https://gulfnews.com/world/asia/pakistan/pakistan-pm-imran-khan-us-war-on-terror-bred-more-terrorists-1.85707355, Sana Jamal (14 February 2022). "Pakistan PM Imran Khan: US war on terror bred more terrorists". Gulf News.

Imran Khan: Cricket hero set to be Pakistan's next PM https://web.archive.org/web/20180802053432/https://www.bbc.co.uk/news/world-asia-india-19844270

Linge, Mary Kay (28 July 2018). "Meet Pakistan's playboy-turned-prime minister". The New York Post. https://nypost.com/2018/07/28/meet-pakistans-playboy-turned-prime-minister/

https://edition.cnn.com/2021/06/05/opinions/imran-khan-world-environment-day-2021-spc-intl/index.html

Qaidi Number 804 is challenging the Pakistani establishment. Who is he?". India Today. 10 September 2024.

https://www.arabnews.pk/node/2491061/pakistan

Imran Khan: The cricket star and former PM who is dividing Pakistan   https://www.bbc.com/news/world-asia-india-19844270

Catriona Luke (3 August 2018). "The enigma inside a paradox wrapped in a conundrum". The Friday Times.

"Imran Khan — from flamboyant cricketer to prime minister". Dawn. 17 August 2018. Archived from the original on 25 December 2018.

https://www.worcesternews.co.uk/news/16382357.former-rgs-schoolboy-imran-khan-declared-pakistan-prime-minister/

https://web.archive.org/web/20180827142511/https://www.independent.co.uk/arts-entertainment/imrans-dangerous-new-game-1615722.html

https://web.archive.org/web/20161203150854/http://www.dawn.com/news/687806

Ahmed, Akbar (12 September 1990). "Mighty lion river" https://www.newspapers.com/article/the-independent/168467483/

https://arynews.tv/imran-khan-was-fired-from-his-first-ever-job/

https://web.archive.org/web/20070929104812/http://www.oxfordstudent.com/tt1999wk5/News/the_interview%3A_anything_he_khan%27t_do%3F

https://economictimes.indiatimes.com/magazines/panache/sex-to-spirituality-the-love-life-of-imran-khan

https://www.telegraph.co.uk/news/worldnews/asia/pakistan/7046650/Imran-Khan-from-playboy-to-politician.html

https://www.thetimes.com/world/asia/article/vip-clubs-and-mystery-blondes-imran-khans-party-years-lwsz5d3rj?region=global

https://web.archive.org/web/20121010004821/http://www.telegraph.co.uk/culture/4705862/Emmas-brush-with-marriage.html

USA: LOS ANGELES: COURT RULES THAT IMRAN KHAN IS FATHER OF 5-YEAR-OLD, https://newsroom.ap.org/editorial-photos-videos/detail?itemid=1967905a9826cb5e0b1a199978b1d1b6&mediatype=video

'Grieving daughter welcome to live with us' – Khan, https://www.irishexaminer.com/lifestyle/arid-30148175.html

https://www.dw.com/en/german-tv-stars-tryst-with-islam/a-5214141

https://dailytimes.com.pk/1168239/imran-khan-jewish-agentmaulana-fazalur-rehman/

Calling Imran Jewish agent was protest against economic system: Fazl, https://www.youtube.com/watch?v=wCce_HwKUkQ

Dr Israr Ahmed Prediction About Imran khan, ttps://www.youtube.com/watch?v=a7EDEFlyP7M

https://theconversation.com/imran-khan-jewish-agent-welcome-to-the-wonderful-world-of-pakistani-politics-13975

https://dailytimes.com.pk/928609/maryam-calls-imran-khan-biggest-fitna/

https://www.google.com/search?q=maryam+nawaz+bashing+imran+khan+as+fitna&oq=maryam+nawaz+bashing+imran+khan+as+fitna&gs_lcrp=EgZjaHJvbWUyBggAEEUYQO

Maryam Nawaz bashing Imran khan, https://www.youtube.com/watch?v=Hhecx-zqwFk

https://www.youtube.com/watch?v=tEYgnIq179E, Kya Farq Hai Imran Khan Ki Aur Dehshat Gard Me | Maryam Nawaz

https://wiki.kidzsearch.com/wiki/Imran_Khan

Books

https://www.amazon.com/Imran-Autobiography-Khan/dp/0720714893

https://www.amazon.com/All-Round-View-Imran-Khan/dp/0701133309

https://www.amazon.com/Imran-Khans-Cricket-Skills-Khan/dp/0600563499

https://www.amazon.com/Pakistan-Personal-History-Imran-Khan/dp/0593067746

https://books.apple.com/gr/book/imran-khans-political-journey-from-cricket-to-revolution/id6740459854

https://www.amazon.in/Rise-Fall-Imran-Khan-PAKISTAN/dp/1836150253

" Khan, Imran (1993). Warrior Race. London: Butler & Tanner Ltd. ISBN 978-0-7011-3890-5.

Clary, Christopher (17 May 2022). The Difficult Politics of Peace: Rivalry in Modern South Asia. Oxford University Press. p. 271. ISBN 978-0-19-763843-9.

Hutchins, Chris; Midgley, Dominic (2015), Goldsmith: Money, Women and Power, BookBaby, p. 173, ISBN 978-0-9933566-3-6

Jaffrelot, Christophe (2015). The Pakistan Paradox: Instability and Resilience. Oxford University Press. p. 279. ISBN 978-0-19-023518-5.

Morgan, Piers (2012). The Insider: The Private Diaries of a Scandalous Decade. Random House. p. 81. ISBN 978-1-4464-9168-3.

Naseemullah, Adnan; Chhibber, Pradeep (2024). Righteous Demagogues: Populist Politics in South Asia and Beyond. Oxford University Press. p. 118. ISBN 978-0-19-775692-8. Retrieved 23 April 2025.

Oborne, Peter (9 April 2015). Wounded Tiger: A History of Cricket in Pakistan. Simon & Schuster UK. ISBN 978-1-84983-248-9.

Pande, Aparna, ed. (23 August 2017). Routledge Handbook of Contemporary Pakistan. Taylor & Francis. ISBN 978-1-317-44759-7.

Qadir, Muneeb (3 September 2024). A MAD, MAD WORLD: The global rise in rightwing populism. Daastan Publishing. p. 50. ISBN 978-969-696-962-4.

Hutchins, Chris; Midgley, Dominic (2015), Goldsmith: Money, Women and Power, BookBaby, p. 173, ISBN 978-0-9933566-3-6

Morgan, Piers (2012). The Insider: The Private Diaries of a Scandalous Decade. Random House. p. 81. ISBN 978-1-4464-9168-3.

Sadiq, B. J. (9 September 2017). Let There Be Justice: The Political Journey of Imran Khan. Fonthill Media. ISBN 978-1-78155-637-5.

Waseem, Mohammad (April 2022). Political Conflict in Pakistan. Oxford University Press. ISBN 978-0-19-765426-2.

Wilde, Simon (17 September 2013). Wisden Cricketers of the Year: A Celebration of Cricket's Greatest Players. Bloomsbury USA. p. 270. ISBN 978-1-4081-4084-0.

Sandford, Christopher (2009). Imran Khan: The Cricketer, the Celebrity, the Politician. HarperCollins. ISBN 978-0-00-731888-9.

Tennant, Ivo (1996). Imran Khan. Trafalgar Square Publishing. ISBN 978-0-575-05936-8.

Bobb, Dilip (15 October 1990). "Book Review: Imran Khan's 'An Indus Journey'".

IndiaToday.

https://www.indiatoday.in/magazine/society-and-the-arts/books/story/19901015-book-   review-imran-khan-an-indus-journey-813105-1990-10-14

"It's a miracle... Imran's notes turn into book". London Evening Standard. 4 July 2008

http://www.frankhuzur.com/imran-vs-imran.html

www.ingramcontent.com/pod-product-compliance
Lightning Source LLC
Chambersburg PA
CBHW071237300726
48975CB00002B/448